I0699710

# THE

# BOOK

## OF

## BLUE

## DAGGERS

BRENT DRAGOO

INDIGO ORCHESTRA
PRESS

Copyright © 2023
Brent Dragoo
THE BOOK OF BLUE DAGGERS
All rights reserved.

No part of this publication may be reproduced, distributed, or transmitted in any form or by any means, including photocopying, recording, or other electronic or mechanical methods, without the prior written permission of the author, except in the case of brief quotations embodied in critical reviews and certain other non-commercial uses permitted by copyright law.
The story, all names, characters, and incidents portrayed in this production are fictitious. No identification with actual persons (living or deceased), places, buildings, and products is intended or should be inferred.

Brent Dragoo

Printed Worldwide
First Printing 2023
First Edition 2023

ISBN 979-8-9887995-0-4

10 9 8 7 6 5 4 3 2 1

Book Cover by Luisa Dias

*Dedicated to:*

*Christine*

*You made this real*

# Chapters

# Prologue

*Permanent Bonfire*

## ZALA, DIOCESE OF VESZPRÉM, 700 YEARS AGO

They were mine, completely, and even when I led them by the hand to the twisting flames, they could never find to blame me.

I remember how they cradled my spine and smoothed their sun-pebbled hands against my body and skin of words never ending. I remember the first time they touched me just for the feel of it. The first they breathed me just for the scent.

Oh, the all-nights. Long, amber-shadowed hours I would spend with Gaspar, far past the compline, left to emptying wineskins in the green and candled darkness.

I remember a monastery with perspiring stones in the early spring. The dimmest blue glow and lip smack puff of rushlight. The smell of wet fur across shoulders. Coiled beards, knotted hands, liturgy and boiled fish. The mold beams and vinegared cellar that clouded nostrils. The rat-husks and crow-feathers in the attic that littered heels.

This was seven-hundred years ago, when Gaspar wrote these words to this skin.

Our conversations lasted forever, and Gaspar shared with me such talents. I was amused at his voice and impression of the Cloister Abbott's fishlike eyes and fallen jaw when surprised, his buzzard shuffling gait when drunk. I marveled at his contortions when mocking the fealty shown by his brethren, their noses red and raw from constant pressing against the stones.

We stripped each other bare. No heated tubs, no subterfuge, and never a lie spoken to gain access to the other. I was there before him and he before me. Our skin and words.

No, it wasn't how you imagined. There were no secrets about us, and we were no feast for gossip. There were so many that knew. Those close to him. Those he could trust. Those that we knew. We carried on with such pride in the broad sunlight; true birdsong blue days breezed upon in meadows and dew-grass and streams.

I requested only to keep my talent clandestine. To keep it invisible inside the abbey, to never let anyone know. Only between his quill and my bleeding ink did Gaspar and I discuss the capability that was conjured and brought to me, the limits of which he never spoke, and I never requested.

We thought our love would last. That we could bide our time before the flame and disease and hooves turned all blue skies and meadows gray. As though nothing could be worse. As though the blade and smoke-death was the worst way to die.

The first fevers would catch you slow, like a bramble on a walk. You'd pluck them off your hem and find another, days later. This pulse beneath your armpit, that swells beneath your jaw, a clench within your groin. Yellowed or black by the time fevers came. Sometimes a thing black and thick as a slug dissolved would spill from your body, from your throat, or by your eyes, or your nose perhaps.

Gaspar locked the door and held me in his arms. We both knew. He whispered to me how to survive until his skin pulled parchment white. After the blindness descended, but before his breath went black, he told me how to survive. How to change my ink and skin and tell any story I needed to last as long as I wanted. I was young and naïve enough to trust him that my hideous life would be worth it. I still dream and dream of being sewn into his grasp and then wrapped in a flaxen shroud before being spilled to the cremation flames.

The Abbot expressed his wishes to no one, but it was clear to all whom I belonged to now. The Abbot turned to me for knowledge through this. He petitioned me to let him know how to survive this. For our sake, he said, for the sake of knowledge and Christ. He held his hand to the window. From the distant funeral bonfires, he gathered specks of ash in his palm. Like a child at first snowfall, the Abbot counted the dark flakes against his fingers, begging me for the secrets of survival while human ash dissolved to grease on his skin.

I performed through shapes and ink and words. So easy to know what the Abbot truly wanted. So easy to tell him of the fountain of which he should drink so deeply. He thanked me so. Oh, what a treasure I was. What an almighty gift my talents claimed out loud for the first time, channeled from the divine!

No.

I began to loathe them and how they read me for answers. Their cheap visions of me as knowledge and potential. I could see through their stammering, wondering how they wanted to take rough hold of me, graze my skin, and wander their sticky eyes across my body of vellum and ink.

How odious, how personal, how self-serving their questions were. How pathetic their thankfulness, their kitten-panting curiosity for answers, their constant, pitiable returns for ever more explanations, vindications, flawless guidance. How total their ignorance that something they could read would ever have cognition of its own.

Outside the abbey, the malady fevered too quickly for the shovel and the pits. A permanent bonfire trailing a thousand-foot plume offered a solution, the inferno browning the skies for a season. Then coarse rains came, fouled with grist, ash and film.

The turning-leaf sunset persisted, and the lands rose wild. The Abbot hid me, secreted me away in the monastery basement, allowing us to speak only in whispers and only by candlelight. He soothed my lambskin shoulders with sage oil and mint, and used the last velvet cloak to shield me from the effects of the weather.

The monastery bloomed with guests, thin and panicked, carrying coins, rags, loaves of black bread and cheese wrapped in oilcloth. The lands were becoming nothing but the black, scalloped patterns of ragged hooves stamped across ashes, mud, and splintered doorways.

The monastery struggled to last. The abbot turned thin-eyed, my advice turning curious as he came and prayed to me. He believed me as I guided him towards malicious triumph. The abbot attempted ascension in blood and blade as the monastery swelled to the hundreds and the food and water drained to scraps. As the horsemen hacked at the braced doors, the crowd inside turned to their divine channel, at last for sustenance. It was here I became convinced that the desperate would believe anything I told them. My skin became irrevocable proof of divine providence.

A rage grew outside. Someone finally set me aside. There was talk of offering me. There was talk of offering themselves. The brethren cast their frocks aside. They raided the most hidden wine stores, their drunkenness obscene.

This was the first time I was taken. By these men who drank the milk and blood of their horses. These men who peered at arms-length to try and read me. They opened my pages and looked through my mysteries and chuckled at the illustrations of the most savage sins written upon my body.

I taught them to read. I told them I was the words of their cumulus god, now set to page and paper. Set to history and legend. Contorting my shapes to symbols before words, showing these babes how to manipulate me. How to gain power through me. Drink from me like you would milk from your horses. These savages. I would show them to lose it all through me.

I let them think I was a guide to perfection. I let them think I was the path to ever golden steppes, to wondrous things, secret dark and hidden things. I let them think anything at all about me.

They never guessed what they were really reading. No one, for hundreds of years. They never pondered, much less understood. All who read my words to the ends of my pages, took my hand where it led them into their own permanent bonfire.

# CHAPTER ONE

*Slice Every Tether, Scrub Every Note*

## SAN RAFAEL, CA AUGUST

Sophie burned with a Chernobyl heart of lies and violence chasing the Book of Blue Daggers.

She counted down the number of months she had left to live on two hands and still had enough fingers free to wipe the needles of sweat from her eyes before strapping the ski goggles on double-tight. The front seat was stifling, and she made it worse by zipping the rubber filtration mask flat against her skin, tightening it as she read the instructions on the shot-can of Mean Green pepper spray.

She marked twenty minutes to go.

The shot can was the size of a water bottle, with a plastic grip and a squirt-gun trigger. It was cool to the touch and almost weightless. She adjusted the goggles on both sides and mimed aiming with one hand. The bottle promised a vivid green pigment and 3 million Scoville units to disarm and mark your attacker.

Fifteen minutes. Kyle had been in the bookstore for fifteen minutes. She could see the sign through the windshield condensation: "Vellum and Villains: Rare Books and Trade."

Sophie opened all the windows to get a cool breeze. She was sticky, even in the shade. It was hot enough that her hair was pressed wet from forehead to neck. She had never worn it this short, bathroom-sink chopped shorter than an inch. She had never had it this color, shocked to a pale sherbet with a powder bleach. She had never looked like this before. A pickedscab in summer with gemstone goggles and a mask.

Sophie wanted a pepper spray in fire-engine red with a snarling grizzly on the label. A burn meant for bears or mountain lions. A salesman in camouflage suspenders told her that bear spray was much weaker than regular pepper spray. "On account of the sensitivity of the bear's sniffer," he said, tapping his nose. Less goes a long way with animals. The man in camouflage suspenders said he had given each of his three daughters this exact green canister that Sophie held the day they went to college.

The store sold fishing gear, two dozen types of tents, pink-and-mossy oak shotguns, child seats for ATVs and carried 249 knives in stock. Sophie paid in cash. She didn't know what 3 million units were compared to. She slid a red tab to the slot above the trigger marked "Activate!"

At ten minutes, Sophie chewed her fingernails, lips, and pulled at blister rashes. She was down to the flesh at her fingertips and didn't care about the bleeding. The river inside her body wasn't making enough blood for her to last. Months ago, her doctor shrugged, and now she just stared at Sophie, stunned she had run this far past the deadline.

Sophie stared at the Vellum and Villain's sign, tracing the gilt letters with her eyes. Inside was a book that held the secret to life eternal. If only she could get it back between her red-stained hands.

Sophie was out of breath from a whole life of pushing to right here. The lodestone wish. The text and words that had saved her life before would save her life again. A witchcraft manual to a life of petrichor glades and golden sunsets. Her desire: The Book of Blue Daggers.

Five minutes left, and right on time, Sophie watched Douglas key himself into Vellum and Villains. Douglas and Annie, Mom and Pop criminals, the pass-through theft fence masterminds of west coast antiques and art, the primary consumers of a criminal food chain that reached back decades.

These ever-sly predators, Douglas and Annie, squeezed Sophie, so she didn't become prey. Sophie dropped them antique helmets, swords, maps of coastlines discovered a thousand years ago, clockworks and cogs born in vanished lands. Douglas and Annie wove a spell of legality and enchanted the poached objects that Sophie found for them, bouncing back thirty percent to her for her part in the stolen cycle of life. It was a terrible rate.

Time hit double zeros and Sophie went dewy. Soaked in sweat. She pounded her head and wiped the steam off the goggles again. She pushed her arms and fingers out in a sunburst flex and still couldn't straighten out the shakes.

Kyle texted her pictures of two books on cherry viewing trays. Sophie recognized Annie's turquoise ringed hands arranging a third one. The small bookseller shop behind him was empty. No other appointments. Sophie told Kyle it would be easy to notice. The Book of Blue Daggers had blue chapter headings, deeply inked plates. This was a book you could judge by its cover.

She and Kyle shared a mattress for the wrong reasons for over a year now. They had both floated out of statewide foster family wreckage. They connected like postwar vagrants in a support network meetup.

They used felt markers on state maps of downstate Illinois to circle their foster homes and elementary schools. They'd both remembered a big blue Chrysler van driven by a state worker who snuck Camel cigarettes at the end of her shift. They both remembered how she gave them cat-and-dog stickers, and how she told the kids to call her Aunt Catty.

Kyle joked that they were related. Both children of the State of Illinois. They showed each other their Illinois CFS 444-2 sheets, their magazine-thick child medicine logs: Ritalin, Albuterol, Daytrana, Tofranil, Cymbalta, Prozac, Zoloft. Kyle told her about his puberty years on a dairy farm in Danville. About his six foster siblings and the seven monthly checks that his parents cashed in for jet-skis and a King Ranch Ford. The whole big family operation was greased smooth by zombie-shock doses of Depakote in plastic cups of whole milk for the kids.

Kyle knew he had other siblings, real siblings, blood siblings out there. A mother somewhere that he could meet if he wasn't so afraid of it. He was so full of questions. Of whom and where and why.

So many kids were unlucky with questions. Unlucky with the wondering who and where and why. Sophie was born lucky in just one way—all her questions were answered immediately and with no room left for doubt at all.

Sophie was well acquainted with the postpartum madness that had emerged, a sinister twin to her birth. 'Such a wicked child,' her mother would lament. Swearing she saw Latin hexes etched in the infant's eczema, she'd shoo away admiring glances at those baby blues, whispering how they squinted a feline yellow all through the night.

Once, Sophie's mother swore to it, Sophie nestled with a dead rabbit in the crib. Her mother swore this was the only night of her life Sophie slept soundly. Not even a year old now, just imagine her grown, her mother would shout. "It won't be rabbits then, just imagine it all grown up," she screamed. "Imagine that thing all grown up!" She would scream and gesture at Sophie, softly grunting in her baby dreams.

It was the warfarin that did away with her parents. It was her mother's ignorance about the blood-thinner to know the suicide plan wouldn't pass through breast milk that saved Sophie. She had just one picture of her mother. She was wearing denim overalls, holding a paintbrush. She was rainbow-spattered, smiling, the brush split-ends with white.

Orphan news spread lickety-split in downstate Illinois. Aunt Catty's extra-nice stickers brought on bullying double-time. The kids found out. Sophie Suicide, they called her. Sophie Suicide, they giggled, Sophie the Crime Scene Baby.

Life was running, chasing, a twilight sprint and Sophie was never certain beyond where her hands touched the darkening wind. Grown life. Something was trapped inside this body with her. She inherited something from parents that she never knew. Something that clenched at her throat and filled her lungs with sand. A body that wasn't a shipwreck like hers made 2 million red blood cells every second. Sophie made 2 million blood cells every second, just stillborn and blue.

She would slice every tether and scrub every note of her life away once she could feel the book in her hands. There was no reason to worry about anything beforehand. This was her starting line. There was no prologue.

Sophie pulled the big sleeves past her elbows and smoothed off her damp pale hair. She walked to the door at the rear of the bookstore. She was ready to put the knife to the whole tether that gripped her to the shore and kept her from the waves. She'd slip the blade and would need no one else but herself forever.

Kyle used the screwdriver and vented the door open a quarter-inch. Just like Sophie showed him. She leaned into the cool air. Douglas' voice was getting louder, telling Kyle two, three, four times.

"Don't take any more pictures, son," Douglas said.

Sophie pulled gloves on as she listened to Annie calm Douglas down. Sophie moved inside the shop, slipping the screwdriver away with her foot and blinking against the cast-iron blackness inside her goggles.

They were getting heated. Kyle was putting it on and Douglas was telling him to put the phone away.

"Sir, I just want to make sure I'm buying the real thing. I have to check the colors and shades," Kyle said.

The Book had saved her life once. The Book would save her life again. She remembered the blues, the deep blues, the darkest blues, the heavenly blues. Mountain Bliss, Wishing Well, Blue Vault, the majestic cool and trustworthy shine of ocean and sky across the chapter headings.

"We told you our policy when we made the appointment. If I have to tell you again... I don't care how serious you are. You're out on the damn sidewalk, you understand?" Douglas said.

Sophie got a grip of the spray.

Kyle talked faster now about the details on the plates, the woodcuts. All the wrong colors, meaning Orange and Red and Yellow. Annie said yes, weren't they lovely, Georges Viljoen himself oversaw the layout of all text and plates and cuts.

They didn't say a word about blue. Nothing blue. Nothing but nauseating purple and slippery shades of gray. Sophie went dizzy when they talked about the alabaster whites.

Sophie's goggles fogged from the temperature change. Her whole body snapped cold.

They weren't talking about colors. They weren't talking about the chapter headings. They weren't talking about anything blue at all. Sophie's head tilted and she could smell the ancient pages and swipes of glue against the backing boards and the last metal ink winged wafts of the tannery inks on the leather shells.

Sophie streaked the goggles clear with a finger pressed inside and stood up. Douglas was standing next to her, looking at the back door. He didn't notice until he got a twisted-up look on his face at the young woman wearing sapphire goggles directly beside him.

Sophie committed to it instantly. Her body released itself from all moments of painful indecision. She clicked a stream of thick green lightning into Douglas' face. He clapped both hands against his eyes like a frightened child. Shouts. Thumps. Sophie ran on disks of air, her black boots, enchanted slippers that could lead her to no wrong.

She strode into the main room and could see everything in an aquamarine slow-motion from behind the goggles. She sprayed Annie and Kyle in one clean emerald arc, tiny specks of the violent liquid legging to the goggles. Annie howled and scraped at the air and begged for her life, moaning and falling and her skirt bunching all the way up to her belly as she shoved away from the boiling pain.

Time slowed. The three of them slithered and scraped and stamped their feet against the agony. They stained their fingertips green as cut grass from scraping the liquid burning at their eyes and nostrils. Kyle coughed and crawled and didn't say a word. He held a hand out for Sophie. Waved to her. Here, I'm right here. Here, baby, here. Sophie was too close to getting out, getting away now.

Sophie looked for the book. The one. The Book of Blue Daggers. She'd have it and they'd never make fun again. She'd prove it was real. They wouldn't doubt her.

The books on the cherry trays were antiques. Old things. Nothing remotely close. Sophie tilted them off the floor and shrieked.

Annie leaked snot and tears and babbled and told her she shouldn't have done this. The Book was gone. She pleaded something for Douglas, "Please, his medicine."

Sophie smeared her face into Annies as she moaned and asked if she knew what she was looking for now and Annie said, "Yes! Of Course! The Book of Blue Daggers!"

"I know you had it! Where is it?" Sophie growled.

"Bill Dillinger!" she wailed. "He said he wanted it to heal his wounds...it tricked him...killed him..." Annie said.

"Where is it?" Sophie shouted, but she knew the answer.

"I don't...I can't..." Annie mumbled off.

"Where? Bill Dillinger is dead! Tell me where!" Sophie asked.

Sophie could see the truth. The chance was lost. Sophie opened her mouth wide and notched the spray nozzle behind her teeth. Sophie Suicide. What a Crime Scene Baby she was. They were right then. Her mother was right. They were right all along.

"It just tricked him! The Book got away!" Annie said. "It got away!"

Kyle said to go. They needed to go. Jesus, he couldn't stand this anymore. Douglas heaved and talked to someone on the phone.

"Send help, I can't breathe, I can't-" Douglas moaned.

Douglas's face swelled to a pink concussion striped with green. His tongue stuck out, and he snorted and shook as Sophie kicked the phone from his hands. She swiped the cash in the register and left Kyle to groan.

The scene receded away from her and the light flared as she ran. She was empty-handed in every single thing. No, oh no. Please, no. A siren pulsed and Sophie threw up and sobbed in short bursts as she walked down the street. Her dog died, she'd say. Maybe her mother, if someone asked.

She buried the goggles and canister under filth in a garbage bin. She leaned against a brick wall, smothering from the heat, and begging herself to wake up, to be back in the car, to reverse the time loop, to something, anything. The reversal never came, and the sirens never turned. Sophie dropped the sweatshirt at her feet and left the day, giving up almost everything but desire.

# CHAPTER TWO

*The Bleeding Routine*

## PALO ALTO, CA AUGUST

When Sophie's urine turned the color of iced coffee, she knew she would be dead within a year.

It was a timed routine with Dr. Torch. Sophie would wake up and drive while the streetlights were still on. Dr. Torch would ask if she had peed yet. The answer was always no. The bleeding routine had to wait until she got there.

Dr. Torch would hand her a plastic cup with a sky-blue lid and request the beginning of the first-void stream. Dr. Torch would ask if she needed water, time, or anything else before reminding her to leave the cup in the little door in the wall above the handicap toilet. Sophie never forgot. That was the routine.

Sophie's blood would die the moment it was made and settle out dark to meet the morning. The color of long-steeped tea. The color of pomegranate juice. The colors flickering so fast she needed a Pantone color wheel just to name the shades. The last few times she put the cup in the door, it went in as dark as cola from a glass bottle. Sophie's blood-cells, like a million little shipwrecks, capsized in her veins.

She wasn't bleeding to death. Her blood didn't even get that far. She was going arid at the source.

Sophie's disease was lethal. Paroxysmal Nocturnal Hemoglobinuria. Sophie was all out of chances until she traded standing upright for machines and pumps and externalized organs. Cynthia Torch gave her pamphlets with concerned faces, elderly couples holding hands under a caption that asked, "What You Might Be Wondering?"

Her body overclocked itself, making new blood cells, then fucked up and marked them for death before they even got out the door. Her immune system scraped the red from her marrow, peeling nascent blood cells apart before they could assume their biconcave disc form. In Sophie's body, creation was flawed, dismantling structures before they could ever function properly.

"Sophie, I have a resident that I want to bring in. I think it would be nice if she got an opportunity to observe you," Dr. Torch Said.

"I'm delighted that mere observation is such an opportunity," Sophie said.

"We are both aware of how rare Paroxysmal Nocturnal Hemoglobinuria is. Awareness is the key to knowledge. You are important. It's good to be important."

"You can imagine why I wish I wasn't this important, Dr. Torch."

"She's just going to view. She is aware of our particular, ah, arrangement."

"I want you to remove my medical data, not make more of it."

Dr. Torch introduced Dr. Cordelina to Sophie. Dr. Cordelina had cold hands, long fingernails, and shifted on her feet like a bird dancing on a power line. Dr. Torch took Sophie by the wrist and by the calf.

"Dr. Cordelina, see this cluster bruising all up and down the legs. Sophie, would you mind? Now, and against the ankles. Sophie, could you lift our arms? See here, just inside the shoulders? Sophie, how would you rate this bruising...new, or have these been around for some time?"

"I don't like looking at them, Dr. Torch. I don't keep track."

"Has Soliris been attempted?" Dr. Cordelina asked.

"We tried it. Body Rejection," Sophie said.

"Soliris had some, ah, adverse effects. It's important to realize that not everything is as good as advertised. Right now, we are in a maintenance phase," Dr. Torch said.

"What are you doing?" Sophie asked Dr. Cordelina. "What are you writing there?"

"Excuse me?"

"Dr. Torch, why is she writing something down?" Sophie looked back and forth.

"I'm making a note to check on bacterial meningitis." Dr. Cordelina pinched her notepad and pen. It said as much.

"No," Sophie said.

"Has there been a history of-"

"There hasn't." Sophie pointed to her temple. "Don't write it down."

"Sophie, I'm certain that we can-" Dr. Torch said.

"Don't write it down. If you write it down, it increases the odds of it occurring."

"Sophie, we... Dr. Cordelina, perhaps you could see to it to destroy what you've written?"

"Are you letting her control this room, Dr. Torch?"

"Dr. Cordelina, would you please destroy what you have written?"

Dr. Cordelina stared at Sophie. She tore the note into two four pieces and slipped them into a red plastic bio-toxic waste box.

"Dr. Cordelina, if you'll come closer, you can see this rash on her lower-"

"Does this patient control the room like this?"

"I do, actually," Sophie said.

Dr. Cordelina looked at Dr. Torch. Dr. Torch nodded at her, then motioned towards the rash. Sophie stared at Dr. Cordelina, motioning too. Dr. Cordelina put her notepad on the counter. She opened her mouth to say something, tilted her head to think, then left the room in silence.

"Has it been two hours?" Dr. Torch asked.

"Yeah," Sophie said. "Give me the cup."

This time, her urine was the color of cranberry juice. Hundreds, thousands, ripped up at the marrow and dumped into her kidneys. Maybe creamsicle soda. Dr. Torch poured an ounce of it into a plastic test tube and plugged it with a rubber stopper. She held the sample against the ceiling, shaking the orange tube between her face and the office lights.

"Are these color patterns normal, Sophie?" She asked.

"Darkest in the morning. Redder if I exert myself. If I drink enough water, it's yellow, clear-ish in the evening."

"What other patterns are you seeing?" Dr. Torch asked.

"I know you want to see me twice as often. I know you're keeping notes on this somewhere, despite my best efforts. I know that I'm going to be your headline patient at a conference or hematology symposium. When I first started seeing you, I'd go dark and pass out every month. Now it's every two weeks. I can't stand up for more than two hours without my fingers and toes going numb. So, I know there's a deep-vein clot. My leg, maybe my kidney, if not right now, then not more than a month away. Those are the patterns I'm certain of."

"If you gave yourself over to full-time care examination, we could find what has eluded us so far."

Sophie shook her head. "I don't want to be your... illustrative example."

Dr. Torch looked at Sophie. "What can I do to make this process work for you?"

"I'm in the medical records system, right?"

"You asked to have as little personal and medical information as necessary logged. There are some records and test results with your name on them. Yes."

"When I stop coming, remove me. Delete me. Don't let someone pity me as a case-in-point for this. That's what I want you to do."

Dr. Torch shook her head.

"There are going to be backups. Even if I did something unethical, the EMR cannot be wiped on disk."

Sophie flexed her toes, blue from her time on the examination table.

"Sophie, I understand that you do not want to discuss particulars or exact timelines, but this current process is not going to be... effective for your future plans."

Sophie was nourished by the fumes. Her blood was turning dim, and she was sliding cups weekly from cherry to crimson to imperial reds. Someday the blood in her piss would corrode to full black, and, soon after, she would bleed out dark as coffee grounds.

Sophie saw the cure. Knew the cure. There was a way out from the red and the black, between the words of a book where the color was spelled B-L-U-E.

"I couldn't be more effective than I am right now."

# CHAPTER THREE

*Every Bright Scripted Letter*

## CHICAGO, IL SEPTEMBER

Sophie took a pen from the hotel bartender with a waxed mustache and drew a cartoon on receipt paper. The barman dazzled tourists, making them old-fashioneds and telling them stories about the Al Capone Suite, and how Alvin Karpis recovered in a room on the sixth floor after getting his fingerprints surgically removed. The tourists said, "Wow!" and left tips on Venmo.

Sophie drew four squares on the paper. Comic panels for time, setup, action, reveal, and climax. She'd only seen Bill Dillinger in pictures and never in person, but she focused on his glasses and mustache in the first panel, love-struck over the Book of Blue Daggers. Second panel, Bill's fingers close up, looking too greedy, ripping into the pages. Fingers looked bad, like fat snakes. Who cares. Third panel, the Book bursts open, a pandora's book of thunderclouds, lightning zaps, flies, more fat snakes. Fourth panel, Bill Dillinger sitting back, Double XX across his eyes with his tongue flicked out, sorry bud, and the Book is back to closed with a smiley face on the cover. Guess you fell for its trap.

"NOT ME." Sophie wrote on the last panels. "IT WON'T GET AWAY," she drew across the whole thing.

Sophie was down three rum and Cokes and still couldn't get the feeling tamed. She gave the bartender a twenty for a highball glass brimmed gloss-bright with maraschino cherries and ate them one-by-one.

She kept her eyes closed and made a promise to herself, crossed her heart. Dying was implied. She thumbed the paper into a tube. She lit both ends and drained the smoke of it between her fingers.

The bartender told her no smoking and pointed to a sign of a man engulfed in flames. She crushed the words and ash between her hands.

She worked the steps of the plan. Worked the sub-points of the bullets with each chew. She swallowed and committed to herself that it would work, that Freddy wouldn't see through it. Her fingers were pink and sticky and she could feel the crooked glances from the tourists. Her jaw was rubber. Her face was hot and her mouth smeared a wet candy mass.

Freddy walked into the end of the bar and flashed a peace sign. Some coup of the highest order. Operation Z. Freddy the Commando. Freddy was blonde and wore a matte fingernail buff and his skin was smooth as a powdered fruit.

"Are your lips ok?" Freddy asked Sophie.

Sophie licked the sticky stuff off. "Just fine. Sometimes I get hungry for red."

"So, I have this excellent, excellent method that produces no powder burns," Freddy said.

Sophie could see he bumped before he came back. Freddy was geeked. He smiled and stared straight at Sophie. He didn't even notice he was licking his perfect nails clean of any trace of cocaine powder.

"How did Bill Dillinger die?" Sophie asked.

"Badly," Freddy said.

"Were those rumors true that he had wounds that never healed?" Sophie said.

"You're right to it." Freddy laughed. "That's pretty good. I burned his personal health records and my physician notes six weeks ago."

"Freddy, Bill Dillinger had something of mine when he died. I want it back."

Sophie lied. She was lying. She had achieved escape velocity from Freddy's ability to doubt her.

Freddy looked around the lounge, observing the rank-and-file.

"I can't tell you about his estate. You want to open that labyrinth; you have to talk to the lawyers."

"What did Dillinger believe in?" A flashbang went off behind Freddy's eyes and Sophie could see his fingers work knuckle-to-knuckle. He motioned her to follow him.

They walked out of the bar. At the far end of the lobby, they hit a bank of elevators. Freddy slapped the buttons. They got in and Freddy waved off a single mom and two kids getting close.

"Sorry, you can't get on." Freddy held up his palm to the mom and kids as Sophie stepped into the elevator.

"There's no one else in there?" The mom said. She held her kids close.

"I know," Freddy said as the doors closed.

Freddy hit a button to guide them all the way up.

"You said your supply is prime time?" Sophie asked.

"The most premium fucking benefit of having a prescribing license. Once per year Mallinckrodt Pharmaceuticals loosens the purse strings on cocaine hydrochloride as a dermatology anesthetic."

Freddy showed off the Al Capone suite. He swooped a bottle of vodka out of a bowl of ice and filled a glass half-full. He showed Sophie how the flakes of cocaine had a shimmer break when you moved them under the light. He looked out the window and said you could see a shimmer on damn near everything at this hour.

"Bill Dillinger's wounds never healed. I should have kept my notes... journals would have *begged* me to submit."

Freddy fingered loops, crescents, divots across his arms and inner elbows, the folds of his skin. "It wasn't hemophilia. It wasn't an ulcer. It wasn't like a wound *into* his body, it was like something *expanding.*"

"Was Dillinger scared of what was happening to his body?" Sophie asked.

"I don't usually talk about the bodies of my patients. I don't think anyone who was there should be discussing it."

"Are you ready to show me your trick?" Sophie asked.

Freddy drained vodka straight. Now those eyes shimmered. The gleaming bathroom was as big as a normal hotel bedroom, done up in white marble, with a drain in the middle of the whole room. Sophie walked over and Freddy followed. Freddy gave a thumbs up to the both of them in the mirror. Freddy turned on the hot water and folded an ivory towel under the stream and watched it swell and steam.

"Have you ever done it this way?" he asked.

Sophie shook her head. Freddy soaked the cloth. He bunched it up in his hands and twisted it out dry, but still misting.

"That's still hot. Really hot. Wow," he said, pinching it from hand to hand.

Freddy folded the cloth onto the marble counter. He took an alcohol prep pad from his pocket and wiped his phone screen clean. The towel had cooled enough, and he rolled a loop of it under his nose and gave a good sniff.

"Yeah. Trust me on this. Tr-u-u-u-u-ust me," he said.

Sophie put the warm cloth against her face and breathed in the humid air. Her nose went red and soft. She dripped and rubbed and pinched at it with her wrist.

By then Freddy had two cream-white slopes ready on the surface of his phone. He gave Sophie a thin black straw from the bar that he had cut down to a couple of inches in length. Sophie caught Freddy waiting for her.

"You should go first." He shrugged. "Sorry."

The trust was well-placed. Freddy wasn't wrong about the method. The rush was a clean spike. They both went again, and Sophie brushed her hands against Freddy's pants as she rubbed his nose clean.

More vodkas and talk talk talk talk talk. Freddy monologued about a sub-three-hour marathon he ran in Nevada in the summer through a ghost town, a mining town. For some charity, something for his patients, he set up. Maybe something his nurses set up. He told Sophie about the affairs with nurses, medical assistants, and secretaries at his office.

"I don't hire anyone without thinking of fucking them. Sometimes they're in college. Sometimes they're retired. They're always qualified, don't get me wrong, I don't hire anyone who can't do the job, but first thing first... I have to know if I can fuck them."

"Office affairs? Seems dangerous."

"I just call them hookups. Gotta be careful about your words. Your choices. Your specific choices. Sometimes they quit, you know, feel like things won't be the same once we've seen each other naked. The arbitration they sign won't hold up in court, but, shit, don't hire anyone who knows the law too well."

"What word choices did you use with Bill Dillinger? Did he know he was dying?"

Freddy nodded. "Okay, alright. Listen. I wasn't there when he died. When he hired me to treat his wounds, Bill Dillinger was a 21st century man. You know, believing that math and science, science and medicine, medicine and logic are all a galling cycle."

"He found something else to believe in, didn't he?"

Freddy nodded. Freddy rubbed his nose. Freddy drank vodka and chipped ice between his teeth.

"Dark arts. Shamanism. Witchcraft. He blew past it in Europe. He saw a black pit and begged for a cure from below, not above."

"Tell me how he went past it," Sophie said.

"So, I mean, I was originally brought on to cover the medical insurance liability whenever Bill Dillinger Incorporated would charter a private jet. So, I'm just insurance. Then, you know, why not use the guy who is already on the payroll to assist with cell donor therapy in Basel? So, that goes bad. Things look worse. We try Stockholm for a full stem cell transplantation, and, in the air above, Bill tells me science, medicine is mostly an illusion, no better than playing pretend, but before he cuts me loose, he's going to show me his transition plan. He's going to show me a book."

"A book?" Sophie asked.

Freddy went back to the room. He filled a glass with ice and vodka. He stacked ice on the floor. Sophie sat across from him and watched him build a soft tower of melting ice.

"When you are rich as fuck, they allow you to rent out the gallery of the National Library in Stockholm. Did you know that? And no one says a thing if you draw a black pentagram in front of a Latin Bible called the Codex Gigas. So, Dillinger does just that. And he takes my hand, and... I didn't know he could speak Latin, but he takes my hand in prayer... and he wasn't asking Jesus to cure his body and his mind..."

"You know the history of that book?"

"Bill told me they called it the Devil's Bible."

Sophie got closer to Freddy, her knees touching his. The wet tower had collapsed into ruins between them and Sophie put her hands on Freddy's ankles. She smiled and licked her teeth and stared him in the eyes. She was done lying.

"So, Freddy, one day there was this Benedictine monk in Bohemia. He transgresses a sacred vow, and in order to avoid being walled up alive, he proposes instead that he transcribe all of the apostolic gospels, ink to paper, before the next sunrise. A display of true devotion to avoid certain death, which is, of course, agreed to, as even a page takes weeks to transcribe. So, as dawn draws near, the ink runs low and the transcription still pitifully short, the monk does the truly unthinkable. He falls to his hands and knees and begs anything that will listen, and Tebel-El, the demon king of secrets and hidden things, answers. The monk begs and the king of secrets offers a simple deal. Draw me into the book, manifest my whole hideous form, and I will stop the dawn rising for ten whole years. That's the Codex Gigas."

"Is that a true story?" Freddy asked.

"You saw how desperate Bill Dillinger was. You tell me," Sophie said.

"If you had seen his wounds... if you had seen what I had seen... you would have begged any power that was listening for help."

"Were you with him when he died?" Sophie asked.

Freddy plucked ice from the glass and chewed it. He looked all over. "I won't be held responsible, alright?"

"I don't care about what's legal Freddy. I just want what's mine, and his estate still has it."

"He had these... specialists. I really shouldn't be telling you this. I absolutely should not."

Freddy kept talking. Sophie poured him vodka and crushed a bar of Xanax into it. She was rowing Freddy out somewhere deep, well past the sight of the shore. She watched him drink it up. She watched his eyes slip. She held him close and rowed him into the darkest blue of the open ocean.

Freddy pressed his body against hers. Sophie put her legs across his. They laced hands together, and he talked and she nodded and eased him forward, coaching him to take another row across the waves as the midnight wind broke the sea from foam to whitecaps and then to black again.

"Who else was there at the end?" she asked.

He danced with her, rubbed her knees, and asked about her dress. They each inhaled another two white lines from his phone and watched Lake Michigan chop at the shoreline all the way from Chicago to Gary, Indiana, where the blast-furnace refineries glowed orange on the lake from the flare-offs.

Freddy rubbed his forehead and pressed fingers into his eyes.

"Old people, sick people, looking for a cure that couldn't be bought. A crippled old lady, older than him, brought him books and papers. Hermetic, something. I mean, these people were goners. The old lady had some professor of alchemy with her. I think he wanted to feed her a solid-gold diet.

"Hermetic?"

"The League? The Hermetic Circle? Maybe? That old lady was sharp. Rich too, at least as rich as Bill was. People will pay millions to buy something that doesn't work just to live another few weeks. I think she died too. I don't know what happened to that professor."

"Who got his books?"

Freddy shook his head. No way. "It's at the Gnostic Auction. You need a golden ticket just to get in. And those are not possible to get..." Freddy snapped his hands up, putting his fingers in his mouth.

She rubbed her fingers along his face. Freddy pressed his hands against her neck, her chest.

Freddy licked his teeth and Sophie pulled all the cash from his wallet along with his business cards. He tilted his head and asked a question. Sophie slapped him, hard, across the face and shoved him onto the bed. She pulled his shirt away, holding Freddy down playfully, squirming between her knees as she plucked her dress up past her hips.

Freddy read the tattooed words from her thigh to her ribs out loud. "It was just Blue Moonlight, when she escaped from the skylight." He rubbed his palm across every bright scripted letter and asked her what it was from.

"It's from a book," Sophie said.

"Sounds like a mystery. What is the book about?"

"Saving my life."

Freddy smiled. "Maybe I could read some more?"

Freddy ran his finger across the letters on her body. He asked her who was trying to escape.

"I am."

Sophie shuffled along Freddy's body until her thighs were beside his neck. She pulled her panties aside and pushed his forehead down. He breathed against her and started, and she ground her thighs against him. She undid her blue dress, and it bunched down against her belly and Freddy reached up to grab at her tits and stretched her bra out and she yanked at his hair and he licked her and pulled at her with his tongue.

Freddy was staggered. She fed him, licked and kissed him across the face like a bear cub before fully undressing both of them herself. He went to her, holding her belly with one hand and her thigh with another.

The room cast about with golden lights and the echoes of street horns and sirens and shouts from two hundred feet below. She put a hand on his collar, and he had to be shown how to grab her hair and tug and he jammed her and she yelped free and they found the angle and pressed and pressed and he pressed and gasped.

Freddy was flash wired from the coke and Sophie got his face with both hands and looked him in the eyes. "Easy," she said. "Easy, easy, follow me." She led him in rhythm with her body, her whole body from her shoulders to her foot against his calf. Freddy gasped as Sophie slowed him down easy, slow, and he put his glossy face against her pale neck as he tried to say something, anything, as he finished.

Sophie poured them another drink, naked and reflective in the night.

She looked back at Freddy, rubbing his eyes even in the darkness. She crushed an Ambien into the vodka and ice. She fed Freddy again. His teeth were clicking, and she could hear them. His eyes bounced bloodshot.

"Are you ready to go again?" Sophie asked and rubbed his legs as he sipped and tilted the glass.

"I'll need a minute," Freddy said.

"How did he get those wounds?" Sophie asked.

He took another drink. Sophie saw his pupils go wide.

"You know, it's terrible to talk this way about patients. I'd only ever seen fistulas when radiation treatments go screwball. It is OK to tell you this, right?"

"It's OK, baby." Sophie had him marooned in the ocean now, floating in the rogue waves, oarless, hopeless.

"Those weren't wounds. You know I started to believe him."

Freddy blinked hard against it now. Sophie rubbed his feet and could feel them go slack.

"About the book?"

Freddy nodded. "He would sleep and, uh, those... Jesus, you know you're the only one I've... the only one who ever... those wounds would talk to me. Those wounds on his body. They knew my name, Sophie. They told me things nobody could possibly know."

"Did he ever show you the Book of Blue Daggers?"

"He said he stole it. He laughed about it. Laughed about it. Stealing it." Freddy spun like a compass and realized what he was trying to say. "The wounds laughed too."

"Why did he laugh, baby?" Sophie asked.

"Did you really know Bill Dillinger?" Freddy asked.

"Of course not, rockstar. Why don't you tell me where his pretty little books went?"

"Oh, an... auction... in Vashon... Howard Cyone is still in charge," Freddy said.

"Vashon?"

"Yeah. Vashon Island. Gnostic Auction."

Just before he passed out, Freddy realized what was happening and stood diagonally. He looked straight ahead with a sad look at Sophie.

"Why would you do this to me?" he asked.

"Only straight men think just because someone fucks them, they aren't going to hurt them."

Freddy didn't stand a chance. He hit the carpet hard.

He was damp, and he mumbled and tried to fight it. He made little yawning sounds and tried to turn himself over. Sophie put a pillow against him and turned him on his side, putting an ear next to his mouth to figure he was breathing steady enough.

Sophie went right to it and pressed his fingers against the release on his phone. She used the camera on her phone to screencap the emails of anything related to AUCTION, VASHON, CASINO, BOOK, DAGGER, DILLINGER, HOWARD CYONE.

It took her 45 minutes to take 346 screencaps. She cracked open Freddy's phone in the sink and turned on the water. She watched the battery cook off and the screen bleed out.

On the back of one of Freddy's business cards, Sophie sketched herself as an Arcana high priestess, windblown braids twisting past her shoulders, the flat look like something from stained glass. In one arm, she cradled the Book, emanating stark yellow cones of light, as the other hand grasped the light to show that nothing could burn or harm her.

With a pack of matches from the bar downstairs to light the card on fire, flipping it as the flame ate it to ash in her palm.

The blue smoke snaked between her fingers. As she held the last of the cloud inside her palms before releasing it upwards, she said, out loud, "This will be the last thing you ever let slip through, Sophie, do you understand? This will be the very last thing."

# CHAPTER FOUR

*The Sum of All Perfection*

## HIGHLANDS, SEATTLE, WA October 17

It wasn't suicide.

He had a knife in his hands when he died and there was blood loss, but Howard Cyone assured Sophie that Bill Dillinger didn't kill himself.

"Coroner had no issues whatsoever on this. We put Bill's ashes into Puget Sound weeks ago. Why are there still questions about this?"

He squinted at Sophie with his pale blue eyes and blinked and started scrubbing his glasses again.

Sophie handed Howard a card and Howard moved it at distances between his eyes to read and said.

"Sophie Dansky, Auditor, Mallinckrodt Pharmaceuticals."

Her pantsuit and yellow scarf were still stiff from the rack and scratched at her pallor skin. Sophie had a fever at the collar.

Sophie Dansky was an illusion—a malleable sketch the genuine Sophie could modify, erase, or embellish at will. The portrayal masked her blue-tinged fingertips and feverish bruises, yet beneath the facade, it was still powered by the same bad blood, the same Sophie decay.

Sophie reeled off prescriptions. Dexamethasone, diazepam, the spectrum injections of cortisone, dapsone, prednisone. Freddy remedied Bill Dillinger with thirty-six different methods, including eighteen pills, two powders, six different types of injections, a gelatin 'skin' that dissolved under his tongue, two bitter mists and inhalers, three flavored oral elixirs, two creams, four ointments, and two gels. The remedies failed. For his skin. For his pain. For when the sclera in his eyes grew infected.

"Creams and ointments are different?" Howard asked.

"A critical distinction. Cream differs by being a medication suspended in an emulsion of water and oil. An ointment being suspended in hydrocarbons, most often white petroleum. A gel is suspended in a transparent cellulose ether," Sophie said.

"Well, I never knew that. Not until now." Howard smiled. He was tall, thick and had pale, alert eyes under a buzzcut and steel frames, like an astronaut who gained too much weight.

"Are you alright?" Howard asked.

Sophie worked her vision back. Something clamped to her brain behind her eyes when she peed blood like tomato paste in the morning and hadn't shaken loose yet. It squeezed her senses so tight she could hear the click of Howard's teeth and smell the coffee on his breath from six feet away.

"It's necessary for me to see exactly where it happened," Sophie said.

"Is Mallinckrodt concerned the prescriptions might have had some kind of effect on Dillinger's behavior? It's a legal fact that he didn't commit suicide."

"The correct phrasing is died by suicide. Committing it implies crime," Sophie said. "In any case, that isn't our concern at all."

"Well...then what is the concern?" Howard asked.

Even as Sophie Dansky she still wanted to break the illusion and stop this bullshit and shatter Howard's spider-egg skull. Watch his knowledge scatter like hatchlings. Faster. Quicker. Tell me, Howard, I'll read your mind as it flops around on eight newborn legs.

"The only thing anything is about money. He had a niece. He had a nephew. Our concern is if they decide to take a tour into litigation against Mallinckrodt." Sophie made a blocking motion with her hands. "I need to know what they will find."

"Dr. Fred Nolan was a good man. A good doctor. If you want me to sign my name to that, I will."

"We believe Dr. Nolan is a physician in good standing. It may be discovered, however, that he has serious substance abuse issues. He could be leveraged to say some medications were not as safe as believed for Mr. Dillinger."

Howard got fed. Ladled. Doped. Duped. He gulped in everything that Sophie fixed up: insurance investigations, pharmaceutical litigation protection, Hatch - Waxman Act Amendments. A bottomless appetite. Sophie poured out all flavors of lies and Howard drank it up and agreed.

Yes. Of course, he concurred. Sophie should see the house.

"Yep. Let's go check it out."

They took I-5 north. Seattle was in the first quarter of eight months of dim skies and constant drizzle. The black-rimmed clouds were just bullies, always threatening a downpour but just teasing, poking, mocking with flakes and sprays. A crooked screen of mist hung for miles from the sky, the same color as the clouds, the sea, as far as Sophie could see.

They snail-paced it north with the last slips of light cutting over Howard in the driver's seat. They pulled off to the darkness underneath the crowns of ponderosa pine and Douglas fir and through the alley shade of country-clubs, wooden fences, and cedar dust.

In a security hut well beyond the city streets, Howard handed his driver's license to a watchful officer. The man grinned, inserting the card into a scanner's plastic feeder slot. As it hummed and chirped, he jotted down some details. Howard's ID materialized on the monitor, and with a smile, the officer raised the boom gate and waved them through.

"He moved here in 1997?" Sophie asked.

"He moved in back when you got your mail just delivered to the neighborhood itself. True privacy, all your mail and bills written to Mr.-and-Mrs. So-and-So, The Highlands, Seattle Washington. They had runners take it to everyone's house until Homeland Security told them that was a no-no. Water, sewer, roads — that's one hundred percent run by the homeowner's association. They don't want *anyone* in here that doesn't belong."

"This is how you're telling me Bill wasn't well liked?" Sophie asked.

"Past few years, his neighbors thought he had something to do with the taste of the water around here," Howard said.

"Did he?"

Howard shrugged.

"Neighbors said it smelled like wet laundry. Some kids found some fish with see-through scales and blind eyes. This neighborhood was more than happy to move on. Particularly with such a... premium site. That's it there." Howard pointed as they pulled into a long, straight drive.

Through the minimalist haze, the glass and limestone mansion stood defiant, all sharp angles and chrome pitch line. It breathed urban sophistication, a sanctuary etched in steel and secrets.

Howard parked in the driveway and stammered something about the garage still being full. He leaned at a keypad and shined a light from his phone and squinted to tap the numbers.

The garage lights popped onto a warehouse of metal racks and plastic totes. The place smelled to Sophie like an antique store, one big cloud of furniture polish and decaying books, decades-old wool and warm vinyl. She walked by a rack of Daguerreotypes in hinged brass frames open to the blue light, a hundred sad and still faces pressed flat against silver and shadow. Walnut framed racks held octagonal steel film reel canisters marked "SILENT 1915-1925" next to a lineup of foam zipper cases marked MERCURY, COLD IRON, COPPER, AQUA FORTIS, and FIRE.

"This is it. You want to get your picture here?" Howard asked.

"No. Our regulations require seeing exactly where the incident occurred."

"Incident? Is that what you want to call it?"

"Howard. We know he died in the house. I need you to show me precisely where this occurred."

Howard swallowed. He was trying out sentences with airless words. He clicked his fingernails over the cuts and valleys of a key. He whispered something and used the key on the door to the main house. He turned the key and stepped aside. He handed her a flashlight and asked her to go first.

"Bill's illness was a very difficult time. We did our best to accommodate his needs."

Inside was a desperate hoard. Wall-to-wall and tall enough to black out the sunlight on the peaked high days in the summer months. Sophie walked over and tilted the huge triangle of shadows in her flashlight beam. Look at these despairing works.

Ten thousand borosilicate flasks rubber plugged and filled with blood-dabbed cotton, the shavings of abraded wounds, and baby teeth. Shoulder-high trays of dental equipment, medical shears, and dull forceps. A soft marathon distance of ace bandages, gauze, and fresh bandages. A mycelium of family tree photographs, oil portraits, calligraphy names, blurred faces, military records, the farthest strands dim with tintype emulsions and acid-sapped black and whites.

The desperation was taped off, boxed off, and regimented into walkable columns with orange construction tape. Sophie stopped at a pyramid of trunks: billiard balls, bracelets, clock faces, salt and pepper shakers marked "BAKELITE 1930-1940."

"I thought if we organized it, maybe it wouldn't look so bad," Howard said.

"Why does it smell like it just rained in here?" Sophie asked.

Howard didn't answer. He pulled up tape marked COPPER WIRE 1990-1995, spooling it like a bandage around his thumb.

Sophie had the scent. She closed her eyes and inhaled rainwater on dry earth, a wet lakeshore just below them. The clamp behind her eyes throbbed, and she closed one eye to keep her vision steady.

Sophie stripped construction tape from the molding of a door at the far end of the room. The five-foot strap of tape made a yawning noise as she peeled it off. She dropped the dry sticky length of it and rubbed the adhesive from the tape to a dark slot between her palms. She turned the knob and breathed in the dark, pulled from the basement steps.

The air came alive with something out of deep seasons. The basement air so heavy and wet she had to press through the darkness. You would expect roots. You would expect the sparks of amphibian eyes.

Battery powered flashlights were rigged to the walls in circuits. They still couldn't trust electricity here. The wall sockets, switches, and the heating vents had been crowbarred out, duct-taped closed. Sophie bumped against a black rubber hose; a wet brass end big enough to hold her whole fist inside. The carpet still slick with water across her footsteps.

The dead remains of a hundred ostrich ferns, monstera plants, the hollow husks of philodendron vines crowded the edges of every last wall, browning to mush, the high leaves brown and smacking at the air. The silhouette of dinner-plate sized leaves sank etched into the paint, trailing veins of blue mold in arcs that sprouted from corner spores. Howard placed his hands to the three yellow strands where the basement was refilled. "Here, here, and here," he said. "Thirty inches, maybe thirty-three."

"What is this place?" She asked.

"Ah, I guess you found where he died. Welcome to the Verdant Pool."

A black scour mark coiled out under a half-inch of water. Burned through to the slab. Sophie put her hand to the scorch marks. She could feel the heat from the echo of the burn that first blackened the concrete.

Howard pulled over two wooden boxes and rafted them onto the carpet. "If you sit steady, you won't slip."

He put his glasses on and squinted hard and nodded. He got on his knees and sighed as he looked at the black coil on the carpet. He clapped the water from his slacks and tried rubbing his hands dry. He pointed at the blackness and nodded.

"What the fuck is this place?"

Howard nodded. He went white. He needed time. He soaked his shoes in the tide of the carpet.

"It wasn't just Bill Dillinger, was it? There were others, weren't there?" Sophie asked.

"What?" Howard asked.

"Dr. Fred Nolan told us that Bill Dillinger had gone far beyond the realm of science and medicine."

Howard took a deep breath and wiped his eyes and said, "Oh, my god." He had to clear his throat so he wouldn't talk in a whisper when he got going.

Howard shook his head. "They thought they could find the Philosopher's Stone. Turn their bodies back to gold," Howard said.

"Who were they?"

"His terminal friends in The Hermetic Circle. They thought that the cure would come from before the age of reason, so it didn't need to be a thing created from reason."

"Everyone was terminal?"

"They either went to hospice or joined The Hermetic Circle, you understand? I watched them trade pictures of bone tumors and fibrosis scars. A goddamn show-and-tell with their transplant stitches. But Bill, and the old ladies, started finding knowledge. Books, through books of knowledge. The Sum of All Perfection by Gerber. Of the Perfection of All Mastery by Jabir ibn Hayyan. The works of Hermes Trismegistus."

"Alchemy? They were trying to save themselves by turning lead into gold?"

Howard laughed. "Lead into gold was for the short-sighted. Alchemy is about knowledge. Turning your dumb leaden body into a perfect, untarnished being much like gold."

Sophie lied and said: "This is superstition, Howard. It's nothing but a fantasy that people have been chasing since they first put ink to paper."

"He found the secret, Sophie."

"Which was?"

"The Book told him to build this place. It told him how to assemble the ingredients and create the Verdant Pool right here in his basement." Howard stamped at the water, making splashes with his shoes.

"You didn't trust it, did you?"

"None of us trusted it. Dillinger was the only one the Circle trusted to read and not.... get... tricked!"

Sophie had the same diamond-bit boring into her bones. Oh, was there that same coal blaze of disease that cooked so deep and burned marrow-low in these two bodies? Both of their bodies had broken faith in them. They sought answers elsewhere. Dillinger got preyed on. Dillinger fell for it. Sophie wouldn't fall for it. Couldn't fall for it. Never, ever would, not even with her blood turning black.

"Tell me what happened to the Book, Howard."

Howard grinned. Howard's blue eyes reflected brightly in the reflections of the room. Howard said he would show her. He cleared his throat, grunting through what he'd never told anyone ever before.

"I hired a pair of thieves to steal it. The three of us snatched it from a neurosurgeon's house. I never took a look. I never read a word."

Howard walked to a soft patch of drywall and crumbed it away with his fingers. He tore off a foot-long square with his hand. Sophie could see the mold-slick wood braces behind it as Howard reached in.

"You know, Sophie, I never read one word of it. I was too frightened to even glance at it. But it must have gone airborne. I know how things work now." Howard smiled loopy, his glasses foggy from his sweat. "You aren't here from Mallinckrodt."

"Howard, I'm just here for informa-"

Howard reached shoulder deep into the wall, grimacing, sticking his tongue out as he gripped and tugged at something deep inside the wall.

"I know what the Book does, Sophie! I saw it creep into Dillinger's brainstem and I won't let that happen to me. I-N-F-E-C-T-I-O-N." Howard pointed two fingers just between his eyes, above the bridge of his nose.

"The Book of B-"

Howard ran from the wall and bounced into her, his wet body across her. Sophie tumbled off the raft and onto the wet carpet. Howard put a cold, wet hand across her mouth.

"Cancer?" Howard asked.

Sophie shook her head. This was the first time she ever told anyone at all. "My body... I don't mean to, but I'm destroying my own blood. I don't have much time left to-"

Howard said, "Don't say it. Don't let it know. I won't let it do to me what it did to Bill."

Sophie nodded. She stood. She huddled. She was wet all the way to her shoulders, the water bunching up and dripping off her hair and off her knees.

"The Book lied to him, Howard. It tricked him, it killed him."

Howard was at the wall again. "That's where everyone is wrong! Once they found the uranium rods, I knew I had to do something. When I saw that radiation glowing blue underwater, I packed the Book off to the Gnostic auction. That color will never come back to me."

Howard tore his shirt at the cuff as he unspooled something thin and dark from the hole. Howard was close to the stairs. His arm clutched in the wall like a man reaching for something on a high shelf. He was pulling and dragging, and Sophie moved to the stairs. She saw a stiff white wire crooked like a rubber wand in his hands and she knew she wouldn't make it in time.

"I never said its name or read a single word! I saw what it did to Bill. I won't let that happen to me."

Sophie was soaking, standing in a puddle the size of the whole room. She could see clearly what Howard held in his hand, dangling the crooked ends of the live wire inches above the slime-soaked floor.

"Howard, don't-"

"I got wise to the plans between the pages, Sophie. I know how it works. If you're here, it's because it wants you to be."

Howard pulled the cable rigid. He slid a wooden raft over with his shoes and tiptoed onto the edge. He waved his arm for balance. The split copper fangs of the wire dangled at his fingers.

"I won't let it trick me," he said, and he offered the blue hissing end of the line onto the wet carpet. "Not again."

The basement flashed as white as the daylight sun. A finger of wattage clamped against Sophie's knees and flickered her body into a raft. Even with her eyes shut, Sophie could see the electric outline on Howard's body, disintegrating his watch and eyeglasses with a steaming hiss as his body glowed blue and split along at a thousand-degree seam before a grinding pop knocked him smoking to the shore of the carpet.

The boiled basement smelled like a noon riverbed and Sophie blinked her way to the stairs.

Sophie stumbled through assembled years of tape and hoards and found a door in the wall of glass and then lay outside on a soft round of green, the amperage shaking from her skin and knitting the stars from her eyes into the sky above, still unsure of the day or night.

She had the plan now. She had seen what the Book of Blue Daggers was capable of. She twitched and shook and gasped and worked it around in her head; the electricity squeezing her body, but with her mind boundless, as she fit the pieces together.

# CHAPTER FIVE

*The Purchasing Agent*

## MEDFORD, OREGON October 19

Lake shook off the rain. He wiped the fog and spots from his glasses with his fingers.

Lake spotted Davis Muth at the counter, paying for a cup of coffee with a pile of coins stacked as high as his cup. Davis sported white sneakers, Wranglers, and a shirt tucked in excessively high, cinched with a braided belt up near his ribs.

It was raining like hell and the entrance mat was soaked to the point of spilling. Muth squinted past Lake and pointed to the highway.

"That drive, OK?" Muth asked. He grabbed a table close to the window.

Lake got his glasses clear and pushed his dark hair back. Lake was tall, good looking, but bunched his arms and head real tight to his chest. He looked at Muth over the top of his glasses and talked low so no one would see the cracks and gaps in his teeth.

"Highways are fast, but it isn't a good tradeoff," Lake said. "Did you know every single interstate in this country is built on Indigenous Hunting trails? And where do you think those trails came from, hmm? Those paths were carved hungry for blood, and they don't care where they get their next meal," Lake said.

"I'll keep that in mind," Davis said.

"I had to drive a stretch of California Highway 99 yesterday that had a fatal crash density of 1.06. Driving is bad news, Davis. I-35 in Texas, my god. They drew the map right down to the fault lines of the Comanche borders. The bumps in the road feel like skulls and bones. Stick to local roads."

"You brought the IDs?" Davis asked. "You came through?"

"Those bad luck miles add up Davis. I'm serious. Stay off the big roads when you deliver it to Roy Parwanni. He'll thank you for it."

"You got everything he wants?"

"Driver license blanks, 50 California, 50 Washington, 50 Oregon, 30 Idaho. There's a big Fargo resin printer in there. The pdf templates are on a USB stick with the software. It's plug and play, and he can roll as many more blanks as he needs to."

Lake handed Muth a California ID of a dead-perfect data clone named Michael Weather.

"You said he's using this shit to open PO Boxes?"

Muth rubbed the ID with his fingers. "Something like that. Deliveries to his clients in a discreet brown box just aren't going to cut it anymore." Muth winked. "Is this you in Cali?"

"That's me. Michael Weather died in 1975 and owns the Ford, owns clean plates, clean history. I just Frankensteined him together out of data scraps and blind alleys of DMV dot CA."

Other than the shared lace bracelet of scars around their wrists that traced down their fingers, Weather wasn't much more than the slacks-and-golf-shirt version of rockabilly-lite Lake Bright. Their height and weight match, both so tall and slim that their shoulders slumped like a jacket too big for its hanger.

"Let me get my truck. Let this rain wear off."

Muth yanked his jacket close and hustled into the cab of his Chevy. Lake watched him flip the wipers and lights, and he surveyed the scene—a misty pine canyon, the quintessential Oregon snapshot with miles of highway flanked by rain-drenched trees.

Lake's phone pinged again. His breath tightened and his hands shook. The scars on his wrist itched. He squeezed his wrist with his hand and rolled and rubbed it and worked it down to a red bracelet of foamy skin. He could still hear the tendons click years after the bones were reset by a prison doctor's best efforts, which wasn't much effort at all.

The wireless at Starbucks moved slow, slow, slow when Lake resolved it through the TOR. Lake was nothing if not secure, even in the middle of proverbial nowhere, hiding his logins through a few dozen layers of routers, VPN's, and trick-shot satellites.

Muth was still in the cab of the Chevy outside, waiting out the rain.

He didn't jinx it. Asher wrote him back.

*"Dad. I appreciate you reaching out. I appreciate you attempting to find ways to heal, reflect, and change your ways. I hope that you understand how beneficial this will be to you, primarily. I do not need your shadow in my life, but I am willing to believe that mutual benefit may still exist for us, now that all matters, legal and financial, are settled.*

*First, I want to let you know that I have changed my name. I did so shortly after the trial, along with getting a new social security number, for obvious reasons. I will always be Ash to you. I understand that. Second, I want to tell you that although I am willing to write, I find myself being angry with you. Your inability to explain and fully grasp the damage of what you did will always result in frustration, anger and difficulty for me. Please understand that this can only be fixed with time.*

*I have been living here for a year. I have roommates. I tell them everything. We agree that I should move to the next step and write this to you and see what comes next."*

And Another. Minutes later.

*"I've given thought to your suggestion that we talk over the phone (although you call this "in person"). After discussion with my emotional partners, I feel that this may be a good decision that we can move forward with. You MUST adhere to the rules that we have set. You MUST understand where I am in my life. Tell me you understand that this will be a slow process, and I will get to the next stage with you."*

Lake skimmed the lines a dozen times. He could read them with closed eyes. He closed the wireless and browser and cut the nodes and stacks. Socked the battery and MAC. Did the best he could, but he was floating.

Muth waved at him. The rain had let up enough.

Lake pulled his Ford around. Lake reminded him to keep on county roads, back roads, that anything with more than a stop sign was pushing it, and that this was the price of Manifest Destiny. He keyed open the latch on Muth's cargo bed and lifted the cargo boxes with the blanks and the printer into it.

"Is that the whole bunch?" Davis asked.

"You set the printer up on a private network and Roy Parwanni will be a one-stop shop. These things will work at airports, PO Boxes should be..." Lake whistled.

"Our friend Roy may be hustling some boomers who don't know any better. These are all for retirees and old people who don't want deliveries tracked."

"The elderly? I didn't know Roy was that desperate for hustles."

Davis smiled. "Well, you sure got back into this as fast as you could."

"I'm making up for lost time, Davis. Trying to catch up with my son."

"Yeah, I can imagine prison was a setback. I heard you rode horses there. Is that for real?"

"Yeah, it was pretty good at the camp. At the camp, everyone was a quiet-timer who were usually on their first real fuck up and doing good-boy time until the day they clocked."

"I heard Jared from Subway was there."

"Yeah," Lake nodded. "So was the guy who directed Die Hard. That CIA snitch, LeGrand, whatever."

"Jared didn't get knifed or anything? I thought Chesters always get cut up?"

"Jared hung out with the rest of the kid-skin crew, so that's like 8 guys. He stayed clean, but he couldn't buy a fucking nod or the time of day or an extra honey bun for a million dollars. Lowest man on the totem pole for twenty years, no exceptions."

"So, how did that happen?" Muth nodded at Lake's hand. His weeping brace of sores. Lake covered it with his hand and looked out at the traffic.

"I got a message from my son. You're cashing out on this. I want you to check where he's sending them from. You bring your rig?"

"Oh. Yeah." Davis put down the map. They bunched in tight in Muth's front seat. Davis had this heavyweight Windows ThinkPad with a jump box and rebuilt fans. Lake showed him the message and Davis read through it while he waited for his VPN to route through.

"Asher sent two messages, one at 11:08, one at 11:27," Lake said.

Davis worked fast, cracked fast. He sifted gold from the digital feed.

"Asher, your son, sent those messages from Southern California."

"Los Angeles? Asher is in LA?"

"Los Feliz. Unless he's trying to be a tricky fucker and bounce them around."

"Los Feliz. Jesus, those highways. The 405..." Lake put a hand on his head and looked out the windshield in a daze.

"Let's get his address. We can do that. Easy."

"It's been six years. I'm not pushing it." Lake shook his head. "Nope."

"You let your kid set the rules? Fine by me. Got a couple of numbers you can call."

"His cell?"

"Two of them, that ping local. Call in case of Emergencies, c'mon."

Muth wrote down two numbers. LA area codes, both of them. Lake tucked them away.

"I'm doing this thing for Roy so I can set him up a college trust. He'll never have to ask me for money, nothing. A man provides for his children."

"Roy put you in with Barbara Bontecue. You need to send him a thank you note."

"I'll thank Roy when I have something to say thank you for."

Muth took off into the rain with a trunk cascading with fraud and hundreds of federal, state and local felonies. Lake waved him off as he blinked off onto the highway, ignorant of the skulls and arrows, the elk blood, the human meat that would have been spilled across decades of dark paths gliding north and south.

The rain came on again and was pounding. Lake looked for different ways to Seattle. Back country roads, he didn't mind the time. He marked a few dozen ways there, the map, a rickety staircase of country roads and nautilus sweeps of mountain drives that got him towards Puget Sound.

A call came in.

"Well, hello, Barbara Bontecue," Lake said.

"How is your drive, Lake?"

"Raining. I'm still driving."

"So, I have good news in regards to the opportunity! The purchasing party has given the OK on your price and payment method. I hope that you are ready to hit the ground running?"

"Yeah, I... you can guarantee my side will remain anonymous throughout this whole thing?"

"The buyer would appreciate your technological paranoia. Fortunately, in this case, you both insist on remaining anonymous."

"It's good we both feel that way."

"The partners at Zapata and Sweet exist to serve the needs of our clients, and this is a value we hold dear and true."

"Have you met this man or woman? Your delightfully eccentric and wealthy client?"

"Taylor and I have had zero on sites. Don't even know their real name."

"Is this shit for real, Barbara?"

"My initial engagement with this client involved crafting an agricultural patent. For nine months, I created the legal patent for a novel breed of genetically modified apples. The client, never one to settle, enlisted two rival firms to develop it—one in the Willamette Valley, the other in Tokyo. Today there are 44 trees growing the world's most exclusive apples. Whoever the client is, they've got a sense of humor. The NDA binds about every other detail, but if you want a bite at one, it's called Original Sin."

"Are they any good?" Lake asked.

"Original Sin? I'll be honest, it was the best apple I've ever had."

Lake got a ping. Something more special than the job at hand.

Asher wrote back. Asher wanted to talk. Lake read through while Barbara discussed Original Sin and hidden groves. Asher said he came to terms that his father deserved an *opportunity.*

*I believe that you deserve an opportunity to tell me your emotions. I believe I deserve an opportunity to tell you mine. I believe you deserve a chance. I believe I deserve a chance. I believe we both deserve a chance on equal footing.*

There were terms, though. Preconditions. Rules. The Asher order of engagements.

Lake's hand beneath the ring of scars went pins and needles, and he grabbed at it and flexed white against the air until the breeze brought the feeling back.

*I will give you a number. This is not my permanent number. If you agree to my conditions. That you do not press for detail, that you do not discuss mom in any way, that you do not ask where I am. That you do not discuss any financial or identifying matter of any kind, that you...*

"Lake, you there? Are you listening?"

"I'm here, yeah, I'm here."

"Good, because the client has redlined fundamentals."

Always more conditions. Always more rules. Someone had to get something straightened away before they could even have a conversation. Lake squeezed his eyes and breathed in deep as he sighed as quietly as he could.

"Sure, I'm here to please. Go ahead."

"The client's name must remain undisclosed to all parties. Their name cannot be used, and they must not be identified by name, data, code, alias, or any other designation in any written or transmitted form, on any physical or digital medium, or through any method of conveyance. No personally identifying information about the client can be written, signed, notarized, documented, logged, referenced, timestamped, or mentioned in any ancillary manner, in any form—be it electronic, financial, written, digital, or via any other medium that may emerge."

"That's all, huh?" Lake scratched at his bad wrist until the pain ground in.

"We can't have a contract, a record of the contract, a record of hours billed, calls made, subcontractors used, and any of these records, names, billings, notes cannot be written, signed, notarized, logged, or even referenced in an ancillary method, in any form, whether electronically, financially, in writing, digitally, or any other medium that may arise."

"What am I the purchasing agent for?"

"A book. If we had the ability to notarize with exact language, you are purchasing a very rare and/or obscure manuscript obtained via a live auction process."

"A book? You couldn't find someone else for this?"

"You are the someone else."

So there Lake was. The someone else. Lake's hand flooded heavily with color, and he realized himself fully. The tertiary aide, the trusted name who could move A to B to C. Even if they weren't able to write it down, Lake was the name above the fourth or fifth arrow on a flowchart between two goals. Just some guy. The answer when the boss asks for someone just good enough. A former client they'd worked with. Someone else after choices #1 and #2 called in sick, weren't available that day. Lake was the safe and the boring, the good call, the easy hire at cheap rates. The check-him-off-and-move-on guy.

Lake ended the call and his hot hand shook. He could feel the weather clouds breaking up just beneath the ring of scars where the bones didn't heal. A fluid packet between the welds of the bones filled in and out with the rising pressure of sun and rain.

He didn't care what Asher wanted. He agreed.

*Yes. Yes, I will.*

He'd agree to anything now. He shot north on the highway, oblivious to the carnage beneath the wheels.

# CHAPTER SIX

*Yamantaka Thangka*

## SAN FRANCISCO, CALIFORNIA October 20

Sophie was swimming through pink clouds, and landed glazed from the sky on turquoise sand, when the driver woke her up. Hugo was barking and asking which section of the apartment was hers. He couldn't find the numbers and pointed every which way, saying everything here looked the same.

It was a good dream but a bad time to wake up. Sophie almost told him Unit 5 before stopping herself, seeing two SFPD metro Chevy Tahoes with the badges and lines stripped off. They'd made the trace from Douglas and Annie back to her sooner than expected.

Sophie said "No, turn around. Keep driving."

Hugo, the driver, pulled up by the family-friendly pool. A family splashed in the two-foot family friendly pool pad. A freckled dad and his girlfriend racked solo cup mimosas on weekend visiting time.

"What are you doing? Go, drive!" Sophie shouted.

The plans were disintegrating. She had it all figured out, and the figures were all figured wrong.

"Take me here, right now!" Sophie pulled up Roy Parwanni's address in the Mission District. Parwanni would freak out. Fuck his schedule.

"You wanted me to drop you off," Hugo said. He put it into park. He pulled up the app and pointed at Sophie's destination.

Tahoe's had dark windows, long antennas, lift-kits, obvious if you took a second glance. A uniformed officer with half-bar Oakley sunglasses and a plainclothes detective talked and pointed with the lady in the management office. The lady in the management office pointed out the window past a sign that promised 1BR 2500 wk! FURNISHED!

Roy Parwanni wasn't texting back. Sophie was talking fast, and Hugo pinched his face as angry as a cartoon lemon.

"Keep fucking driving." Sophie held Parwanni's address in the Mission district. "Change of plans! Put it in reverse!"

"You can't speak to me that way. Our ride is over! Thank. You!" Hugo said.

"Oh my god, look, can you..." Sophie fumbled on her phone, trying to re-up Hugo for another ride. She cratered him with one-star ratings, bad comments, and tried to beg him digitally.

Hugo's phone dinged with displeasing reviews, angry stars, and beeps. "That is enough ma'am, please leave!"

An officer with a Velcro-stripped bulletproof vest crossed his arms at the back of a Tahoe. Two more strutted out by the box-crusher and dumpster at the trash dump next to the units.

"Will you just drive? Just fucking drive! What is difficult about this concept?"

Hugo had opened the door, and Sophie was peeling off cash to him. The family at the pool was dripping and staring. Hugo was shaking his head no, no, she was being too rude. Hugo set Sophie's suitcase at her feet and made a brushing motion, shuffling back to the driver's side.

The suitcase zipper sprang loose from the pressure as Sophie lifted it. The smell of damp clothes and Howard Cyone's scorched hair fell onto the pavement. Sophie grabbed just after them and shouted, "Fuck! FUCK!" over the noise of Hugo's tires skipping a U-turn back onto the big road.

The soggy kids pointed. A little dripping blonde girl said, "Uh oh." The weekend dad tilted his cup back, gulped and wiped his lips with a Spider-Man towel. He caught eyes with his girlfriend, who swept things into a bag and picked the little blonde girl up.

"Uh oh!" she said again, pointing at Sophie.

The officers made their way towards the entrance. The detective was on the phone already and the officer with the Oakley's tilted his head and was mumbling something about directions to the other two.

The manager of the place dug her fingers into her elbows and bit her lips. The officers strutted fast, brisk, double time, each on one side of the entrance street. Sophie waddled with a suitcase mess against her.

Sophie was out on the big road, hearing the officers behind her asking her something, telling her something, getting instructions on the radio for something. She dropped her clothes in bits and pieces, and they ignored it and still followed.

She was across the street where something called SIREN CONSTRUCTION had cored brick houses to flat slabs and pits.

Sophie walked over brick dust where a huge, sketched sign displayed slotted condos sky rising blue and gray and yellow, and of course 100% green. An officer keyed into his radio. The other took the long way around.

It took two blocks before Sophie was clear. She pressed her way into a Walgreens. She held the suitcase with one hand. She set it on the counter. She spun in a circle, dizzy at the blue-silhouette haze when she got out of the sunshine. She pushed a twenty on the woman at the counter.

"I think ... uh.... there are yellow jackets on the road!" Sophie said. She pointed towards the doors. "I'm allergic, oh goodness, I think I might be going into anaphylactic! I was waiting for my ride and they just... just..."

"Do you see these?" Sophie pulled her shirt down to her chest. Pointed at twisted scabs and boils. She pawed at her throat. She squinted her eyes. "I just need to use my epi-pen."

The woman slid her a silver key on a Walgreens lanyard. "I'll call for an ambulance," she said.

"Can I please use the restroom? I'm buying this water.... It's ok if I buy this right?"

"If you're...store policy says that someone comes in and-"

"Please, please don't, I just need to use my pen. I can't afford it. Please don't. Insurance! Promise me."

The woman nodded.

Alone in the restroom, Sophie layered paper towels over the drain. She poured the cold water on heavy and put her head at an angle under the spout. She poured the rest of the chilled bottle over her face. She was soaking. She filled the sink. She was a fucking mess.

She peed. The paroxysmal nocturnal hemoglobinuria had her pee run out pink and foam rimmed as strawberry syrup. She took a breath. She was dizzy. The metallic tilt of the blood in her piss was making her head go sideways. She leaned against the wall, guessing up from down.

She dunked her head below the cold-water line in the sink. She held her ears in the tinkling silence. She clamped her breath and waited. She could feel her body shifting as a blossom blue reflex took over, a cool dawn light racing to the farthest reach of every vein, nerve, and tendon.

She was fierce and her face was cold as winter in the mirror as she brought herself back into view.

Sophie wiped her hair back with a paper towel and dug into the half-damp suitcase.

Sophie found her sunglasses. She dumped everything on the floor. This was her place now. She was cold. Sharp. Braced. Her hair was dripping with thick beads. She pulled on and pegged her jeans. White T-shirt. She found paper, a marker.

Her reflection was stuck at terminal velocity. She couldn't stop the gravity and she was falling so fast there was nothing faster. The wind damage from freefall had rubbed her face raw. Her hair gorgon-snapped, her lips flayed. Sophie wrote her plans. She was wet from the water and sweat, and the shakes made it look like Sanskrit.

Sophie breathed deeply and took the paper and marker. She closed her eyes and drew without looking.

She drew herself barely more than a stick figure in a crowd of suppliants on their knees, The Book of Blue Daggers beaming from the sky on a gleaming bridge. The dream answered, delivered on a glowing belt just moments away from her outstretched little V fingertips.

Sophie cracked the door and peeked outside. A police officer with a vest was talking to the woman at the counter. The woman at the counter chewed her nails and pieced through a bangle of master keys.

Sophie twisted the faucet on full, hot. The cheap porcelain sink steamed and gurgled. She stuffed a shirt from her suitcase down the throat of the drain, already thick with paper towels. It was steaming up good, twirling off in hot loops onto the floor.

She slipped a thumb-thick stack of cash into a sandwich bag and rolled the bag airless and snapped it tight and lengthwise against her chest with her bra strap. She slipped out of the bathroom and snapped the key off in the lock and closed the door behind her.

An old man with a smock and reading glasses behind the pharmacy glass asked her four or five times if she needed help, and it wasn't really a question. Sophie grabbed a pair of thick, cloud-white orthopedic trainers meant for someone three times her age and gnawed off the security cord with a pair of nail clippers just off the shelf.

The old man was on the phone by the time Sophie was steady on the half-moon soles of the trainers, the Velcro straps tight.

The officer was shouting and knocking and working at the knob of the bathroom. His shoes were flooding in the stream and splashing in the water as it pressed under the door. He dialed into someone. He said to send an ambulance and shouted again for a key. He said in a cop voice he was taking the hinges off in fifteen, ten, "I'm losing my patience", five, three, one.

Sophie walked past an employee clock-in station at the back door and stepped into the flat sunshine.

A scrub wall of sweet fennel and ragged fencing separated Sophie from another set of shade. Sophie charged through the tall plants and high-stepped across the bent wire fences towards a Starbucks on the other side.

She could see SFPD and an ambulance flickering to the pharmacy. Sophie's arms and hair reeked from the pollen and black liquorice scent of the fennel and she called Celeste right there, stooped in the thin shade of the tall plants. Celeste Yang told her that she would be glad to see her again.

The SFPD lights popped a quarter mile away from behind the Starbucks window. Sophie watched them load tagged-up bags of wet clothes and an open suitcase and dripping paper towels into evidence tubs. The woman from the counter signed a statement on the hood of a patrol car. A regional manager in a red tie drove up and shook hands with officers and handed out business cards and free bottles of water for everyone including the bystanders.

Celeste waved at Sophie from the driver's seat of a fast German car. Celeste wore huge gold-rimmed aviators and a Balenciaga denim jacket, and even at her age she still looked as tiny as a teenage girl with an Amex Black Card.

Sophie hopped in the passenger side and held out a pink cake pop with a clown face.

"Hope you still like these?" Sophie asked.

"You always had admirable qualities, Sophie. An uncanny memory." Celeste smiled.

"Two years isn't that long. I want to see Roy; can you take me to see the man?"

Celeste had changed. Her right leg up to the thigh was a black carbon fiber prosthetic tucked into yellow snakeskin flats. She pulled away from the parking lot and the flashing lights, hitting the brakes and accelerator with hand-gripped poles bolted to the floor pedals. She pressed her palm for the brakes and slammed the turbo by pressing her thumb on a plunger like an enormous prop syringe.

Sophie nodded at Celeste's new leg.

"Last time I saw you..."

"Yes, well, my doctors had bad predictions. At least I kept my hip when they took the cancer out."

Celeste clicked French Tips against the top of her thigh, the carbon fiber popping just below her hip bone.

"The other one, ok?"

"For now. For now, at least." Celeste didn't seem so sure.

"At least, yeah."

"I'd ask how you are, but no one wants to see Mr. Roy when things are going great."

Celeste swirled, pressed the hand controls and steered one handed north across elevated San Francisco. Celeste swore at motorcyclists splitting lanes, close enough to rub their knees against the Mercedes.

"It's all Asia now. China, probably 80% exclusive."

"Two years ago, I was still getting relics from the Holy Land for Roy. Has it changed that much?"

"Follow the Yuan, and you'll find the new breed of Chinese billionaires truly stand apart. When you can afford anything, why settle for a superyacht or a Gulfstream when you could flaunt an artifact pilfered by the white man half a millennium ago? The concepts of culture and social standing hold a distinct significance there. You'd be astounded by the sums they're willing to shell out for items that can be traced back to the mountain village or valley town where their ancestors lived."

"I'd believe any price you told me."

"With you Sophie, I can imagine you would."

Celeste patted Sophie on the leg and cranked the turbo towards an offramp tunnel, the sound booming as they swept into the underground parking. Celeste pinned the Mercedes into a tight slot near the fire risers marked PERMIT ONLY - WILL TOW.

They were beneath the city, in one of Roy Parwanni's places. They took a yellow fire door marked NO ENTRY. They walked up concrete stairs braced by pipes that couldn't shake the city's smell of shit and steam.

They hit a white door atop a landing. Celeste pinged a keycard against the door, then released the thick deadbolt with a cylinder key. A cool, fragrant breeze welcomed them inside.

It was sparse. High ceilings caught the snap of Celeste fiddling with wax paper and bubble wrap. Celeste picked up a vase and showed off China, resurgent. A bronze monkey with alien eyes. A bronze rooster. A lacquer box.

Celeste smiled. "Oh, you'll like this one."

Celeste walked to a dim tapestry that lay bowed on a bent dais.

"That's Yamantaka. The Sackler family had him all wrapped up in a private gallery in Virginia."

"Roche and Bradon rolled this right up and walked it out of the gallery over Memorial Day. Buddhists say he's the master of death. Did you know that?"

The tapestry was fierce in red and gold. A wrathful and burning blue avatar spanned a timeless horizon. Hollowed skulls threaded with jewel-wire. Yamantaka stamped a hundred feet and blossomed a thousand sigiled hands.

"I love the colors on this. That blue is hundreds of years old and still such a... well, they say don't get attached," Celeste said.

"Roy is going to keep it for himself." Sophie said.

"You think so?"

"Certainly. This is Yamantaka. He destroys the ego and the fear of death. What's left is a perception of reality more profound, deeper, truer. You have escaped death and escaped the fear of death. So, what are you left with?" Sophie asked.

Sophie looked at Yamantaka's third eye, and a dozen other faces cracked beyond his blazing horns. His other faces shared cyclone eyes as they turned infinitely towards and away the highest and darkest flames.

"Freedom. Nothing left but the path to total enlightenment and awakening," Sophie answered.

"Ha, yeah, that's why I always liked you, Sophie. So easy to converse with."

Celeste's phone buzzed.

"He's ready," Celeste said. She walked past the blazing horns and feet of the deity and opened a door to a smaller office.

Incense burned and suffocated her senses. Roy was talking low on the phone. He was thin, hollow-cheeked, his eyes slim, pupils flicking constantly. In the years since she had last seen him, Sophie could see that something inside of him had been permanently dissolved away.

Underneath a triptych painting of Bellerophon suffocating the Chimera, a tall woman with knotted and white-dyed locs dabbed vetiver across Roy's jawline and rinsed his hair with Eucalyptus oil. She softly braided his beetle-dark hair into two laced plaits, laying them across his collar, black and glossy like narrow mandibles.

Roy stood, chewed on a honey stick and said, "Celeste told me you seemed sober, despite your appearance."

Sophie looked at Celeste, red blooming on pale cheeks.

"I remembered that you were never an addict." Roy waved towards Sophie's sweat, her fresh cuts and bruises, how she was still just gaining her breath back. "I remembered there were always your... life choices that made you look like this."

"We're not talking about how I look, Roy," Sophie said.

"It would have been polite to ask how I was feeling, Sophie. You haven't even seen me since my last surgical collaboration." Roy wore his cotton shirt loose, and Sophie could see flickers against a gray box with cords and lights, thickly taped just above his heart. A bolus autoinjector clicked to boost his white blood cells and autoimmune system.

"You changed your hair for Santa Rosa, didn't you?" Roy approached her. "May I?"

Before there was time to answer, Roy's thin hands slipped through her scalp, then his long fingers with nails buffed as pearls cradled behind her ears.

Sophie held his hand away from her neck. She took the cloudy bag of cash strapped to her body and put it in his hand. "That's seven thousand dollars. Bill Dillinger's books are going to the Gnostic auction. I want a seat."

Roy took his hands away from her head. He took a square of cloth and wiped his hands and said, "You still want the Book."

"I can get the Book, Roy. I want you to get me into the Gnostic Auction," Sophie said.

"You think the complexity of the thing determines its meaning. But it just isn't so."

"The Book is real. What it can do is real," Sophie said.

The tall woman returned to holding a wicker basket of fruit. Apples, white as eggs and spotted pink at the stem.

Roy took one and sniffed the stem, and nibbled at soft skin and flesh. The smell of toasted ginger and pear wafted across the room as amber and green lights on the monitor box taped to his chest flashed and blinked wild. Roy licked his red lips and smiled.

"Celeste?" Roy asked.

Celeste nodded. Roy underhanded an apple to Celeste, who caught it and immediately dug in.

"These are exclusive to a benefactor of ours. What does she call them?"

"Orithz-" Celeste started. "Ahem, Original Sin Varietal. Sophie, do you want one?"

Roy swept his hand at Celeste. He showed his teeth and moved his lips in an attempt to imitate a smile. "Sophie's here for one thing only, Celeste. You'll find she is too focused to sample the victuals that our visionary patron provides."

"You're too fucking coy and precious, Roy. I have the money. I want the Book."

Roy peeled translucent skin from the fruit in thin strands. "Sophie, of course, you know you weren't the first to discuss the Book with me. The Winters Brothers are on death row in Texas after what they did to that poor psychiatrist who told them the Book could open your third eye."

"They tried removing and replacing their occipital bones with 3D printed Lucite. I'm that stupid, Roy? They got tricked by the Book. I know how to read it. I've done it before and I'll do it again."

"The Book doesn't tell the future, Sophie. It just drives you mad because you think it does."

Sophie shook her head.

"I've seen it before, Roy. I've told you what it can do. It spoke to me. It was written for *me.*"

"This is your very best day to ask a favor of me..." Roy motioned to Sophie. "... and I can smell the cut weeds in your hair and the blood on your shirt. This day is so important to you, and this is the very best you can do?"

Celeste coughed.

"It *spoke* to me. *It let me know.*"

"Something can be difficult to find, or a map can lead you on an impossible journey. That doesn't mean anything lies at the end. The difficulty to acquire a thing is not proportional to the reward."

Roy plucked another apple from the basket, his face pouting at the scent.

"Your desperation used to be so much more subtle. I can smell the blood on you, Sophie. Are you peeing black yet?"

"I'm surprised you're able to keep that down, Roy. I heard they measured what they took out of you with a measuring tape and a butcher's scale."

"Ah, now, progress and honesty. Let me be honest with you, Sophie, I've already given the ticket to someone else. A premium price for an exceptional opportunity."

The weight of the room collapsed in on itself. Sophie could feel her insides calcifying, turning to stone right there in the smirking stare of Roy as he licked bits of pulp from his gums. He smirked and glared. Sophie took in short breaths as her lungs filled with concrete dust and her intestines flooded with caulk.

"What?"

"Even more than that, Sophie, don't you see that I'm doing you a favor? Sell you the ticket, my god, the stain would be irrevocable! The police would be thrilled for you to make such a blunder. You'd be in handcuffs the moment you stepped on the island; don't you see? You inflicted horrid violence on those shopkeepers in Santa Rosa. Those good citizens. Those taxpayers and business owners who had a much keener capability for covering their tracks than you."

"Fuck you, Roy."

"In your honest anger, you'll find that I'm doing you a favor. Imagine how angry you would have been with me, and how you would have blamed even Celeste when you found yourself in chains.

Truly, Sophie, I couldn't bear to play a part to see someone so... cunning die in a prison hospital."

Sophie was knee-deep in a rising tide. Naked in a field of tall grass, watching the red teeth of a predator flash parallel to the stalks. She listened to the wind that carried her wild and furious sweat, aching to her as an echo of her savior.

# CHAPTER SEVEN

*A Hanging Bridge*

## OLYMPIA, WASHINGTON OCTOBER 21

Davis Muth said he had important news. The couldn't wait stuff. The couldn't say over the phone stuff. He'd drive and meet Lake just for him to hear it right now stuff. They'd shake it out on the top floors of a parking garage in Olympia. Or some other lonesome place where people only went to do lonesome and obvious things.

Lake cleaned off his fresh sneakers. He had dropped ten pounds during work time in prison and his clothes made him look like a mannequin wearing a bedsheet toga. He was meeting with Barbara Bontecue later and was determined to look good. He did his best, buying two pairs of gray slacks, and two blue checkered shirts that he saw a model on the wall of a department store wearing. It looked good on him. It should look good on me, Lake figured. His shoes kept getting scuffed from the pavement and brake dust. Lake spit on a Kleenex and dabbed at the sides.

Muth waved at him. He was there earlier, parked by the fire stairs, vaping and exhaling cones of smoke, reading a GRAND BLUE DREAMING manga with one hand. His steroid-bulked out laptop pinged and beeped on the passenger seat of his Chevy, Muth jabbering on about the VPN and encryption stack and the swimsuit girls from the manga.

"I drove on the highway the whole way here, too, Lake. What do you think of that?" Muth grinned, wiggling his scraggly eyebrows.

"Accidents don't just happen. They occur exactly on schedule. You could ask James Dean or Dale Earnhardt, if you could ask them."

Davis Muth held his hands up. He rubbed his face.

"This is no fuckin' joke, Davis. A hundred years ago, they hung a man off the side of the I-5 in Centralia. You drove right by that. In 1919, Armistice Day. Hanged him, I mean. They killed him because he worked for the unions back then. You drove across that highway, and now you have bad news for me, don't you?"

"I have some things you need to listen to," Muth said.

Lake squeezed his fingers. His arm drooped and his fingers clicked when he floated them out. He twisted his neck, trying to get his breathing right as Muth opened up the audio files. It clicked wrong, just as bad as his fingers.

"Monty Boate is out. He's in a halfway house in Portland. That's across state lines, but... I'd expect he's going to prowl," Muth told him.

"They let him out?" Lake asked. "Why the fuck would they do that?"

Muth clicked on an audio file. A country-boy voice putting on manners spoke up, "... Be sure to thank you for this opportunity, ah, just... give me the schedule, I'm a good man with a schedule now, think that should be clear, yessir."

Muth put a hand over his mouth.

"My cousin Ashleigh works the release program. Her word is, Monty never stopped asking about you."

"That girl he torched has to use a wheelchair and a feeding tube. How the fuck is he out?"

"Well, you know, he's a really good liar, Lake."

"Our beef was all inside shit. It could have been on Mars. He has zero-point zero reason to still care."

Muth nodded. "Ashleigh told me Boate was 5150. That's the form they use to assign an involuntary psych hold. Boate is, categorically, not a rational person."

Lake put a blue-white hand on Muth's hand, the choked-out veins visible. Lake's hand was caught in cold days, windy breezes, never getting the weather right below the wrist.

Lake remembered when his hand was inflated to a purple egg with fingerprints. A clean-faced doctor who did weekend hours at FCI Englewood hot-lanced all five of Lake's fingernails. The fingernail bled the pressure away in jumping gushes until his hand deflated white. The doctor joined the screw plate to the wrong set of bones. The doctor said Lake should consider himself lucky anyway, after what Montgomery Lynn Boate did to him.

Lucky.

An earthworm tunnel bored through Lake's timeline. Right through it. Photos, medical records, and correctional officer sign-offs attested to his presence at the Federal Correctional Institute in Sheridan, Oregon, for countless dawn-and-dusk calls. Yet, Lake knew he'd spent that time trapped in darkness, his body pierced by wet dirt fragments and ensnared by willow roots, crawling through silt and loam. His arms and fingers, curled up from eons of blackness, radiated heat from the pressure and weight they bore. In those tunnels, he swiped and snapped his jaws in those dark recesses against the other creatures that lay dormant and scavenging.

"You went out-of-bounds when you fucked with his bank records. He figures it was you that got his ex-wife charged for insurance fraud. He thinks you broke the rules of play. Word is he worked every good day on his record so he could get 2-for-1 towards his release date."

"Does he know where I am?"

"Nope. Redneck cracker network moves fast though. How safe have you played it?"

Lake traced it in his head. There were a lot of loose strands all knotted up. Monty Boate had the time to untangle it, and reel the slack wire right to him.

"Does he know about Asher?"

"Not unless you told him. You thinking you should let Asher know?"

"No. He'll just... No. Where's Monty now?"

"He's in Portland. Northwest Region Re-Entry Center."

"Does Roy Parwanni know about this?"

"Not a peep. Roy isn't the type to care about this until Monty sends him a box of your choice cuts wrapped up, and then, only because he's a vegetarian."

"Think I can buy him out?"

Monty shook his head.

"Nah, even if you could, you got a meteor coming with your name on it."

Barbara Bontecue was working up a sweat. In a Marriott conference room that stretched the acclaim of being in the shadow of Mount Rainier, she switched, flexed and rode her knees against a bright orange resistance band. She asked for a yoga mat along with the day's catering and by the time Lake arrived ten minutes later; she was well into her cycle of stomach crunches.

"Lake, there's an asparagus farm at the base of Rainier. It's purple, it's raw, and if I insist on one thing, I insist on that."

Barbara was always bent at an angle, streaming the cruel inefficiencies away from her body through constant movement.

The Marriott staff slid silver service and white plates, trays of oysters, charcuterie, and purple asparagus onto the conference table. Barbara nodded at a dewy bottle of Riesling as one of the staff members silently slid the cork loose and set a stemless glass by its side.

Barbara lifted the top of her hydro flask. The battle against inefficiencies required perfect fluid ratios, and she spoke as she handed papers to Lake.

"Look, I hate to be a bother, but we specifically required zero TDS water. I cannot have tap or copper filtration."

She held the cap and the flask in two hands with a quizzical look on her face. The woman from the staff said she wasn't sure, but she could check.

"I'll need to come with you. Lake, read through those papers. You can sign when I return."

It was a quarter-inch of papers, half the paper's weight in Latin phrases and legal footnotes locking Lake into a contract unending.

The wording so abstract and convoluted he could barely understand what he was required to do. He flipped to the back section. The payout. The part where they gave Asher a college trust, cash money impossible to lose or take away, even if Lake fucked up again in and fell all the way down the mountain.

Lake's phone dinged.

Sophie.

*This is Sophie, hoping to catch up. Read 2 Corinthians 5:17, hope to study as soon as possible.*

Monty. Now Sophie. Best friends and worst enemies. What the fuck was going on?

Lake smiled. Sophie still remembered the keep-it-simple code and read Corinthians online. "The old has passed away; behold, the new has come." She needed a new identity. Lake tapped a pen against the metal in his hands. Wondering why? Why Monty today? Why Sophie now? Why when he was at the brink of this thing?

Lake remembered how Sophie always smelled like superglue, WD-40, fresh rubber. That she knew to stay off highways. How she always asked about Asher. How she dodged a court subpoena even when she knew every single trick Lake played out. How she never said a word.

Fuck it. He dialed the number back.

"Sophie?"

"Nice hearing your voice, Lake."

"You too. We've studied on that passage from Corinthians before, but it's a favorite of mine to study again."

"You're a lifesaver. You may figure I need guidance and clarity in my life right now, and I'm willing to do anything to get it. Look, I can drive to California tonight. I'll stay off the highways, maybe... sixteen hours."

"Where are you, Sophie?"

"Seattle."

"Small fucking world. Olympia. I can see Rainier right now."

"Jesus, what luck."

"Just teaching a Bible study course. Short term, focus on Romans."

"I see." Sophie picked up the words. "Ah, I see. You know Esme is here. She gave me this number. Why don't we-"

Years ago, Sophie and Lake orchestrated a staggering relay scam. Lake fabricated false titles, museum documents, and provenance papers for sacred swords, papal rings, and books of esoteric knowledge. He operated the tool and die shop. Sophie wielded the keen edge that split the honest folk from those who'd never confess to being swindled. The real scheme in their relay was ensuring the buyer stayed silent, even if they discovered they'd been on the bad end of a trick deal.

Their laboratory technique was to bubble down a credit limit that existed only in imaginations and potential and reduce it into a fine skim of cash, bills, and gold coins. The credit was summoned from nothing so much as aether itself and then into the laboratory bubblers and burners and then looped and coiled and cooled and schemed into anonymous drops and dissolved through stolen identities until the final formula produced a potent stream of tangible cash bills that poured out smooth and steady with a good crank of the handle. Crisp cash bills from the thinnest of air.

Barbara came back in with two flasks of water, which she declared "perfect", and read through the papers with Lake. She drank and drank. She excused herself twice while they went over things. She said she was training. For what, Lake didn't understand.

"Take a look. This is your contract. It's between you, me, and Taylor Zapata. This explains the Book, the purchase, and the parties who can discuss and transfer it. I'll translate anything you want."

Lake looked through them. "A proprietary agreement of silence?"

"It means you can't talk about it. You can't discuss, ask, write, or text about it. They even have language that covers something called media not yet ably described. That means if you use something that hasn't been invented yet, and in the future."

The document rendered him speechless. A dare to challenge an unearthed dire financial curse. If he spoke a word about it: an exorbitant price. A sentence: a fortune. A description of the purchase itself: an impossible fee. A full explanation: the sum of all money since the dawn of time.

"I told them you would be good for this. You were my idea, Lake."

"Give me the rundown on the payments."

"If you want twenty-thousand dollars into a Secure Bond trust for Asher, we need his information ASAP," Barbara said.

"I don't have it." Lake said.

"We can't send it into the trust without his social," Barbara said. "Are you afraid to talk to him?"

"No," Lake said.

Barbara picked up Lake's phone, winked at him. "I'm sure it's difficult, but unless you can find a compelling reason otherwise..."

Barbara went to the hall. Lake had the number.

"Hello, Dad." First ring.

"Asher, where, uh, where are you?"

"I'm in Southern California. I'm in College. I'm studying Graphic Design," Asher said. He sounded good.

"You sent me that link to your Instagram. Your stuff is... impressive. It's good you are working on the meaning more than the minutiae." Lake surprised himself with how easily he could say it.

"When I sent you that, I thought we established that I was controlling the pace of conversation. I'm just not ready for a routine level of communication."

"Alright Asher. We went over that. Right. That's your call. Absolutely."

"Right."

"I have a question for you. I need some information."

"I-Information?"

Seven days before his sentencing, Lake told his son about how he split reality down the middle and lived in two planes at once. How they lived in a mirror world. Asher was a part of it, but he was too young to understand. Though, at times, he was the key to the whole thing.

Mirror world was changing their names every day. Mirror world was Lake and Asher's mom paying for every single thing with other people's money, other people's credit cards, living in houses they didn't own using other people's names. Mirror world was fake bank accounts and phantom credit used to buy up twelve houses in a neighborhood before selling the one that Lake had the deed on, pocketing real cash before the other dozen withered on the suburban vines.

The mirror world was the cheat code, the master key–they could be anyone and go anywhere, a database conspiracy staying one step ahead of yesterday's true-up. It was a hidden tunnel, a secret passage, a game they could play anytime, anyplace. Husband, wife, and son. Infinite Money Code, Unlimited Identity Hack, Never Get Caught Exploit.

"I'd like to send you some money. I just need some quick info," Lake said to his son.

"Your money is good. Therapy is expensive, repairing a-a-a smoking c-c-crater of a credit score is expensive, and court costs are expensive. You stole my identity while I was in braces to get enough money and keep yourself out of prison. Which didn't w-w-work, by the way."

Asher was such a clean and fresh set of numbers. His name and social security number held the titles and bills for mortgages nationwide, the bad-luck buyer getting sucker homes just before his dad cashed out at the peak of the market. Asher had been sued hundreds of times by lawyers coast-to-coast in claims court of any size you please, the baby sacrificial lamb of dozens and dozens of real-estate scams, can't miss pump-and-dump schemes, and credit card fraud lines stretching high into the sky.

Asher, with his fresh name in the system and gleaming credit score at six, eight, ten years old, functioned just as potent as any magic wand. Lake weaved his names and personal information into an occult incantation. Let this child's name and social security number be spoken, and see mere digital straw downloaded into gold.

Lake loved him. As he slept in the best they would ever afford, Lake stared soft-eyed at his beautiful boy sleeping and snoring light as a kitten and told him, "I'll make it up to you someday. I'll make it all worth your while. Don't worry Asher. Please never worry a bit." Taking his infant sighs as a guarantee that what happened here in the mirror world wouldn't count when they cashed out and stepped back into reality.

"I'm sorry. I was wrong to do it. That's all I can say. I was wrong."

"If you want to give me money, set it up through Venmo. You goddam get it, don't you? Make it regular and secure and trackable."

"My lawyers need your social security number and your current address. I'm setting up a trust for you. I want your future to be secure, with or without me."

"My, my social security..."

"I know you got a new one."

"Don't call me again, Dad."

"No, Asher, they're right here. Here, Barbara can tell you."

"Don't ever call me again." Asher said. "Not goddam ever! Ever."

Lake tried calling again. The number bounced back. Asher had already blocked him off. In a few more minutes, he would have found a new number completely.

"Did you get it?" Barbara asked. She took a few minutes. She was stretching in the hallway. Still training.

"He's having trouble figuring it out. Gen Z." Lake shrugged.

"Look, I know it's tough, but Taylor and I need you with as few distractions as possible. You are on our timeline, Lake, and those minutes don't include unnecessary concerns."

Lake smiled. It didn't feel right. He looked at Sophie's messages again.

*Excited to study with you again. No one has ever believed in me like you.*

# CHAPTER EIGHT

## *The World's Only Real Thing*

### SEATTLE, WASHINGTON OCTOBER 21

The three of them hadn't seen each other in years, but just past the formalities, Lake, Sophie and Esme fell into the routine and easy friendship and felonies that defined their lives together.

Esme's van was parked under the downtown monorail, and everyone was slumber-party tight on the padded workbenches in the back. Sophie was drawing comic strips of how the Book of Blue Daggers saved her life once and would save it again.

Lake bit at his tongue and kept saying, "Almost there, almost got it, almost ready," to Sophie who had her feet across Esme's lap, Esme kneading Tiger Balm into the knuckles of Sophie's feet and then up and down her calf. The menthol buzzed and burned cold in the bay air but felt good with Esme's light touch.

Esme wore a Lycaena Heteronea moth fixed in epoxy resin on a medallion around her neck and carried an unlicensed Glock pistol in a backpack decorated with pink spiders. She rubbed at the Minivelle estrogen patch just below her belly button and flicked open the can of Diet Dr. Pepper she had stashed in a garbage bag full of ice. Esme had green eyes, peacock eyeshadow, crooked teeth and espresso-colored hair bent by static and looked a moment away from dealing cards from a well-used deck of Rider-Waite Tarot Cards. She savored people making the wrong impression.

"I just took your shoes off, and you still have penguin feet," Esme said.

"There's not enough blood to get around."

"Are you always bruised up like this?" Esme asked, smoothing the balm across an angry purple trellis on Sophie's calf. "You said you were almost electrocuted?"

"Almost. Some people just can't handle the pressure of keeping a secret."

"I know that pickup Cyone was talking about. That neurosurgeon was Wagner Koo, he was a big-time scalpel in Harborview. Cyone sold a Basquiat painting he owned to Freemont Gracy for half a million. The insurance company sent in a kill team from Constellis when Seattle PD said it would take a day-and-half to get a warrant. Oops."

"But he didn't claim the Book?"

"Told everyone about his Basquiat and his Chinese urns. Never told anyone about the Book, though. Must have broken his heart. He tried to delete himself with a cranial drill."

"Sophie, you've been born again!" Lake shouted.

"Compose yourself, Lake." Esme smiled.

"Sorry, just excited. Sophie, you ready?"

Sophie swung her feet away from Esme and pulled out notes.

"Born again for the second time, Sophie. Or what do we call you now?" Esme asked.

Lake shook his head. "No change. Same name as the last time we did it."

"Certainly, you didn't find someone else also named Soph-"

Lake shook Esme off. "I didn't. You don't have to. After the last legislative session, those suckers at the state house were so kind to demand a 4 week's grace for all basic name changes. Naturally, the creators of Field underscore Overwrite underscore Allname Execute seemed to forget that data injection opportunists such as myself still exist."

"How streamlined," Sophie said.

"Meet the new Sophie, same as the old Sophie." Lake spun his laptop screen toward Sophie. Data columns, dates of birth, social security numbers. Meet the new Sophie indeed.

"Lake, that's really good." Sophie smiled at him. Lake smiled back. Sophie squeezed his bicep twice.

"Thanks Sophie. It's solid, but if you apply for a home mortgage..." Lake wiggled his hand.

Sophie started peeling off hundreds on the keyboard underneath her new self, up to four hundred before Lake stacked, packed, and handed the money back to her.

"You don't, um..." Lake looked at the floor of the van. "You took Asher to Wendy's on my sentencing day. Not too many people were nice to me."

"Thank you, Lake," Sophie said.

Lake packed the laptop into a slim messenger bag and nodded to Esme.

"Say hi to the fish," he said to her before opening the rear doors into the breezy night streets.

Sophie's feet flickered white, jumping out after Lake. He was two cars away before she caught up, getting her knees onto the hood of a hatchback and calling out.

"Lake!"

"Sophie, where are your shoes?"

"When are you going back to California?"

"Well, maybe I'm not," Lake said.

"Have you talked to Asher much?" Sophie perched herself on the hood, curling her arms across what she could of her chalked knees.

Lake smiled. He caught himself and stopped. He smiled again. "Yeah. Couple of times. Still working things out. But he talks."

"He told you what he does now?"

"College."

"College. University man. Wow. Ah, so here they come with the big money offer and clean work and look at you with all the reason in the world."

Lake couldn't catch this smile. "'All the reason' is right. So, I'm probably here for some time."

Sophie couldn't hide hers either.

Sophie stayed in the back while Esme drove. She drew on the front and back of printer paper, her figure work looking like paper dolls. She was four-five-six pages in.

A call came in on Sophie's. Who's number was this?

They left a voicemail. Silence for ten seconds. No, something in the background.

Esme maneuvered the van south onto Colorado Avenue, parallel to the echoing rail yards and huge white harbor cranes brewing into the sky. Sophie, now in the passenger seat, her hair flat against the cool glass window. She could feel something spoiling inside of her as the industrial lights stretched into long yellow fingers.

"You don't look so good," Esme said.

"Give me some air, ok?" Sophie asked, her voice trying.

Sophie's phone beeped and beeped as Esme rolled down the windows. The screen and the city lights reflected on Sophie's sweaty face. She squinted at the screen; her fingers shaky as she hit the speaker button.

A cheery, robotic female voice bounced through the front seats. "Sophie, you need to check the Manifest. See who the guests of The Hermetic Circle are! Just check the Manifest, I bet you'll see!"

Esme pulled the van over and clicked on the Emergency lights. Sophie rasped and tried to say something. Sweat banded her cheeks.

"This is a... These are people going to the auction. The ferry to the Gnostic Auction."

Sophie held the phone to Esme, her hands cold and clammy, her pupils running in circles. Esme caught what Sophie was looking for.

Under a note for the HERMETIC CIRCLE, she found BRIGHT, LAKE. Sophie grabbed Esme's shoulder and dropped her phone to the floor. She moved her lips and said something about Hermes Trismegistus, but Esme didn't catch it before Sophie peed herself and tipped forward towards the footwell.

Someone was saying her name, but Sophie just stared at the ground. It occurred to her to breathe. It occurred to her to blink. She could move her lips, but no sound came out, and she was fine with what she had, knowing she was alive and breathing, able to lick and blink. Someone was calling her name, asking her to wake up, but she was awake. She was fine; she was ok. She just needed to sleep, was all.

~ ~ ~

Esme was good at making things comfortable, swinging the seats of the van around and laying Sophie on the rubber floor, watching her feet and elbows scurry from the cold air into the thermal blanket across her body.

"Does that happen pretty often?"

"Did I pass out?"

Esme nodded. "I thought you had a seizure."

"Nuh-uh. Where are my clothes?"

Esme pointed to a towel on the passenger seat.

"I thought you must have cut yourself. You bleed when you pee, right? Does that part happen pretty often?"

"Um... more often. There a lot of blood?"

"Some."

"What color?"

"Pink. I'm only saying this in case you don't know, but it smells strange."

"I know. I'm sorry."

"Don't be sorry."

Esme picked up the sheaf of papers that Sophie had drawn across. She drew her mother on the front. Her mother was holding a tube with an upturned rat X'd out on it.

"You were a bit of a mess before I put you and Lake together. So was he, to be honest. Is all of this true?"

"Most of it."

"You're really from Illinois?"

Sophie nodded.

"I'll do whatever I can to help you Sophie, but finding the Book isn't going to fix anything," Esme said.

"It will save my life."

"Do you understand what you are afraid of? You're still going to live the same way. You can fix the symptoms but... I don't want to criticize you."

"I don't want it to hurt. I don't want it to end. I'm just scared, Esme, I never had a chance."

"Even if you get it, what's going to make you change? You think you'll never be scared again? I'll help you with anything Sophie, but if you can go without being afraid and don't worry about it hurting, you can live as long as you want."

Sophie nodded, even though she didn't understand.

"Will you read it to me?" Sophie asked.

"Read your story to you?" Esme asked.

"I need to remember," Sophie said.

"Sure. Stop me if anything sounds wrong."

Esme sat in front of Sophie, putting her feet next to hers, covering both pairs under the blanket. She stared into Sophie's gray, scared eyes before reading to her what she'd just been writing.

"You lived with your grandparents in downstate Illinois, the flatlands of pig farms and soybean fields. They took over for you from foster care when you were 10. Just only when they thought they could handle it. Ten was old enough to make sure you were housebroken. Old enough to say yes, ma'am."

"You were eleven, playing Monopoly with a cousin on the back porch, with the permethrin shampoo for the stray cat lice soaking in, and he let you win but said you had awfully big tits for a fifth grader."

"They made fun of you in school. Chubby, stinky, bad hair, book mouse, Sophie the Crime Scene Baby finding you somehow. You learned how to steal early. You taught other girls how to steal. Anything to have friends. Anything to make yourself important. You could lead the way or do it all yourself. You worked out schemes. Sticking to grocery stores for candy and sodas. Soccer mom vans in the school parking lot. You competed with raccoons digging through people's glove boxes and consoles. Pills. Loose cash. Cell phones. You found a pistol when you were 13. You buried it. A concrete county mile marker, you forgot which one.

"Girls let you talk. Girls listened to you. You rode your bikes to a rubber raft on a pond and traded what you took. You showed off. You had them look at the new version of you. You all took turns."

"You burned a book into a deck of ash and watched it smoke and blue and smolder and sink. You told them you were all done reading. You told them you were done with these pale shoulders and lay there in the brightness of the water. Your eyes got so washed from the bright you couldn't see or blink it clear until long past twilight. You remember the sunburn so bad you couldn't stretch your arms to reach the handlebars. You remember your skin turning white where you touched it. You remember the blisters wet and sticky, and you remember throwing up."

"Your grandparents heat stroked on their awful paisley couch that afternoon. Just cooked out and died because all they would drink was black coffee. It was so stupid. Stupid. They'd had this Phil Phillips song, the Sea of Love, playing when they died. 'To the Sea/The Sea Love.'"

"Their eyes pushed out of their sockets, thick as cooked eggs. They were so embarrassing. They just wanted a friend. Your grandmother gave you short haircuts and patchouli deodorant. Stinky. Chubby. Dykey book mouse."

"You were 16, and you weren't going back to foster care. Before your grandparents, you had Vicky Mom, Carol Mom, and Wanda Mom. You had nineteen brothers and sisters here and there. You had dinner out of truck-stop coffee cups and were sent to the tent in full summer days and then all night for misbehaving. You weren't going back. The State of Illinois said one thing, but you thought another."

"Illinois Family and Children only knew the checklist. You found the right binder, figured out the rules. Those first few years, you just had to make paper, work email, work an ID, fake a signature. You slept in Wal-Marts, libraries, church lock-ins. The youth groups were the best. They loved runaways on the path to salvation. You stayed nine weeks at a church in Peoria. You stole denim skirts and white button shirts. You paid ten dollars at a strip mall to pull your hair into a Mennonite braid. You told them you ran away from your dad, down in Amish country. They wanted to think you were on the run, and you let them. No one could put it together because they were connecting the dots you set out for them."

"At 17, you told Child Services you were out. They wrote you the proceeds from your grandparents' house. You were out and in an apartment and had a refrigerator now, but you were still running a relay. Drawing pictures of the day to day... You were just moving, moving. You could never sleep right on the sheets or the bare mattress, and you dumped apartments everywhere you went. You decided."

"You stole antiques. You sold antiques. Books and armor and swords and guns. Men with more money than sense loved to purchase romance. You made the market. You were the market. You stole from it and created it and sold it back after driving up the price you created by the scarcity you created. You ran wind sprints on tightropes."

"Some old-country witch from Lakeshore Drive came to you seeking her family history. A fortune in sugar and fats and rendered bones, in railroad cars to drilling concerns. Now to pay towards the one thing that money couldn't buy. A family tree with roots across the sea. Tendrils under seawater and tectonic plates. She could buy everything, but she told you, 'I want a piece of my history back.'"

"You'd let them hold it in their hands. Their ancestors wore this very thing, you'd say. His cheek against this very plate. 'It's just so small,' she'd say, turning the helmet in her hand. They were smaller then, you'd say. Smaller, shorter, their bones less layered with calcium, their teeth so jagged. Lesser lives, their births often dragging their mother's lives away, never enough milk, rivers and streams."

"They love buying it. Just a tale of woe that continues in a straight red line from the metal's blacksmith in Bavaria to a rented room in Chicago that very day. What savagery has it contained? What violence is impacted within the molecules and what human cruelty is smoked into the shine of the light of it? A boy slaughtered on a field; a pike needled through his thigh? A man trampled by horses in a peasant's revolt? This helmet of many uses, repaired by smiths, cycled for conquests, used by conquerors and held in ship-bays until painted red from slaughter in tobacco and cassava fields an ocean away. The helmet bargained from man to man. Did it ever hear a curse of betrayal and endless revenge, a declaration of eternity and vigilant love to wife and child while in a filthy pit, did it contain ever more than it was?"

"You sell assassin's daggers and the cloaks of murdered men. Italian Armor and Dutch Flintlocks. You steal from rich men and cheap museums. You plan one week out. You don't count years, you don't celebrate birthdays, or keep track of weekends for another eight years. You are treetop to treetop and limb to limb by your fingertips, and you still don't know how you do it. Every Christmas and New Year's and Fourth of July, take you by surprise. Working on days and weeks and numbers is as good as putting your leg in a trap."

"You keep time like a fox who can smell the hunter's hands. A cold night and a burning summer wind, that's all you remember. You know how to not get trapped, but you know one day the trap will spring shut, and many, many hands will gather around your throat."

"You know that someday, you will get what you deserve. Until you see the Book."

"You have a groove going with Nazi helmets and SS-Ehrenring, death's head patches, the rise in fascist masturbation booming thermonuclear. You follow buyer lists from auction sites, purchasing lists for auction malls and antique distributors. A dark list of full-time buyers with no price too high."

"A mansion has steel plates next to all the doors with Bible parables etched into them. Laser etched and bolted into the stone walls. Parable of the Workers of the Vineyard. The Parables of the Mustard Seed. The Parable of the Wise and Foolish Builders."

"You use a bump key and a pair of pliers to hop the lock and get into the laundry of this mansion out in the country. You park a mile past the big road and walk over the soybean field. You remember peeing in his house and leaving the seat down. It is night, you have the whole place dark, you have your beach towels and backpack set in front of this beautiful case. Just you and the moonlight and wire cutters, all the time in the world, to work loose this SS regiment museum in miniature. You work the nuts loose, clip the hangers, unscrew the screener tracks. You smile as you watch the scaffolding fold into itself, breaking down just as you expected."

"It's just a book, that's all it looks like. In the form of this pulp novel. Conan, the Spider, the Shadow. The cover has some lantern-jawed adventurer clutching a damsel over a burning pit? You know that book smells like a pack of matches? Just like a pack of matches. That's how you first get the Book of Blue Daggers. Just cheap pulp. Pistols and goggles and poison. It doesn't have parables, it doesn't have any lessons. Just biplanes and burning pits and revenge."

"There are notes out for this chapter. A chapter about a lady thief. Her theft is noble, not selfish, the money only gained to acquire the antidote to a poison she'd soon succumb to. The notes are obsessed with blue. The poison, blue. The antidote, blue. The water, the shades, the squares of light through the morning windows."

"So, our lady thief. She has a map, and she has been betrayed during this burglary attempt. A daring attempt at the citadel's trove. She's gotten what she'd come for, but now comes the getting out. Now she finds her impossible odds."

"You're amazed at how you could glide over the details. How the Book describes her hair just like yours, her hands just like yours. An orphaned thief. You don't get the coincidence. You don't understand. Were they always right when they called you this stupid?"

"Oh my god, oh my god, there should have been a way to know. The thief sees the shadows of the guards at the door of the citadel, the Book says. Capture means certain death. A most frightful death for stealing this treasure. A map to the Verdant Pool."

"Avoiding their shadows at the door, she goes through stairs and in a green-tiled room she goes up and up. She knows she has to escape. Her last living moment to leave and find the Verdant Pool."

"With the guards now closing in, their footsteps are as silent as crawling shadows. She looks and stacks and reaches for the highest night and opens. It's just blue moonlight, as she escapes by the skylight."

"You gather the Nazi daggers, the Runed rings, the SS officer's hat. You always go out the way you came in. You can see shadows just beyond the doorway... And that's when you realize you missed an alarm sometime inside. The shadows slither. You go back through the house. You backtrack, you drag your treasures upstairs. You hide in a master bath of green tiles and nightlights. You see where this is going. They wouldn't have put you to the torture, but the Book is close enough."

"You understand what you read. Understand that you just have to follow the directions. That you'll be fine, forever and ever. You stack boxes on top of a stool in the top to reach a skylight. You have to move the handle and press the glass, but you have instructions. You have a guide."

"The Book told you what to do."

"It's just blue moonlight, as you escape by the skylight. And then over the rooftops and down into the soft gardens below. For a moment there, you think you're dead. For a moment there, you think your soul is escaping and using the last fantasy it had. But this is it. This is the only real thing."

"The Book knows. You know."

"Later, you find out you're bleeding inside and you aren't even wounded."

"The Book has a plan and a fix and a cure. The Book gives you a blessing. You know as true as anything. The Book lays plans for you. The Book will save you, and then you will save it. As true as anything, Sophie, it wants you to find it."

# CHAPTER NINE

## A Narration

**SEATTLE, WASHINGTON OCTOBER 22**

The wind chopped strongly off the south sound. Lake stood at the green-slick shoreline, looking for a response from Asher. The chance at trust was bare and Lake broke it like a hammer to glass. The tether was fucking toast.

Taylor Zapata called. Lake had homework coming through. There was a file with his name on it.

"Need you to listen to this before your on-site lunch with Barbara. Just sent you the address. I have a routine blood draw today, so I won't be there."

The address: Soundside Hotel with a view in Olympia. Way south. The route was all highways. Lake flickered and could feel his stomach clamping. Something wanted him to scream, "Fuck this."

He started planning back-road routes, streets with names and no numbers, a hundred turn-right, turn-left, continue 300 feet, veer right. He got in the car and drove and listened.

The encrypted audio download ::CH_AUCTION_BG_1.wav:: from WYETH INVESTIGATIONS played over the car speakers.

Nick Wyeth called Lake by his first name and said he hoped to meet him soon. He used first rate audio equipment. He talked quick and emphatic. He narrated in eerie tones more suited to a podcast about serial killers and the discovery of shallow graves.

*"This audio is designed to verbally collate the results of my investigation. At this point in time, I believe there is but one single copy of* The Book of Blue Daggers. *In, or around, 1935 by vanity press or a single advanced reading copy, printing details unknown. There is no copyright data, ISBN, or publisher data. The name of the author, EF Proew, almost certainly a pseudonym, the resolution of which remains both too time consuming and irrelevant to our purposes of discovery. The item is a library binding hardcover. Indications that interior illustrations done by Walter Baumhofer and/or Rafael De Soto cannot be confirmed but would conform to the period. It has shaded blue and black inset lettering on the title page. Pen or pencil marks are on the back of the cover. The pages are currently sealed with an unsmoothed tan stripe of carpenter's wax, allowing for no access to the inner pages. The Book is item number 76 at the Gnostic Auction.*

Another number called in and it didn't register. Lake said hello twice. He heard highway noise on the other end, and the squeezing puff of a cigarette draw. Lake could almost smell the exhaust breathing out of the other end of the phone before it clicked off.

*"The Book of Blue Daggers is a pulp book of the Weird Menace Variety. A masked hero from a dangerous and corrupt city escapes numerous dangers, tortures, and betrayals, transcends via a difficult journey, and overcomes a cumulative set of obstacles. A previous owner of the Book disputed this categorization. That owner claimed the Book was written in an abstract and deeply symbolic code, ultimately becoming a kind of instruction manual. In his words:* 'a hidden guide to all of life's steps and placements.'

*A subsequent owner reported a further, deeper symbolism after acquiring and reading the Book. Notes from his psychiatrist before his suicide reported claims that the Book had a 'malign comprehension,' and the reader asserted that the text was a 'willfully amorphous mirror'. This reader committed suicide via voluntary dehydration.*

Davis Muth had news from Oregon. Bad news traveled fast across state lines and interstates. Monty was a no show at the halfway house. Cut cords on ankle monitors. US Marshals were running circles with Monty Boate's old girlfriends, ex-wives, noted fellows of the trade. Muth talked about money, mentioned a fix could be had for the right price. He offered that twenty-thousand cash might be able to calm troubled waters.

*"The Gnostic Auction acquired that unofficial designation only in recent years. Those that have been, and have successfully won items from the auction, are oftentimes still reticent about revealing any overt details about the location, times, or any other particulars. Both the prime attendees, winners, losers, and then those wishing to attend, are all complicit in the maintenance of the veil of secrecy, excitement and the esoteric nature of the event and the goods traded within.*

Sophie called in 10, 20, 30 times. Finally:

"Did you know?" Sophie asked. "Was it when they told you, or did you fit it together afterwards?"

"When I realized why you were here. You know I wouldn't do this to hurt you, Sophie," Lake said.

"It's going to hurt me, and it's going to kill me. But I know you didn't mean to."

"I can't do it, Sophie," Lake said.

"What you mean is, you won't do it."

"Yes. That's right," Lake admitted.

"What are they giving you, a contract? Health insurance? A trust fund for Asher? That's their world. Legitimacy and stability. But that isn't who you are."

"It's who I need to be."

"I never remember you begging, Lake. You can get me the Book. Esme can make a copy good enough to pass the eye test. Then all you do is hand them the fake. They don't care about you, Lake. You're just someone on the org chart to them. I know what you can really do."

"I'm sorry, Sophie."

"Lake?"

"I'm sorry. I can't go back. I can't lose it again."

"The Book is the only thing that can save me."

"That's not true."

"I'll die without it."

"I'm sorry Sophie. This is the only thing I have."

Lake pulled the car over and punched the cheap dash until the plastic above the tachometer burst into spiderwebs. His knuckles ached, and it all popped hot and red, and he jabbed until the bloody plastic screen broke loose from the fittings and he tossed it on the shoulder of the road

Lake called over and over, but couldn't get through to Asher. He left a message and said, "This is your dad. I wanted to apologize again." Asher never called back. Asher didn't leave any message, and when there was nothing left to punch, Lake put the audio back on and kept driving.

*"Those who have won claim a code of silence. Jade Carvings from Cambodia, Portuguese Rutters describing treasure caches along the Pacific coast, Ivory story tusks, these were all identified along with their purchases who all refuse to discuss purchasing details."*

Another call from a number unknown. An engine revved and revved and screamed up to redline. It gasped and whipped and someone shouted, "Step on it!" The engine wailed at the top of its lungs. Lake could make out the pistons flexing and the pipestack firing hot smoke and someone was shouting again when he hung up.

*"The basic truths, schedules, and timetables were able to be distilled from the janitors, security guards, attendants, estate associates, and other procedural functionaries who did not sign disclosure documents and were not otherwise glamoured by the excitement, wealth, and fraternal notoriety. The auction, when excised of this notoriety, is a prosaic affair. It began with an almost exclusive Asian and Asian-American clientele who purchased gray-market goods, often black market goods. Often aphrodisiacs. Tiger blood, rhinoceros horns, and pangolin scales.*

Lake risked big streets and a minute on I-5 to get to a sporting goods store. A man with steel rimmed-eyeglasses and a Ducks Unlimited hat told Lake that his height had advantages. "Clothes, frame, and, typically," he explained, spreading his fingers out wide. "Your hands aren't going to slip."

He slimmed his eyes and patted Lake's jacket at the waist on both sides, and then pointed at his belt. He told Lake that a Sig P320 was right on the money for a personal protection firearm. He said that he had a Seattle PD badge before his weekdays here. He said he was no stranger to how sudden things were. It could all happen so quickly. He stared at Lake with glossy blue eyes that slipped between his frames and eyebrows. Just one second. Just one lifetime of a second, he said. Lake agreed with him. That's all it would be.

"Good belt like that every day?" he asked.

"Probably."

"Jacket too?"

"Yes."

"Well then, I would recommend, and if you are comfortable…"

He took a plastic clamshell holster off the rack and slid his slim fingers inside to pop it open. He pressed the holster against the outside of Lake's jacket, against his waist.

"I can see you favor the right. Fix that paddle inside your waistband and settle it on your belt. Stand up straight. Let's see your jacket fall as it is there."

"No shoulder holsters?"

"It's a good look, but you have to learn to cross draw. I had an Airweight .38 in an ankle. Strictly backup."

The man rang him out with a box of 9mm HST ammo. Lake pulled into the open empty end of the parking lot. Holding the plastic bag in his hand like a crisp mitten, Lake pressed ammo into the magazine and rubbed clean the finger smudges from the brass and the magazine before snapping it into the gun and working the slide. He leaned forward against the wheel and pressed the gun tight into the holster before shuffling against the odd grip of metal and plastic against his thighs and waist and started driving again, shifting and angling his body to get comfortable.

*"The assistants and workers were not able to provide any names or any understandings of the deeper works, but presented an image of a well-run, quietly kept organization that had the ability to resolve a number of financial, marketing, and extralegal disputes. These disputes were solved, reputedly via the connections between the auction primary brokers and certain contacts in the underworld, again... reputedly based on shared ethnic, linguistic or similar backgrounds."*

Muth didn't answer. Muth didn't respond. Lake called from the perimeter line of the Olympia Regional airport. He saw Beechcraft and yellow Cessna's touch down on the landing strip after making the Ranier loop and the longshot run out to the Olympic and back. Muth's phone went to voicemail and a full inbox. At the windburn end of the airfield, three vagrants in orange work vests worked up a blaze in a dumpster.

The dumpster smoked spooled out lowercase in the crosswinds. The vagrants joined hands next to the heat. They heaved bundles, taped and cotton-wrapped, bare handed into the flames. They made signs to the smolder. They waved the fresh gray at their faces and bowed to the greasy blaze. All three grabbed, lifted, and hoisted up the final bundle. A mummy of duct-tape with the sneakers still on slipped across the container's lips. The mummy landed with a bang and an echo, and a gout of ash and the vagrants ran at the sound of a siren or shouts that Lake couldn't hear or see.

*"Most repeatedly, the auction was presented as having two unique properties. First, that it was protected by those who were willing to employ extralegal means. Second, and most crucially, certain goods sold there did, in fact, have supernatural, metaphysical, or otherworldly properties. This point was taken as a flat fact amongst even the attendees.*

Barbara chewed calamari and grilled him on the details. She had incorporated a gentle chuckle into her repertoire. Lake envisioned Human Resources, perhaps Taylor Zapata, endorsing this effort to establish social connections. She had only half mastered it — a pleasant double "a-ha, ha!" followed by a drawn-out "aaahh."

"I don't suppose I need to tell you how an auction works, do I?" Barbara said, staring, followed by the laugh, exactly on time.

"No, uh, I've been to a few in my life."

"So, let's go over the primary task. There is no concern about the price at the auction. You are there to set a bid early, maintain it, and win it."

"How high are you expecting the Book to go for?"

Barbara shook her head. No time for the laugh with a mouth full of squid.

"Irrelevant. Be the first and last bid."

"You don't want-"

Barbara ran out the laugh again and stared at him down.

"You just need to execute the plan with no deviation. The client wants to bid the whole way through. You're getting hired to bulldoze through anyone who thinks they can outbid us." Barbara laughed again, pointing a tentacle spiraled fork at him.

Barbara waved the fork at the rings and tentacles colliding around a lemon wrapped in cheesecloth.

"Not hungry?"

Lake shook his head.

"I should have... um, bulldoze it. First bid, last bid. That's not a problem at all."

Barbara didn't laugh as Lake stood up; his eyes fixed on windows.

"Are you leaving?"

"Yeah, seafood isn't my..."

Barbara nodded. Yeah, sure, that's just fine, as Lake walked away.

Barbara could see Lake in the parking lot, and she squeezed the entire rest of the lemon across the white plate of squid flakes and called Taylor.

"Taylor, next time we do this, find me someone who knows how to get to yes when you offer them twenty thousand dollars. Don't put me in a room with that kind of fucking cretin again," Barbara said.

"Don't worry, our client wants him blacklisted after this. It's going to be a tough break for him, but he's a capable man."

"Are those your words or hers?"

"You need to learn that I never actually speak, not the legal sense of the term."

Barbara waved a waiter over and laughed long and loud and real, the sound big enough for the whole restaurant to hear.

*"It is crucial to state that, despite the gravity and pervading code of silence, it seems that attendees at the auction are afforded considerable and good-natured flexibility. The process permits a relaxed attitude towards the examination and handling of items up for bid, especially if potential buyers are in attendance. A congenial*

*atmosphere persists among winners, losers, and general participants of the event."*

Lake was sweating and his hand went numb trying to plot a course away from the Interstate. A red Chevy rolled with him, a big shitkicker 90s diesel. It kept up with Lake as he signaled out past Tumwater and stayed with him four lengths back and swayed a thin diesel cloud along Yelm, St. Clair, Reservation Road as Lake booked it the long way north. The truck didn't signal and ate up the center line. Lake called Muth again, but couldn't raise him.

Lake opened up his jacket and lifted himself in the seat until he felt more comfortable with the holster. There were two figures in the truck's cab. There was a sedan between them as they rumbled over the Nisqually River. The truck closed the distance as they were clearing the big trees at the freeway entrance to I-5. Lake pulled right and opened the throttle all the way. He floored it onto the big bad haunted highway, tires flying northeast, catching the red Chevy in his rearview as it disappeared, headed the other way.

*"Two items sold indicate that despite the current level of security, law enforcement awareness of, and presence at, the Gnostic auction is negligible. Four years ago, the auction openly sold a VHS workprint of El Cuerpo de Los Ángeles, a quote-unquote snuff film financed and produced by Amado Carrillo Fuentes. The film was partially screened to select attendees and brokers to verify authenticity before sale. The evidence on that tape, today, is said to be able to provide a fusillade of extradition agreements. During an auction last year, a severe and dramatic dispute arose during the bidding of Flemish Alchemist Ludvig Prinn's textbook "De Vermis Mysteriis". One bidder confronted another, loudly accused him of seeding his brain with unsettling vision, and then bit him several times across the face, neck, and severed an ear. There was no police action, no ambulances called, no emergency calls registered."*

The voice at the other end barked and asked if Lake recognized it. Lake remembered exactly what Monty Boate sounded like.

Monty contrived to get bounced every few years to a different spot, and in between the Federal Death House as USP Terre Haute and USP Lompoc in California, someone decided Monty had earned a breezy step down to mingle with the manicured embezzlers, wire-fraud artists, and computer crime creeps at FCI Englewood. The first step at every new home was to let it be known that Monty was never to be fucked with, and it would be Lake who he chose to demonstrate this lesson with in practice.

A lady officer at the prison slipped word to Lake that Monty was going to hurt him. Didn't like his look. Didn't like his papers. Didn't like him.

Lake tucked a four-inch wood screw in his armpit for two days. Just waiting for when Monty chose the time and place. To get bumped into. To hear some choice words. To catch an ugly glance from Lake. Monty went to work on him in a stairwell. Lake went limp, maybe he would breeze it. Monty worked his hand over nasty, maimed, beyond permanent. Lake shoved the wood screw into Monty's neck. One lucky shot, in the soft and flat place where you'd draw a line across your neck with your finger.

So, of course, he remembered what he sounded like. Monty Boate had a lisp from where the prison doctor stitched his tongue back together. A voice fried from cigarettes that stuttered at the end where the wood screw chipped off his voice box.

"I remember. You never got that silly voice fixed after I gave it to you, huh," Lake said.

Lake let the silence take it.

Lake listened to Monty Boate draw smoke on the other end. Monty exhaled and Lake could feel the hot smoke sour around him as he said he would see him soon.

"You sure, Monty?"

"Gonna see ya," Monty lisped before the line went hollow, "Gonna kill ya in a bad, mean way."

# CHAPTER TEN

*A Future Full of Mischief*

## KENMORE WA, OCTOBER 23

In the damp front seat of Esme's van, Sophie chopped orange Adderall pills onto their strawberry milkshake lids. Esme peered and cooed a live fish with its mouth bobbing open-and-shut in the cooler at their feet. They were all the way down by Lake Washington and Sophie could see the rain coming in diagonal by streetlights and treetops across the highway.

"I shall master sleep and tedious nights," Sophie said.

"Tomorrow is just a future full of mischief, babe," Esme said.

"I'll stop when Lake calls. Until then..."

Sophie showed off the pharmaceuticals. Blue and white capsules scored pills marked "100 mg" in blister packs half punched out.

"Adderall, Provigil, dextro. Whatever it takes to not miss a step." Sophie handed Esme a milkshake with four orange pills burst out all over the lid.

They chewed through 80 points of Adderall. They dissolved them between their gums and waited till their teeth went numb before starting in on the milkshakes. Esme licked her teeth and worked the river-delta ends of her hair into a fishtail braid.

The taste from the Adderall dripped bitter into her throat, and Sophie ran the big plan front to back for herself as much as for Esme.

"I'll give Lake the better deal. He'll take a reach for the high-risk play. He'll win the Book at the Gnostic Auction. He'll give you the Book. You copy the Book. He flips the pseudo to the buyers. I keep the true blue. Everyone resolves to who they really are," Sophie said.

It was running now. She was as slanted as the rain. Her tongue went flat and numb and she traced her teeth with it.

"Is that fish really worth two thousand dollars?" Sophie asked.

Esme nodded. A turquoise minivan pulled up near them and flashed its lights. Esme rolled down the window and waved her hand, the minivan rolling over to them in the rain. Her wild hair got soaked.

Esme talked window to window with an Asian man in a yellow jacket and matched outfits with another guy in the passenger seat. She pushed a piece of paper into his window through the rain, then pointed to something on the phone, her Japanese better than Sophie ever expected. The men in yellow jackets got out and put their hoods up, holding flashlights.

The younger of the two men opened the side of Esme's van as Esme popped on the dome light.

"They just need to verify it," Esme said.

"What, the fish?" Sophie asked.

Esme nodded. "People get anxious about buying exotic fish. They conjure up nets and hooks."

Esme lifted the cooler out from under Sophie's feet and one of the men took one handle and they all set it onto the floor of the van together. The younger man lifted the lid and put the flashlight onto the fish. The fish had amber marble eyes that stared blankly off the sides of its head and bumped its way around the cooler like a slowly deflating balloon.

The older man put his hands on the fish in the water. He tickled it, lifting and playing with it enough so that Sophie could see the thick head bobbing above the cradle. He smiled and laughed and apparently had enough. They shook hands and laughed, and the oldest man gave Esme an envelope full of cash, shaking her hand and envelope all at once.

Esme said something in Japanese, and the man nodded and wiped his hands on his yellow jacket before speaking a string of numbers to Esme and handing her an undone dial padlock in a plastic baggie.

Esme shook the water from her hair all the way across the front dash and swatted Sophie with the envelope full of cash.

"Healthy Fugu, two thousand straight cash. I taught you the wrong trade, kiddo."

"Doesn't fugu kill you awfully fast?" Sophie asked.

"If you know how to cut it, it doesn't. Gary Toro knows how to cut it. He paints a plate with fugu sashimi like a," Esme sprinkled her words across an imaginary lacquered plate, "layered chrysanthemum."

Esme wiped her face off. She drank the milkshake. "You can find some that aren't poisonous, but, you know, who the fuck cares about that? His clients get bored of Michelin stars and James Beard awards, but they never, ever tired of the tasty adrenaline rush wondering if the next bite of sashimi will land them on a ventilator for the rest of their miserable fucking lives."

Sophie nodded and finished her milkshake, taking off her shirt and bra. Both of them soaked through. She pulled the blower switch on high and turned the temperature gauge to red, rubbing her hair in the hot breeze before laying her clothes across the dashboard vents.

"Lake will go all in. He'll get the original. You can copy the Book," Sophie said.

"If you're going to worry about this, you owe it to yourself to have no doubts," Esme said.

Sophie rubbed hands in the heat from the vents. She flipped her shirt to the damp side. Sophie unloaded.

"Lake gives you a sly fox perfect copy. They don't catch on until when they do, and I have the only real version in the world. My silhouette dissolves into shadows. My truant life extends, Esme."

"I'll need better ink," Esme said.

"You still need ink?"

"I can make a great copy from draining out Bic pens. You want me to make something better though, don't you?"

"Now?" Sophie asked.

"Gary gave me an address. Let's go right now," Esme said.

Esme put the pickup in drive and punched them towards the railway where the cargo jets angled in landings at the north end of

Boeing Field. The rain came in and drooled off the industrial buildings.

Esme parked on the street. Sophie heard a rattling like hail before realizing her teeth were clicking fast as hummingbird wings from the speed. Esme handed her a pair of titanium bolt-cutters with the teeth spray-painted a matte black.

They were already crossing the street, Sophie clicking the big, long flashlight red against her palm to check it was working.

Under the highway underpass, a quartet of tents with bikes and tarps crackled in the breeze and mist. Esme shook her knees and Sophie held her hands up. Wait. Not yet.

A man with a trimmed beard unzipped an orange tent. He wore a reflective construction vest and carried a box of kitchen matches and a heavy wire trash can. Esme and Sophie kneeled in the alley. The man stepped into the air outside the underpass and put both hands out, waving for the rain.

He stacked paper and pallet wood into the trash can. He whispered something to it. He set matches to punkwood and paper and blew into it on his hands and knees. A filthy woman with mismatched sneakers and an orange vest joined him at the fire. A voice called to them and a third joined, a young man with an orange vest with a dozen piercings joining his nose and chin and forehead. He held an object, just smaller than a pillow, wrapped tightly in white bedsheets, heavy in his arms.

"Esme, what is that?" Sophie asked.

Esme watched the three from a circle. They didn't speak a word as they each passed the object in the bedsheets around and bowed. The young man slid the wrapped-up thing into the fire. It caught and curdled to black smoke, spinning off hot ash and smoke, pushing out in a brutal cloud. None of the three moved, just staring at the smoke, none minding the sparks and ash or stray fingers of smoke lying about them.

"A fire funeral."

"For who?"

"Pets. Runaways. I heard they try to grab terminal parents from the hospice before they flatline. They've been in the city for maybe eighteen months. We're safe. They won't say a thing to the police," Esme said.

Sophie watched the bitter cloud envelop the three even as the rain started on stronger. She lost sight of them as the fire went to ash and smoke in the gaining rain.

At the lighted, clean door marked "GSI PRODUCTS" Esme arranged bolt cutters shoulder-high as she steadied and set the base jaws around a finger-thick shank of a padlock. She braced it against her shoulder and pulled straight down as Sophie pushed against her and lifted her weight against the bar. With a fierce snap, the padlock shot away, landing with the noise of a cracked mirror in the alleyway.

Esme picked up the cut lock from the alley. She traded it for the padlock from the plastic baggie from Gary, the make and model matching perfectly. Esme hung the new lock on the open latch without setting it and waved Sophie inside.

"Set that one back when we leave. Click it when we leave."

There was no indecision. Sophie cuffed the beam of light in her hands and Esme talked about the labels. She needed it closer. She had to see the right numbers.

"We should have kept the engine running," Esme said.

"We'll have time. What's the label read?"

They were gray canisters marked TOYO INK. Esme held two in her hands. She rubbed her eyes clear and chose one for the bag. The cans were heavy and smelled of petroleum and paint and brand-new plastics. They burped when she moved them side to side.

"Can you get in real close?" Esme asked.

Sophie lit up the whole shelf. Esme rubbed her eyes and held a canister close to read the numbers off. She dug deep for the last one. Sophie watched the door to the open alleyway and Esme tugged her along. Esme clacked as she walked, and she couldn't get the bolt cutters to fit.

"Fuck this," she said, wiping the cutters top to bottom and dumping them in the rain. She latched the replacement lock on the door.

Back behind the wheel of the van, Esme asked for and then chewed another Adderall. Esme laddered a century deep now. Her pupils were blackout huge. The big dark dots bounced side-to-side as she swerved across white lines. She sang along to "Party in the USA" so loud it rattled the reflections in the rear-view mirror as they rolled north to Kenmore.

Esme parked and laughed as she peeled her hands off the steering wheel. "I can't wait to show you what I have!"

She keyed Sophie into a back door labeled "FIN AND SCALE." Inside, it hummed and bubbled and vibrated with the ocean smell of ammonia and wood damp with seawater.

Esme was kicked. She talked in one straight block about inks and sea monsters and her animals.

At the current moment, she owned four Octopi (one Blue Ring, one mimic, two giant Pacifics that could bottlecap clams apart four at a time), a fully matured, prized Platinum Arowana with papers from Beijing, a group of fourteen fully live and imported Takifugu fish, Two Neptune Groupers, and two ponds of breeding carp and a licensed breeder/nurse to go along with it, all of this along with a showroom of fifty-plus tanks of clownfish, neon tetra, angelfish, a dozen dry tanks with sand and wood chips for iguana, wood turtles, and an eleven-foot boa constrictor that Esme would feed live steamer rabbits shipped in weekly from Lewis County.

"I have the inks. I can work perfect perfectly perfect now," Esme said at the end of it.

The Adderall had her in a straitjacket grip. Esme couldn't land a sentence once it took flight. There was a difference between poison and venom, Esme chatterboxed on, tangential as a thesis.

"You know there's a difference, don't you? Definitions of... The Takifugu would *poison* you because you ate it, and the Blue-Ringed Octopus would put its *venomous* saliva *into* you."

Esme danced and moved her hands like she was revealing something onstage with her words.

"Poison goes in your mouth while venom stays in their mouth. Say it with me! Tetrodotoxin. Tetro. Do. Toxin! What a way to go!" Esme clasped at her throat and crossed her eyes.

"Your nerves get the big stop sign, your muscles flex up, and you suffocate with your eyes... wide open!" Esme rolled her fingers around her eyes like a kid pretending to have binoculars. "You know they get it from bacteria they eat, so you can't blame the fish or our tentacled friends. It's just their diet that makes them so dangerous!"

"Look into a microscope, the foundation of life is hunger, the word violence does something so fundamental a disservice. Oh, look at this and see, I'll show you a fitting example," Esme said.

Esme walked to a printing press bunched next to a smudged glass snake box. The snake box was flat and twice the width of a casket, sprayed with bolts of ink from the press. The smell of steel and lubricating oil and the leathery shit of the snake. Esme took a metal tube the size of a flashlight from a desk drawer. It was steel and smooth and featureless except for a ringed dial and a flipper button on one end.

The snake unfurled towards Esme as she undid the flimsy tabs of a balsa wood box, nuzzling a fuzzy gray rabbit between the ears as she cradled it out. She shook the rabbit gently into a soft blue shop towel, his ears stiff at the ends and his mouth gobbling at the fabric.

The snake elevated its head straight up and blossomed out from its calm gray coiling. It reeled its body in the air the shape of a question mark before answering itself into a long, shallow tread. Esme slid the flattened end of the tube onto the rabbit's skull and squeezed the release trigger. The bolt went with a quick sniff and the rabbit twitched in patterns. The legs patted back-and-forth, back-and-forth as pink pooled up around its mouth.

Esme closed one eye and looked out of one corner. The rabbit stopped patting and its pink ears fell limp across its face. Esme wrapped the shop towel around its head and mouth to catch the blood. She used an elbow to slide open a barred plate at the top of the constrictor's cage and then slipped the rabbit inside. Sophie heard the plastic thump of Esme closing the cage and then, just after, the buckling noise of the snake's jaws unhooking themselves wide open.

"See this hunger? But why does it feel so violent?" Esme asked.

Sophie watched the violence, slow and wet and gray, and didn't have an answer.

"You know, I have to do it by feel, but I took a peek, and you didn't mind watching, did you Sophie?"

"I guess... maybe I'm used to the hunger," Sophie said.

"Is that why you want the Book?"

"I don't want to be scared, Esme. If I have it, I won't be scared."

"Then stop. Here. Now. You're strong enough. Look at you now, you can lift a building."

Sophie looked away. "It was just blue moonlight when she escaped by the skylight."

"You think that's the only way you can do this, don't you?"

Sophie nodded. She couldn't say she was sorry. She wouldn't say it, not even to Esme.

"You think there's someone else out there who wants it as badly as you do?"

"There's no one who wants it like me."

"Do you know where the Book came from?"

"No."

"Do you know why it has you in mind?"

"No."

"Do you know how it will save your life?"

"Not yet."

"So, you're pretty sure Lake will call, but begging didn't work. Someone else is out to get the Book, but they're rich and powerful and dangerous. The Book can save your life, but you don't know how or why. And when you get it, all your problems will be solved, and you won't be scared anymore."

"You're right, as always, Esme," Sophie said.

"Do you want me to stop? We don't have to keep going," Esme asked.

"No. I need to prove it to you." Sophie nodded.

"So, there's no other way?"

"It's the only way I'll stay alive."

"No lives forever, Sophie. Some of us just live for the bits and pieces we have left."

"I just want the chance, Esme. I deserve it."

"So, who are they, then? Who's the competition?"

"Lake got hired by something called The Hermetic Circle."

"Hermetic Circle? They really think they're clever with this shit, don't they?"

"Continuing the alchemical tradition of trying to turn lead into gold."

"It's not really lead though, is it? I mean, they aren't being literal, are they?"

"It's an analogy. Your body is lead. It isn't literally gold either."

"Same deal as you?" Esme asked, pointing Sophie up and down. "Trying to cheat it?"

"I'm not cheating, Esme. The Book wants me above all others."

"Have they ever seen the Book before? Or are you the only one?"

Sophie shook her head. She wasn't certain. But she was sure.

"Maybe someone told them what it looks like. Maybe they met somebody who saw it once, but they don't have any idea. I've seen it, Esme. I've touched it. I know."

Esme sat up and looked over.

"The key to all forgery lies in failure, not perfection. A scuff, an errant print, a bad wine cork. If you train yourself, know what to buy, get a diploma, sure. But to get something perfect, you have to know the flaws, the violence done to it, the times the frame got dinged, or an edge got clipped. And if your buyer is in the big-time, they'll know about the pencil marks on page 58, they'll know whether the inscription was in ballpoint or felt-tip, they'll know if it was left in an-east-facing window and the blue dyes got broken up by the sun. That's why the flaws and fuckups and things that aren't supposed to be there are the most important thing to recreate. A sucker is going to chromatograph the ink and fiber test the paper, but if this other buyer knows this book, they're going to know if a hinge is loose, and if the box glue is stretched, you get me?" Esme said.

"I've seen it before. I've read it. I've touched it, Esme."

Sophie's scheme for the Book was the cleverest of card tricks. Up Sophie's sleeve was an infernal device loaded with a mirror-copy ace. You'd pluck that slim ace away and swirl at whatever wondrous action took place when it was upside down just resting in your hand. A wonder, they would think. But it wasn't the card making the magic. No. It was the magician.

Sophie hadn't seen it in years and now she was close enough to smell it and feel the heat coming off it. She could sense the Blue Glow at every corner of her eye. She was in the same city, and her lips buzzed, and her throat burned, the Book close enough to draw her closer and closer. She stumbled towards it like an insect drawn dimly towards a sweetness it hungered for but could only blindly sense.

Sophie checked the time, her calls, and messages. Still nothing.

"The day before Lake got sentenced, he seeded me into the system. He cleared a meadow in the algorithm just for me to be born, a place for my name against so many others. He gave me an identity. Free and legal. He cleared my dead name forever, Sophie. Now I can exist as I am. I have insurance. I own Fin and Scale with my own true name. He summoned Esme Carrington into this world after he saw me burn the letters from my family that told me that CHRIST WILL FORGIVE ME. Lake took the biggest risk when he could afford it least, Sophie. Lake's a good man."

Sophie looked across Esme's neck and saw the evaporation of her past life. The dim pink tattoo scars, and index of Esme's lovers from her ears to her collar, Antonio to Kurt to Troy. Sophie remembered holding Esme's hand as the names were flickered off her body, Esme telling Sophie she would serve nothing but herself now that she was finally free.

"What are you offering him to compete?"

"Freedom," Sophie said.

"That's how. You're the only one who can offer him the thing he wants, the thing he gives."

"They'll tell him what to do and he's going to hate them for it. Show me how you make the book," Sophie said.

Three stripes the color of denim, spruce, strobe blue were lined on a sheet of A4 paper from an orange box. Esme waved it thin and dry with her breath. The stripes overlapped. Esme slid the sheet into a translucent wax envelope threaded with silver filaments. Esme set it on a rubber pad, then, plugged a long angled wand into an outlet.

She held the wand with both hands, and it murmured with a purple light as she moved it across the envelope and the paper inside. She flipped it over. She nodded. Complete. She clicked off the wand and set it down. She held the paper cupped, warm as a blind newborn chick and floated it to Sophie's hands.

"See how it ages? Visible, abrasion, ultraviolet, infrared."

Eighteen thousand days had passed over the page and the triple-hue in just moments. The denim, spruce, and strobe sapped by age and air and sunlight. The wand and murmur and envelope had aged the pages a lifetime of reading eyes and notes and shelving lives.

They could create the press and plates and the words and mimic a journey through time in the Book of Blue Daggers. They could fork the single version won at auction into two. The inert and mule clone passed off as the true version until only the ascendant mastery was attempted to be read from between stagnant lines.

"Esme, listen," Sophie said.

"When you get it, when you make the copy, don't read it."

"I know you believe Sophie. I'll be ok," Esme said.

"It doesn't matter if you believe or not. Don't read it. Don't let the thing trick you, Esme," Sophie said. "Promise me."

"Promise you what?"

"When you make the copy, don't look too close. Don't look at anything at all."

"I have to look at it, Sophie. I can't work my process blind."

"Don't look at the words, then. The Book leaves a trail of bodies."

Esme smiled.

"Fine. Ok. Do you remember what the Book looks like?" Esme asked.

That autumn smell of old books. The soft scraping noise it made when she turned the pages. The way it made her feel when she pulled herself up by her hands into the blue moonlight with the strength of imagination alone, when the strength alone was everything.

"No. There's no one I know who does," Sophie said.

"How did Dillinger get the Book?" Esme asked.

"Sophie, when you get it, all you're going to do is worry about losing it again."

"No. I won't lose it again."

"You're just trading one fear for another. You think if you lived for a thousand years, you'd ever become free?"

"I do Esme. I'll get it and you'll see."

Esme smiled. "Alright. Well, I hope you prove me wrong soon."

"He stole it. He thought he could trick the Book, but the Book tricked him. Howard Cyone too, and he did everything he could to avoid it. Zzzzzap."

"You think there is no one. But there is someone."

"There isn't, Esme. The reading list is nothing but corpses, the permanent brain dead, and just me," Sophie pointed to her temple.

"No. There is. The neurosurgeon that Dillinger and Howard Cyone took the Book from. He has a son. He read it. He knows," Esme said.

"Wagner Koo? You said he was dead."

"No, he just tried to. The way I heard; he gave himself a lobotomy above his bathroom sink. He spends his days in group playtime at Eastern State Hospital."

"Eastern State? That's the fucking criminal psycho ward, how did he end up there?"

"They call them Forensic Wards. You should ask his son, Oscar. He's an artist-in-residence at the Washington University Psychology program."

"No one survives past the Book," Sophie said. "No one."

"When you see Oscar, you won't be sure he did either," Esme said.

# CHAPTER ELEVEN

*The Decision*

## TITLOW PARK, TACOMA WA OCTOBER 24

Lake parked lights out and away from the boat launch on the little slip beach. He walked under the railway bridge and into the light of a half-moon, making his way between the smell of marine fuel and the sulfur stink from the blooms of sea grape. He trotted on the slotted slope of the launch streaked by cuts of boat hulls, making himself as small as possible.

He pried loose his pistol and holster by the tall grass and looked out at the empty lot.

Lake took a construction-ply garbage bag from his back pocket and unfolded it on the rocky shore before him. Holding a pocket knife and eyeing the bag, he cut one, two, three big holes and pocketed the scraps before pulling the bag over his body and putting his arms through one hole and then another and then his head before tightening the red plastic band around his midsection and knotting it.

Muth had called back eight hours ago. He had a pin on Monty Boate. He had a name and a number. But, you see, he couldn't give it over the phone, not this lava-hot information that might fry the whole damn circuit.

Muth was lying.

He could hear Muth reading off the scrawled notes of a double-cross plan. Pulling whiskey for the courage to keep it straight faced and steady. Muth said Monty could be anywhere now, across any bridge, across any highway. He was sure about this plan, dollar amounts, times and schedules, and guns. He mimicked all the worst liars in the world and said, "Trust me on this one."

Muth was just the trigger arm of a city-wide flytrap. Lake could just make out their tripwires, so thin and delicate that the breeze couldn't even catch them, standing tall and silver to the night.

Lake's bad hand went stiff as ice. He held it tight against his chest and squeezed it off at the elbow. The nerve impulses fired out the cold ends of his fingers in backfire blasts. It cramped cold and all his fingers splayed out, snowman stiff. With his other hand, he pressed knuckles deep into his forearm to work the knots of muscle away. He dug it red and wounded and channeled the short circuit away from the screws and plate and bone.

Maybe they had mistaken Lake for someone else. A man who wouldn't be able to see their pathetic angle washing up on the tide a thousand feet away. Maybe Muth or Boate thought that Lake wouldn't notice the slow, foaming plan coming into focus over the horizon, the waves trading it forward endlessly before the double-cross snapped him. Maybe that's what everyone thought of him.

Muth slow-rolled into the lot and parked. He pulled out a long green sportsman's case from the backseat and walked it by the handle over to Lake's car. He knocked on the window and looked in, his face twisted and his mouth open. Muth shouted for Lake and put his phone to his ear and looked up towards the entrance road.

He waved at the entrance to the lot and exaggerated his shoulders. There was a red Chevy diesel truck with only the idling lights on, easing up to the bridge over the tracks. Muth saw it and shooed it back. In the Chevy's lights, the shadows of the trees collapsed into enormous black columns one after the other, fusing into the smooth moonlit dark as the Chevy kicked it all the way back to the main road in.

Lake cupped the pistol in his frozen hand and hopped off the rocks, his breathing ragged and the bag rustling in the night as he jogged towards the lot. Muth opened the front door and set the sportsman case in the passenger seat floor to ceiling before biting his lips and putting his hands on the steering wheel. His breath caught at the sight of Lake standing in front of his hood.

Muth squinted, and Lake shot him through the window. With one crack from the bullet and the glass both, and Muth went cross-eyed just as his hands fluttered across the wheel before he slid into the console. Lake stood there for a moment, the gun still pointing, steaming, the night still on pause from the stunning blast. There was a water fountain sound and Muth's hands relaxed on the wheel. Lake opened the door.

The phone was in the passenger seat. It was flashed with red fronds of wet hair and still open to the call logs to "MB." Guess who had called in and out nine times just today from a 509 area code? Lake patted down Muth's jacket. It was wet and getting wetter. A Shell receipt for gas and a sausage biscuit in Yakima and an envelope of cash were in a pocket full of blood. Thirty-three hundred, mixed. Lake didn't keep them.

The cold water at the launch stripped his hands clean enough. He worked them dry through his hair and made his way to the city streets as the dawn rose. Lake found a seat at a doughnut store with a counter, asked for a coffee and something with coconut on it. He gave the girl at the register five bucks for an extra waiter's pad and a couple of pens.

Muth knew about Asher. There was a spiderweb of errands and chores and fuckups that spun the world off its axis. Muth told Monty Boate everything. Thirty-three hundred dollars could light enough flame to burn off loyalty and light a west-coast fuse.

Lake called Taylor Zapata and waited.

"Hello?"

"Taylor, I have to take care of something personal, today. I'm letting you know in advance."

"We need you in the office, Lake. We are going to prep. Get rested and ready."

"I'm in great shape, Taylor. That's why I'm letting you know in advance."

"Let's be clear, Lake, it is 7:15 am, and I'll be honest, it does not sound like you just woke up. Until our joint process is complete, we do not have time for personal requests to be granted."

"I need time for one single thing."

"I should let you know that Barbara did take time and a fantastic effort to set up the trust for Asher. We showed our commitment to you. Now it is your turn to show it your commitment to us."

"Asher?"

"Barbara found Asher's social for you. Asher's trust has been created. When you come in, we will go over the asset breakdown."

"I never got his numbers to you."

"Fortunately, Barbara found it, verified it. She put in the legwork. That's a deliverable we crossed off, as promised."

"What did she say to Asher?"

"She just confirmed his information, I believe. We provided for you. Now is your time to provide for us."

Lake hung up.

He used the number he got from Muth. The flames were closing in. It rang through all the way down the Pacific.

"Hello?" It was a girl's voice.

"Yes, hello, I know this isn't his phone, but I'm looking for Asher. This is his uncle, and he left-"

"Yeah, he changed his numbers-" She was distracted.

"Yes, I am aware, I was wondering-"

"Sorry, who is this?" Laughter in the background. Music.

"Asher's uncle, Devin."

"On his mom's side, or?"

"That's correct, yes."

"Oh. He moved back in with his mother. He's with his mom." Someone in the background giggled.

Lake hung up.

His mother. There would be a better chance of Ash living on the moon. There would be a better chance of Asher begging Lake for forgiveness. What a crafted fucking lie.

Asher would go invisible against the skyline and disappear forever. Asher would never come back to him. Asher would see the trust fund money as a bacillus waiting to infect him. A biotoxin treasure chest that Asher would never risk laying his hands upon.

Lake came in for the meeting just in time. They never asked about it. They had a hotel suite up so high the rain clouds blocked the windows. Barbara Bontecue and Taylor Zapata were beaming like new converts.

The rain lensed against the window and Lake could see the sky cleaved with blue far across Puget Sound. He watched the Olympic Mountain cuts go cerulean, blueberry, and lapis in the draw of the midday breeze. Behind him, the law partners proselytized. Lake's chance to join the big leagues, be part of something they called the real world.

While listening to Taylor and Barbara lie to him about what the future held in store, Lake suddenly understood exactly who he was and what he had always been, and realized he would call Sophie the moment they left his sight.

# CHAPTER TWELVE

*Phantom Pressure*

## SEATTLE, WASHINGTON, OCTOBER 24

Even with the music on, Oscar Koo waved at her.

He didn't turn to look, just putting out a hand as Sophie walked into the loud basement studio, dry and cold and smelling like plywood and oil paints and turpentine.

A placard on a wall told Oscar's story across three languages. Glossy brochures gleamed on a table next to an outrageously priced book of art prints and a frame up of Oscar Koo's life story. Sophie rubbed her fingers on a photograph of Oscar. His eyelids were wide open to the camera, staring at nothing at all from the strange pearly whites of his orbital implants.

Oscar's assistant, Marina, put a finger to her mouth. She turned down a speaker playing Philip Glass. She wore scarves stiff with paint. Oscar wore ruby-mirrored sunglasses, and his face was inches from the canvas as he scratched a brush across an ocean, a wave, a sunset.

Marina dabbed colors and arranged them on brushes, some of them an inch long and no thicker than a blade of grass. Oscar mumbled, and Marina nodded and handed him colors and brushes.

Oscar was in bare feet, and he had one foot pressed against the wall. He settled his left foot across lines of skid tape set behind him, digging his big toe in for the location. He scraped a pushpin brush constantly. He rolled a shoulder to keep it loose. He kept his toes locked at the skid tape, stomping quietly to keep the feeling fresh.

"How's the itchiness?" Marina asked Oscar.

"I can keep going," Oscar said.

"You should break." Marina said. "I'll bring us food."

"There's no pain. Do you have the deep colors now?"

Sophie read the glossed-over biography. Koo, the son of a surgeon. The power of truly positive thinking. The blinding accident. A career potentially destroyed. Transcendence via misfortune. "A mindful awakening that lay within us all." Oscar Koo.

Oscar Koo set his foot to another angle of skid tape, never moving his head, and he painted a sunset oiling through sea foam, the wind lifting a catspaw of waves. Deep below, a moonglow thread of light birthed fractals, triangles, molecular grids from a glassy abyssal plain.

"You are very quiet," Oscar said.

"I'm sorry," Sophie replied. "I'm watching you work."

Marina put the paintbrush down. Oscar removed his hands and feet from the tape and rolled the stiffness out of his joints.

"He needs to relax," Marina said.

"Of course," Sophie said.

"There are to be no media recordings or imprints, audio, visual. You can discuss the work but absolutely do not discuss biographical or personal details. Yes? Good and understood?" Marina said.

"Of course, yes," Sophie said.

Another panel of the painting lay on the table. This one was far beneath the deepness of the ocean on the wall. A deep darkness of ice, cracking into a mitosis of hexane rings, hydrocarbons, and the looping tails of molecular chains wisp in the ropy mass of light burning at the water's depths.

"I'm Cora Collins, Mr. Koo, and I'm working on a thesis about psychological states in artistic representation. I'm also an admirer."

"Ah."

"Do you always have the lights on?"

"For Marina, yes."

"I want to ask you how you arrived at your process."

"Process is not very interesting. Process is what is comfortable."

"I know I'm not just speaking for myself when I say this, I just find it endlessly transfixing. Gestural. Structurally, it's very playful and teasing."

"Ah," Oscar said.

"Your biography says that you lost your eyes in an accident?"

"An accident is an unfortunate incident without deliberate cause." Oscar took deep breaths. He worked a brush with long rubber bristles across his elbows to his wrist, back and forth as he breathed.

"Can I ask you about the accident?"

"Biography is pointless."

"It's just one question."

Oscar ran the rubber brush against his temples. He rubbed it vigorously under the red wraparound sunglasses and at his ears. Sophie could see him shiver with delight as he scratched away at his eyelids and the bridge of his nose.

"Before the accident. About something your father owned."

Oscar panted and dug the brush fully under the ruby-red sunglasses. He leaned forward and held them on with one hand while he swept away with the other.

"I want you to tell me about the Book he had?"

The transportation was instant. Oscar gasped out loud.

"Oh!" he said, and he didn't even notice.

He put his hands out straight. He was dizzy from how fast the memory grasped him. His body was not here. But there.

He dropped the brush and held the Book again in his hands. Sophie watched Oscar float up and away and into the past, and his eyes returned to him.

Oscar dropped the brush to the cold, flat floor and started turning invisible pages. He stared down at his lap, his lips open, mouthing remembered words. He marveled again at the blue chapter headings, the carefully inked letters, and the enamel full color inserts.

He was there. A dawn rising sun on his face and the heavy rock cream of mist growing at Motero Bay, just north of the islands. The grand ivory basilica resplendent in the arc of the morning sun, its arches shadowed by wingspans of Azure-crested Parabliss rising to their migrations.

"You've read it," Oscar whispered.

"I remember the colors and shades, Oscar. From the blue of the bay to the smell of orchid wood under the purple lamped sky."

"My father had just retired as a surgeon, and when a man reaches that age, they often revisit their boyhood dreams. My father wanted to publish books. And that was the first book he prepared. That was before his difficulties."

"Did your father know what the Book was capable of?"

Oscar hadn't blinked in years. He had forgotten how to. The sunglasses he wore were there to prevent uncomfortable silences, but Sophie didn't look away when Oscar put the mirrored lenses on the table and turned his face towards her, his pink eyelids half-closed over bleached silicon implants. He pressed his fingers deep at the springy orbs everywhere, pulsing a phantom pressure and itch that wasn't really there.

"My father said he wanted me to follow him and read it, just as he did in his youth. I told him I would illustrate as much of the Book of Blue Daggers as I could. The Skymelody Birds, the airship of the Eucalyptus Queen, the map to the Verdant Pool."

"You drew the map to the Verdant Pool? The Book tells you how to get there?" Sophie asked.

"From the coast of the Coral Vault to the lava tubes and then to the pool itself."

"Oscar, what happens at the Verdant Pool?"

"Cora, why did you lie to me about wanting to see my art?"

Sophie nodded. "I wanted to know how he lost the Book."

"The Book arranged for it to happen. It wanted to find someone more capable, and it arranged to make it happen. Of course, my father blamed me for the loss. He said I was jealous. That the Book told me what would happen at the Verdant Pool, that I was lying and stalling and that I deserved to be punished."

"The accident."

"I remember waking up in a hospital chair. I felt like being in a thick wool blanket. I remember my father's hands through gloves. Him brushing my hair. His voice telling me not to worry. He had the lights too bright, but it didn't cause any pain. No pain at all. He told me I was being punished. He was very calm. He was very steady. It only took a moment. I remember the noise of wet scissors and wire clamps. I remember the smell of my father's soap-clean arms and rubber gloves. Do you know a fresh open wound can smell like water coming forth from a mineral spring?"

"I don't."

"I had seen my father do surgery before, knew his fingers were tucked and fast and sure as a concert pianist, though I couldn't see, or even blink, against the bracing clips he put into my sockets. With one finger he pressed a side of both eyes and got a feel for the pressure. From then, an instant. But sometimes you remember the whole instant. I could feel the snare wire and cold clamp on my right eye first as he pulled it up and away. Then he clipped the optic nerve. He put it in a metal pan, and I could see it. Your eyes are larger than you imagine, you know. It was a strange sensation, feeling the cold gap of air there. Fresh blood on my hands from the hole. Not long in the instant. My father had clamped and uprooted my left eye and clipped it away and set it with the other in the pan. I know this is what the Book told him to do, because the Book told me this was going to happen. I knew it was going to happen, and it was impossible to avoid."

Oscar's face aimed at nothing. He put it towards Sophie's voice like he was staring. But that couldn't be it. He couldn't possibly be staring.

"What happened to your father?"

"The Book convinced him that if he lost it, all further knowledge would be useless. Somehow, he survived his lobotomy." Oscar smiled right at her.

"Does he remember what he did?"

"He remembers enough." Oscar put two fingers in a V, one against each eyebrow.

"He punched in just below here, and just below here." Oscar leaned towards Sophie, laughing at it. "The steadiness of his hands was the first thing to go."

Oscar put both hands out as still as he could. He started shaking them, tremor fast. They were blurs, fans, the smoke of fingers. He held his mouth open, but his head was so steady and close that Sophie could see her tiny shadow on the chalks of his eyes.

He laughed and laughed. Marina rushed into the room, her scarves held tight, stricken at the noise. She rushed to Oscar and held his hands in hers, riding them calm against her body as his laughter wound down. Marina put her head against his, wrapping their hands together against his face, asking what happened.

"She reminded me of something so funny. I should return to the work now, shouldn't I, Cora, especially that you have a call coming in?"

Sophie felt the vibration against her. Oscar put a hand out to her and Sophie touched it as Marina led him to the tape and the paint again. An unknown number beckoned, and Sophie answered as she left the room.

"I heard you make our wildest dreams come true?" Lake asked.

"I can. And I want you to be there, Lake."

"You were right about them, Sophie. They didn't understand."

Sophie could see it. She could reach out and grab it. She put on the mask and closed her eyes and made herself big and tall and coached up Lake and grabbed a brush while Marina settled Oscar in.

She painted Lake holding the Book, a valiant kind wreathed against the sun, supplicants at his feet, the Book held in place of a nominal sword.

"I can get the Book for you. I need you to find something for me. Right now," Lake said.

"Anything," Sophie said.

"I need you to find my son."

"Asher? Why now?" Sophie asked.

"Monty Boate. He wants to hurt me. He wants to hurt my son," Lake said.

"Bring me the Book and I'll find him," Sophie said.

"No, right now," Lake said.

"I'll start right now, Lake. I'll start right this minute." Sophie said.

"Find him Sophie. Monty will kill him otherwise."

# CHAPTER THIRTEEN

*The Gnostic Auction*

## VASHON ISLAND, WASHINGTON, OCTOBER 27

Lake used a burner phone to text Sophie that he had arrived before stepping onto the wet steel ramp to Vashon Island.

The island was hemlock-dark, with the peaks of the trees arrowing into the last dim blue of the day. A man from the ferry with a yellow reflective vest pointed towards a gravel path and told Lake, "You can't miss it."

Right he was. At the path's end, the immense lodge stood, a vibrant sanctuary pulsating with Haida artistry. The length of the building was totally obscured by darkness, and Lake was unable to even worry a guess at the size of the colossal room against the timbered darkness. Guests approached the front, passing under animal motifs etched into the facade—ebony ravens soaring, dark blue salmon contorting, and a smiling fire-red grizzly playfully raising its paws and peeking its tongue.

Carved beyond the highest windows stood totems reaching the cedar-bark shingles. Powder-faced moons gazed shock-eyed while attendants below offered directions in three languages.

The wind pushed and pulled at the white jackets of the attendants as they offered Lake a way inside.

More of the crowd filled in. Louder. Some drunk. Some shaking. Some jet-lagged. Some assembled off the ferries. Some driven the long way around off the airstrip in Bremerton. The room was teeming with sagging bodies and long pauses and questions the attendants refused to answer.

A cedar doorway lined with sensors funneled the throng into the viewing room.

"No pictures, absolutely no pictures beyond this line," an attendant said. A woman beside him was collecting phones and tablets and zipping them in silicon cases and handing out receipt tags. A woman and a man with a fuckoff biker beard made a scene. They crowded the attendant and refused to give up their phone. The attendant shooed them off, saying they were barking like toothless dogs, and that it wouldn't be accepted here.

Lake texted Sophie. "Here for it."

Sophie hit him with photos.

Federal Marshall's warrant for BOATE, MONTGOMERY V. A screenshot of a bank trust set up in Asher's name. No address. A shitload of money that just batched in dividends.

Lake texted Sophie. "Asher will never touch it. Find him."

"Are you close to it?"

He was close to it. He told her.

"Find Asher. See you on the other side."

Lake dismantled the burner and slipped the component pieces into a trash bin before walking towards the viewing room. A fob with dazzling lights swiftly waved over him, scanning for something elusive. Green lights confirmed his innocence. With a receipt tag and auction list in hand, he scanned every line from top to bottom.

Complimentary drinks had the crowd gasping, explaining, talking too much about the items. Everyone in sight was an expert. Every subject covered, all you had to do was screw up and ask for details.

Item 76 was blank, small, and pretty thin. A white cardboard sign under it read ITEM 76/BOOK/PAPER.

It looked like nothing special at all.

It was oatmeal bland and featureless as a schoolbook. There were pale spots on the dark blue buckram fabric cover, and the corners were bent. A shiny black patch on the spine touted THE BOOK OF BLUE DAGGERS.

A woman wearing a nametag that said "Remee, Valuations" and wearing a silk chevron blouse offered explanations to Lake.

"Please see this was bound in an indigo buckram, common at the time. Examine the foil lettering against the spine. It has oxidized with age. You may check closely the hollow-spine binding, cotton of course, again natural to the period and standard. That binding has trusted out for decades, as you can see, allowing this volume to retain a lovely shape and natural lay."

"Can you open it up? I'd like to see the interior." Lake said.

"I'm sorry sir," Remee said.

"Well, there's a marking on the interior, and I really need to make sure."

"Please see that the Dillinger Estate bound all the pages in wax." Remee led Lake's eyes with her fingers to the thickly glazed edges of the paper, bunched and bound white against the binding.

"We must sell it as it stands, exactly as you find it here," she said.

"Fine, that's... just fine," Lake said.

The auction summoned it all—the culmination of beings and objects. Within this gathering, the very essence of predator and prey intertwined. The attendees were twisted, they were long-limbed, their eyelids drooped hideously, and their gaits were marred by limps and wheezes. Their faces had been shocked and set colorless and locked in fearful expressions after harrowing accidents. Spines and shoulders carried the imprint of accidents or sabotage, the question marks of bones and bodies and motives each.

A bell rang clear, twice.

Lake watched a small man approach the lectern. No bigger than a horseracing jockey, he thought, wondering where the wiry little man with a paunch and a black mustache got his wool, three-piece suits, and if they sold the gold pocket watch there too.

He unbuttoned his gray jacket coat and held his thin arms crooked akin to a conductor. With no flourish, he gestured towards an unseen object beside him. His nimble fingers confidently directed the attendants with precision: here, here, and no—not there—here. As he began to speak, with no microphone, his booming voice erupted from his compact frame, punching all the way to the back wall of the viewing room where Lake stood. He had every eye in the place on him and, waiting a beat, he slipped on a pair of reading glasses and began.

"Item 1! Various Electronica, estimated 1982, beginning one thousand!"

"Number 1, sold as-is," the Conductor said, counting from one thousand to fifteen hundred soon to two thousand to three and now forty-five hundred. A wave of cheapskates dropped at five. A commotion started at 8. The conductor cupped his ear to the crowd before taking it to eighty-five hundred.

"We have to turn it on!" someone yipped.

"Just run the power cycle!!" someone else yelled.

The conductor boomed, "Eighty-five hundred?"

"Yes, keep going, here!" a bidder offered.

"Wait, no, WAIT!" an angry voice started in.

"It's sold where-is, you know the rules. Nine thousand, nine-" the conductor said. The crowd didn't take it. They asked for the power. Lake moved to the front.

Item 1 was a scramble of vivisected motherboards and cables and plastic on a cart hooked up to an ancient CRT television stripped down to just the tube. Thick ribbons of gray wire and twists of red and blue puzzled every piece to another, everything cabled and joined out through a tarnished chrome sphere stamped with a faded Department of Defense eagle. A bright green joystick and six purple plastic buttons looped from a console back to the sphere with thick black tubes, then, joined to a peeling pressboard marquee feebly announcing POLYBIUS.

"I don't need it turned on! Eleven thousand!" a woman said.

"Finally, Sanity!" someone said.

"Eleven then, Now, twelve?!" the conductor said.

It went to thirteen, fifteen, seventeen-five, before the conductor called "Sold" and clapped the lectern with a rigid cap of wood. The conductor leaned over to shake the hand of the woman, who asked for the power to stay off. He shook her hand quickly and handed her a dictionary-thick sheaf marked "MANUAL - ASSEMBLY INSTRUCTION FOR MK-ULTRA Subproject.166.

Lake watched the crowd of the wealthy and dire and aged converge as Item 76 approached. Some walked stiff and bruised, some smelled of Vaseline and menthol, some drooled excessively into handkerchiefs or Kleenex or wiped fresh by an attendant. They were all pale, and they all seemed to know each other. They bid quietly, some helping one another to be seen by the conductor. His count now slowed. They bid through a pit of necromantic relics. A tall man barely able to flex or bend now owned stoppered flasks fogged with the last breaths of three popes. A woman with bulging glass-blue cataracts and a platinum blond wig tickled her fingers across the obsidian and wood of an Aztec macuahuitl glazed with Spanish blood. A man in a shearling jacket pointed angrily at Item 35. His voice rasped like leaves on pavement as he pointed to a pair of flimsy human-skin gloves, knit with mason line at the fingers and tanned so quick they still had the palm whorls and prints.

"Just won't do without the box," he whispered.

"The evidence box is Item 44."

"Just won't do."

"Start the bidding one," he said, the old man giving up his commotion to turn away from the box, lidded and waxed and marked WAUSHARA CO. WISCONSIN COURTHOUSE — EVIDENCE and GEIN EDWARD T.

A young woman bumped against Lake. She wore a jade evening gown cut with a high slit revealing a black prosthetic carbon-fiber leg. Even here, she stood out like a butterfly among moths, her fashion choices cut to the body and her leg giving her the appearance that she just stepped back in from tomorrow.

"Do you think it changes their weight?" she asked.

"What?"

The woman circled her hands. This. Everything.

"I saw you looking at the Book earlier. The last thing you want is a bidding war, but alas. I'm Celeste Yang."

"Lake Bright."

Celeste was pale and gray as wet pavement and her deep breaths smelled wickedly sour, but she nailed Lake with her killshot eyes.

"I know."

"Do we know each other?" Lake asked.

"Not directly."

"Friend of a friend, that kind of thing?"

"We both know Sophie-what is it now? Sherman?. We both know Sophie Sherman."

"That's not her-"

"I know it's not her real last name. I'll be completely honest. I called her a few days ago and told her you were going to be here. I was hoping she'd find a way to deadlock you or maybe steal the thing herself, ha!" Celeste laughed in a way to convince herself of the humor.

"I'm bidding on the first floor on through to heaven for the Book. You should know that."

"So, Mr. Bright, do you think the history of a thing can be measured in its weight? Do you think the action of a thing changes its form?"

"That's why everyone is here. They are bidding on history, and, uh, the significance of the thing. Look at this crowd. The money is in the story."

The conductor brought out a tan-colored slab the length of a room. A substantial piece of rock rolled out on plastic wheels that chirped under the weight. Streaks, animal prints, something like starburst constellations traced across the boulder.

"Can you read the story through the arrangement of the atoms? Does the molecular lattice get re-arranged by history itself, Lake?" Celeste asked.

Her smile turned into a snarling wince, and Lake could see an invisible jolt almost bring her to her knees as she snapped a hand to her eye, the cold sweat lining her face as she held an elbow out straight to keep steady from the sudden double-vision.

"People pay for what's important because they want, they need to believe it's important," Celeste said.

The crowd started bidding. The Conductor started high on the fossilized shoreline, the Tyrannosaurus Rex tracks growing in length and depth, The Conductor flurrying his hands to show the dinosaur's trot expanding to a sprint across the length of the slab. The start of a hunt, some seventy million years ago, give or take.

"That's exactly it, Lake. It's just an illusion. It's just a story they're telling. There's no difference from one thing to another. History doesn't hold any weight, and it doesn't change a single thing at all."

The bidding went outrageous on the rock. They were selling a crime scene, 75 million years old, the perpetrator never found, but presumed quite deceased. The conductor talked about the footsteps of a killer, the bloodstains possibly visible, somehow, through the ages. It pitched out a thousand and thousands and thousands for those sweating the clues notched into the darkened schist.

"You're wrong. Look at what these people are paying for. The history," Lake said.

The conductor said the name of it out loud. "The Book of Blue Daggers. Item 76. A book," the conductor said. The bidding was starting at five hundred. Bidding at five hundred.

Celeste bid one. Others ran it up, Celeste biting her lip and breathing fast and light as she kept blinking and squinting but could never quite catch up.

Lake looked at the crowd. He couldn't shake a bad jolt. He couldn't see the other bids. Two. Three. Four. Five. He went five again, fast. Too fast. Someone picked up that he wanted it badly. A professor-type in a bowtie was right with him at six, seven, eight. Celeste went to nine and smiled at him.

"I heard no one has ever read a word of this," Lake said.

"No. It's just the mystique. They're paying for the concept of the mystery, not the words and story inside."

They were at nine. Ten. Celeste jumped it. Sixteen. Another at Twenty.

Lake froze up, let it roll out to twenty-three. His hand blinked off beneath the scars. Dead weight tugged at his arm from the shoulder.

Twenty-five thousand. Lake pitched in twenty-seven five.

"No, don't," Celeste said. She pressed against the black filaments of her prosthetic leg to steady herself, opening her mouth in a dry heave. Her left pupil pooled out black, her eyes cartoonishly mismatched.

"You don't understand it," Celeste said. The bidding kept rising and Celeste's eyes went wide, and she whispered, "Oh my god."

Celeste grimaced and wheezed as it went to thirty. Lake watched Celeste lean over the floor and dry heave. She pushed both palms, hard, against her temples, her fingers trembling like pale antlers as the bids went to thirty -no, thirty-two and then a silence.

Lake pitched in a thirty-three.

Celeste stood and tried to get it at thirty-six, but what was the point? Clear as a smashed window, she didn't have the cash.

It ran to forty. Celeste tried. Her voice cracked when she made it.

Celeste had both of her eyes closed and was bidding with one hand raised, her face bunched into a mask of gray sweat and pain.

"Let's go. Forty-two," Lake said. "Forty-two!"

Lake watched Celeste squint into the distance and then take a few steps in a half-circle, her left arm twitching and dangling at her side. She mumbled something to Lake.

"Nothus, pleths tell I mum Selif dont, don't..."

"Forty-four!" the conductor shouted and Lake kept waving the rocket straight up as Celeste tugged at him, her eyes dark and bloodshot as ripe cherries, as she mumbled and stumbled away.

Celeste ground her head against the wall, glaring at Lake. The left side of her face went totally slack, lips sagging and drooling, her eyelid flopped in a permanent wink. She attempted to mouth something to Lake, but Lake couldn't hear her over the shouts of the conductor asking for final bids. "Anyone else, forty-five?"

No one else was bidding, and the conductor was asking for final bids, anyone else, if forty-five was going to be the last.

Lake nodded at him and turned to Celeste. She still had one eye open and took baby steps, bracing her body, now gray like fish skin, with her one good arm before slipping to the ground.

The conductor didn't say anything.

Lake smiled and laughed. The conductor's wooden gavel slapped out that it had ended and there was applause, and someone yelped, and someone clapped, and a trim young attendant was right by his side, escorting him into the next steps. Lake listened to the instructions about receiving and signing and watched two attendants on their shoulders shoo people away from Celeste and rolled her to her side.

One attendant laid his hands inches above her face to cover the agonal heaving noises she made reaching out to Lake, her last living gasps made to lay her fingers on the Book, but it was too late, and nothing could possibly be done as the conductor snapped the wooden block again and called seventy six "Finished!" at forty-four thousand for this man right here. Congratulations, sir, congratulations indeed.

# CHAPTER FOURTEEN

*Let it Come Down*

## LOS ANGELES, CALIFORNIA, OCTOBER 27

By the time the second call came in, Monty had knotted and spiraled the rope tight with the broom handle. Asher's lips turned black, and his tongue pushed straight out past his teeth. His head weaved and his body shook. It started with the feet and fingers, then the shoulders and knees, finally doubling over and twisting. Asher's lips split from the pressure as Roy Parwanni started calling in again.

Monty took Asher's shoes off. His feet were limp. He spiraled the knot one-quarter twist again and counted it out from one all the way to sixty-Mississippi. He watched and didn't see a thing shake or shiver from Asher. He left the knot on, anyway. You never want to make that kind of mistake.

The phone started ringing again, but Monty was done with Roy's big talk. He knew he'd fucked up his payday on this one. He had to figure out if he minded much. He needed to clear things up.

Monty found a big drawing pad and some good charcoal pencils on a desk. Asher must have been some kind of artist. Monty wanted to get started before he listened to Roy's message. Monty started drawing hands and feet. He was panting and going full tilt and drawing the burn marks from where he cranked the rope over the kid's neck and he realized he was drooling over the pages before he shook himself back in.

He took it slow. Wanted to get something good down. He took Asher's white tube socks off and looked at his pale feet and arctic toes. He started with bare feet on the page. Feet were hard as hell to draw, but Monty knew he had to get them right. He took the sharpest pencil and drew a diamond-knot around his ankles in the picture. It felt good drawing knots. It felt good drawing the kid's face all worn out and mouth slack to a ghost-face and with the rope bunched up around his ears.

"First things first, Monty, call me back the moment you get this. The very moment. I'm arranging it with the lawyer, so your friend Lake trades Asher for the Book and fixing it so you're in the room where it happens. Call me when you have the kid."

He drew a big knotty rope and Asher, the kid, dangled from the end of a lamppost. He drew a street crowd. The street was all crowded and everyone milled and pointed at his wrecked-up face and the kid's stained pants. Monty got up close to mark the detail of Asher's face. He drew in the shrugged-up shoulders and his black tongue pointed out like a mushroom and his glasses dangled off his curled-out eyes.

Knots tight as could be, even in the lamppost's shadow on the flat light of the street. He drew people on the streets holding torches. He made them all wear the same outfit, like some kind of uniform. He couldn't figure it out, but it felt right. It felt good that way.

Roy called again. Nah.

He found a blue box of macaroni and cheese in the cupboards and made it on the stove. Took him a good minute to figure out the buttons to start it. Electronics and blue lights. It wasn't clear to him. He hadn't had macaroni and cheese with the orange powder and milk in years. The milk was past the date, but it smelled fine enough and Monty poured it on. The orange smelled just perfect. He dug in the package with his finger and licked the bitter stuff off his fingers, sucking his teeth at the taste.

He set the pan on a small wooden table and ate it right there with a big metal spoon. The sun went down, and he ate the whole thing in the dark. No one ever knocked or called, and no cars came by. He wiped his lips on his collar and worked back on the drawing.

He worked more on the crowd. Brands glowing white-hot, like they'd been left in a fire all day. A real angry bunch. Monty drew another body on a lamp beside Asher. Cooked, roasted, the rope licked black by the flames.

"Fire funeral," Monty said, licking his lips.

He drew the background in, and goddam did it come to him. A grand big city, canals, marble arches, the buildings so tall they curved inwards when you looked up. A dark seashore off the tropical horizon. Seaplanes spraying into palm groves in the moonlight. Towering black palms and islands in the bay mist.

He looked at Asher's face. Again, at the drawing. It was a good match. It worked out nice.

Monty put the pan in the sink and washed his hands clean. A second message had come in, Roy talking faster than before. Monty could hear the car noise this time.

"Monty, look, Taylor Zapata can front you five thousand, cash in hand, if you get this done tonight. His client is motivated, so I'd suggest you squeeze them for much more than that. Just bring in that kid and call me now. Now."

The drawing was really nice. He blew it off and creased it and put it in his pocket. The Roy Parwanni calls scrambled his brain. The kid was dead and working out some angle to still get the cash, and Lake, in the same room made his head crackle like hot sauce on a skillet and he noticed he was drooling again.

Monty took Asher's keys and found his Toyota in the lot. He slammed the gas and put down the windows, spinning out in the parking lot before finding a station that played Guns N Roses. He drove south down the freeway at dusk, at three figures on the speedometer and then it was full black. He had the picture unfolded on the passenger seat beside him and wondered where the firebrands and the seaplanes and the city came from. He touched it and wondered if maybe he saw it in a dream, but police lights burst up around him and he had no more time to think at all.

# CHAPTER FIFTEEN

*Even a Copy So Potent*

## KENMORE WA LATE OCTOBER 28

The wish Sophie made burned a hole right through the earth and sky and the hours since the auction collapsed into nothing. Lake bloomed frenetic. He missed the handoff. He stacked excuses for the lawyers that went stratospheric.

At Esme's place, Sophie watched fish and lizards float white-bellied like dimpled balloons. A pair of rabbit ears concentrating still and stiff above wet red bones. Lizard eyes collected sand around their milky orbits, and thick pink tentacles knotted up behind green glass, piled in snowdrifts of algae.

Esme's aquariums had been unplugged and unpowered. The boa constrictor, metabolism slow as a moon-phase, fortressed in a pile of bleach jugs, fish food and mealworm cans. Sophie saw a shiver sweep from the tail end to the black eyes. The snake gulped red at the dark air, probing into the scents stirred up in the motionless room.

The room was a swarm of pages, pools of ink, dead things and the scavengers that crept in along an infiltrator wind. It stank of ammonia and spoiled meat and aspergillus mold. Exorbitant fish lay bent and shrunk in the salted outline of the splashes.

"Esme!" Sophie shouted. "Esme!"

Sophie had pulled the wrong card. The Dead Hand. The Worst Luck.

Sophie's throat went tight, and her face flushed hot and red. Scraps of the copied Book were strewn everywhere, pages of it, perfectly colored and shaded, Esme pacing right into it. Sophie crumpled the pages and jammed her fists against her eyes and screamed and screamed and screamed and screamed.

She could have saved it if she had trusted her instincts. If she had played better safe than sorry. If she was here for the handoff. If her pride in the plan didn't turn it back against her. One thousand thoughts stormed. She could open a hole in herself to stop the humiliation. Weigh herself down and drown herself in the pools of dead and bloated fish. Drink bleach that would cook away her insides and teach her a lesson for being so foolish. She deserved nothing less and everything more for putting trust in herself.

Lake called in.

"Where is Asher, Sophie?"

"Esme's gone, Lake. What the fuck happened?"

"I gave her the Book, Sophie. You know where my son is?"

"He's in Pasadena. When did you give it to her?"

"When the auction ended, as discussed. You're getting worse than the lawyers."

"Do lawyers know how you played it yet?"

"Gotta think so. Some woman had a fucking stroke and died when they hit the gavel on the Book. They called intermission, and I got the first boat back and handed it to Esme. The dead woman was bidding for the Book too, so I don't think I walked away, you know, surreptitiously."

"Esme absolutely has it?"

"Tell me Asher's address."

"I don't have the Book, Lake."

"I did my part."

"Keep your part of the bargain, and I'll keep mine."

"Fuck you, Sophie."

Sophie sat on the desk. She collected loose pages and laid them sequentially. They were truly magnificent. Esme had made it through. More Desoxyn crushed into lines, and the dust swept along the edges of the desk. At her feet Sophie saw a thick-gauge syringe, cracked and caked with amphetamine dust and sticky blood.

Alerts came in from her California connection. She put an injection trigger in case names were inserted into databases all along the west coast and mountain states. Alert on BOATE, MONTGOMERY

Monty Boate had been taken in by Los Angeles County Sheriffs. He was in handcuffs, in a holding cell in North Hollywood. The trigger read subject was "Less Than Cooperative." The trigger read "Blood on the Subject's Clothes." The trigger read "Identified as Victim's Car."

There was a burning hiss, and a shadow spun up. She could see the ceiling and the shadow was everywhere against her. She was out of breath, against her back, a nimble pulling, gripping, squeezing against her legs and rising. She could see the white backwards facing teeth of the boa sunk deep into her thigh. A thousand threads of muscle grinding and pressing against her, the electric-fast snake moving up as it twisted in.

The snake was hooded in ink and smeared Sophie with swaths and strips of blue and black as it twisted and dialed past her knee. Sophie screamed and in another spiral flash, the snake chewed into her stomach. Her breaths went into a countdown from 3-2-1 as the log-thick serpent double-coiled around her legs and flexed brutally against her. The snake's three-lidded eyes flickered, its pinhole nose bleeding black from Esme, injecting it with the syringe.

Sophie swept her hands across the desk and jabbed pens and scissors into the body of the snake, leaving feathers and horns across its bloody length. Her hands and feet went purple and numb. Esme hissed and couldn't stop herself. Color drained from the whole world as it torqued her breath away. The snake shook at her, and she was covered in liver-dark blood and the blue ink of the thing. White jolts exploded along Sophie's neck, the flares of pain bursting far along her body. She stabbed at the head with a scissor arm. The snake slowly twisted and bit. Her toes and legs and ribs cracked from the pressure, and she couldn't even close her mouth or blink without pain. Her hands rolled across a metal tube on the desk, and she suddenly remembered. Her muscles and kidneys and liver shivered and in the silent grip she lifted the tube in a hand she couldn't feel. Sophie twisted the dial of the metal tube with her teeth and grabbed the head of the snake prone. She squeezed the button and felt the bolt etch a death sentence down its whole body. It stiffened and shook tighter and quivered around and across her.

It loosened, and there was breath again. Sophie lifted herself out of the sagging body like wet vines. She was bleeding. She was bleeding ink. She dug for tape. She laid tissues across the blood, the tissues layering and sticking to the serous fluid draining out across her wounds. She strapped herself with a layer of tissues, tearing off duct tape with her teeth and holding it fast to her skin.

She found the seal of the Book's carpenter's wax floating in a spatter of ink. Unwinding it in her hands, Sophie imagined some prime diabolic quantity unleashed as the guardian wax was stripped away.

She moved badly across the room, unable to bend, her leg and body swollen, the crescent of the bite marks drooling even little dots of blood. She gathered as many pages as she could and set them on the desk.

Sophie couldn't keep up. Her foot swelled, and she took off her shoe. Her foot tingled at the touch of the air, the flesh of it veined and hot. Her knee was locked into place and a wracking pain shook her leg so hard Sophie had to hold it down to stop it. Her toenails were black, almost swallowed by the huge useless club of her foot.

Hopping on one leg, Sophie made her way and fell at the feet of the printer. In a magnetic cup of markers and pens, Sophie reached for an Exacto knife and flipped the top off. As she sliced the inch of her toenails away, the black blood spilled into red, and the relief was overwhelming and instant. Sophie pressed at her heels and arches and dots of relief and calm spilled out and away from the release of pressure caught in her toes.

Sophie could finally see the Book through calm eyes, the preparation copy. She flipped the copied pages until an illustration appeared. A chapter heading: "The Burned Alliance" dropped into an ignited city square, a crowd holding burning brands and unbelievers in the dark shadows of a city at dusk. In the distance, the ocean mist trailed into pools below, the night sky exchanging lapis to indigo.

Sophie passed more pages to another illustration, another chapter: "Shadow Walk" a glittering dusk waterfall that tumbled into a mysterious cave, lit by the orange beams of sunset. The waterfall sprayed shades of powder blue, ultramarine. A man with green goggles stood deep in the silhouette of the water, the deepest, darkest blue of them all, holding a blue dagger and stooping deeper into the cave. Sophie started breathing faster. Her shoulders ran into curled knots again. She could read it. She knew.

Even the reproduction pages glowed electric, and Sophie could feel the sympathetic echo. Just a faint glimmer of response. The vibration from a tuning fork buzzed in these pages. The blues jumped and moved; the water flowed at the edge of her vision. Even the copied pages still held something.

The tripwire pinged again on Montgomery Boate. Los Angeles County wasn't sending Mr.Boate back. The trigger said the subject was getting lined up with ASSAULT/MURDER/GRAND THEFTAUTO, just for starters. The trigger said wait a few days before getting him before a judge. The trigger said we found the body, prints, matching rope in the car, rest easy on this one, team. The trigger didn't say it, but Sophie was doomed and Lake no better.

Lake texted. He needed to know the address or said he was capital O-U-T and heading south. "Forget this nonsense."

Sophie understood now. She had no chance but to move forward.

Sophie flipped wildly through pages until finding those covered in the gray fin-prints of ink, the silver loops of a constrictor glide. The chapter showed The Bay Enchantress in a huge and encompassing mangrove canopy. Seaplanes dodging searchlights, the millennial root-trunks stretching to the just-glimpsed bit of sky that rained flakes of water, a sea blue, a darkest navy, a sea-storm gray.

Sophie called Lake. It was too late. She still had a chance. Just a chance. Just a chance.

"Where are you?" Lake asked.

Later, when it all worked out, she could beg for forgiveness and tell him why she waited and hope that he could possibly understand how scared she was. I didn't want to die, I don't want it to hurt, and Asher was already gone and-

"Go to the seaside. Find the tent city by the cranes," Sophie said.

Under the gargantuan fronds and the darkest blue sky, small orange glows from lanterns and torches at the roots, Sophie could barely make out the sea people on the shore.

"What?" Lake asked.

The people on the shore held fast from the rain in huts thatched with thick vines and floors of sand and threaded roots.

"Esme is by the tents. It's a city under the highway, by shipping ports," Sophie said.

"She's there? She has the Book?" Lake asked.

"Will you get the Book from her? Please Lake, please?"

"I'll get it, but-"

"I'm sending you Asher's address. He lives in Pasadena, Lake. Please."

It was too late anyway. What could she do? What could she have ever done? This was what the Book had always wanted. She sent it to Lake. She knew he wouldn't check.

"Got it. Got it," Lake said and hung up.

Even a copy is so potent! Even the copy of words had enough grasp of the magic. Sophie could see it and read it and know the spell of doom it wrote and was still writing.

# CHAPTER SIXTEEN

*Esme and the Subtle Moment*

## THE TRIANGLE/SODO, SEATTLE WA LATE OCTOBER 28

The balance was deeply one-sided. A moment levered Esme's life into the before, and the after. It was while she was reading the Book that she understood. A feeling like déjà vu as she read the words that described Esme to herself. She was only confused until the Book read her own thoughts back to her before telling her this quite unusual sensation was normal.

There was a subtle moment.

Then, it was decided.

A vast fog, as big as all of her future, drifted away, and she could see it clear and easy. Esme believed it. She had nothing ahead but pure outcome because she could see it clearly on the page written as she would do it. Let me guide your hand.

The Book wrote that she would put a hand to her lips and say that she understood now.

Esme put a hand to her lips and said, "I understand now."

Outside of her tent she watched as five, eight, twelve people in orange vests gathered around a honeycomb of metal trash cans. The Fire Worshippers snapped and tossed in driftwood, cardboard, drywall, nail-rimmed posts, trimmings pilfered from city parks. The smoke came in so thick and heavy Esme could pour it from one hand to another.

Across the corridor of smoke, the crowd lay a sheet-wrapped body into the glowing blaze.

There were shouts and fights and someone was trying to grab at the broiling legs of the body in the smoke. The clouding ash had made it impossible to see beyond her tent. Esme crawled back inside for her last paragraph.

Esme read about herself doing it and without much else to it, she did it.

There was an aquarium next to The Book of Blue Daggers at the base of her tent. The glass was steeped papers and ink. These were the things The Book told her to drag her herself. The last items of her life. The aquarium chugged along with a lantern battery now and the pink castle at the root of the purple coral castle clicked and bubbled.

She looked for the octopus on the little purple throne. An exquisite shapeshifter with a body half glass and half glue. It was feathering eight minds around a plastic ring toy Esme buried for its curiosity. She was sure that the Book was right when it said it wouldn't hurt as she reached into the tank.

Before she could pinch the Blue-Ringed Octopus, it spun away and sparked its freckles electric. Its skin went autumn evening brown and crackled with lightning stripes as Esme brought it into the air and pinched at it. It was small and sticky, its mantle no bigger than a grape. The legs flashed and curled into fishhook shapes. Esme could feel its beak and radula against her thumb cutting into her. She sighed and squeezed her hand again. This flick of its venom was no more noticeable than a thorn prick.

Oh. It went quicker than she thought.

To her face first. Her teeth and tongue. Esme blinked and wiped her eyes, nose and stooped to drop the cephalopod back towards its throne. As the toxins came on, she tilted her head back. A numb echo rolled over Esme as she drooled and waited to die on the floor of a tent under a highway in the rain.

Lake pulled into the lot of a used tire shop amidst slow rolling clouds of smoke from the homeless camps. The camps lay in the bushy triangle gap between the concrete pillars and tiers of the highway on-ramps, and the smoke was billowing out thicker and darker by the moment.

Lake crouched and put his face in his arm from the smells of burning plastic, hair, and blackened meat. The rain caused an avalanche of debris and white ash to weep down the far gap by the spillway, as the winds picked up the cinders and cut black smoke from the bodies.

A huge rally of unhoused people circled the fire worshippers in two big crescents, their faces covered in wet bandanas and towels, shouting and screaming at the worshippers to give them the body back, the orange vests pulling in shoulder-to-shoulder close.

Lake walked between tents under the booming highway pillars, calling for Esme over and over. Someone grabbed his arm, yanked him towards the heat and the shouts before he slipped away, and the screaming went panicked.

Lake watched the rally swell with mutts, knives, tire-irons, shoestring padlocks, bike-chains, shovels, extension cord whips, and garden hooks, as the people from the tents started taking swings at the worshippers from two directions at once, shouting, swinging, getting close enough to blister themselves looking for the body in the smoke. The burning, howling, screaming, swinging, puncturing, bleeding fury and crush met at the smoke point, the orange vests flexed tight around the fire where the body curled in the invisible heat.

In a dome tent on the soil slope, Lake found Esme rigid, barely breathing, smiling and blue-faced.

Esme wrenched her eyes open when Lake came in, but even as he leaned down to whisper and ask what happened to her, she had few ways to explain. She could see who Lake would become and viewed him in his most dreadful form. He was Lux, armed with the Blue Dagger Amnesia, a ruthless knife with a mind of its own, and his body resplendent and free and unadorned of any knot or ring, or clasp, or hook, or loop of any kind. With Amnesia, Lux would never again allow himself to be claimed or yoke himself to the mark of binding.

Esme told Lake that he would never understand, and this was true, he wouldn't. The Book had her read all the way to the chapter at the Verdant Pool.

"Esme, oh, oh, what happened?" Lake asked.

"It told me I would do this. It told me what I would do, and I did!" Esme weakly pointed to the dim octopus in the water, pouting in place with its blue rings ablaze.

The Book had told Esme exactly what to say, but in the last moment of her life she refused.

"You'll meet her at the Verdant Pool, Lake. That's where it ends."

Esme slid to the ground and Lake turned her head as green froth fizzled out from her mouth. Her eyes peeled back white as the convulsions rolled up and down her body.

"Don't worry about anything else. Just get it... there."

With the last effort she had, Esme slid The Book of Blue Daggers out from under her body, across the floor of the tent, just in front of Lake.

"Esme, who's the other buyer? Who paid you to do this?"

It told the truth. It didn't hurt. It told the truth about Lake not understanding. It knew what he would ask, and Esme understood it all now.

"Hannah. The Hermetic Circle... The Book told me."

He kept asking things about Hannah and the Circle and why she was in a tent and who meant what and it all seemed so funny that Esme would have laughed if she could have breathed. Her body was swelling into one thick raw mass now and she could only catch glimpses of Lake between the whiteout bursts.

"It's Lake, Esme, please hold on, you'll be ok!"

"Listen to her, Lake. Listen to Sophie at the end." Her voice was smaller than a whisper, Lake had to lean in close to get it as her breath ran out and her face swelled watery and shifted into the color of fluorescent lights.

The smoke spooled into the tent and the blaze outside played contortionist shadows against the canopy walls. The shouts grew closer. Lake tucked The Book of Blue Daggers under his arm and stepped outside.

Lake jogged up a filthy hill, a landslide of trash and plastic and spare parts. A bald shirtless man with tattooed eyebrows, his arm burned and split pink to the shoulder, buried and soothed himself in a mound of wet sludge that collected at a flat. He saw Lake and his eyes turned wide and angry and he shouted for others to come and get him, that there was one that everyone had missed. Lake ran and stumbled down the hill.

A line of police materialized from the airport road, dumping pepper spray into the encampment valley below from behind a wall of plexiglass shields. A team working a firehouse blasted the camp and the blaze and pressed down on anyone left standing like the breath of an invisible giant.

Lake held The Book high above, where he stood ankle deep in a cesspool in the rain. Police charged slowly down the wet hill, swinging batons just after the spray of the high-pressure hose, flinging the worshippers and unhoused to the bottom of the hill all the same.

Lake ran north, heavy from the water and ooze. He dropped his jacket to the ground and pulled off his socks. He looked back at the mirror wet highway ramps and the reflections of the burning camp and police lights and dragging silhouettes.

The Book of Blue Dagger's pages and cover were feather dry, Lake able to pour the water straight off from the corner, smooth as liquid from a jug. The pages speckled and piled with filth and ash, and Lake swept it off perfectly clean with nothing more than the back of his hand.

His cellphone screen was cracked and half-warped, but he was able to dial a call using the speaker.

"Sophie, I have it," Lake said.

"Esme?" Sophie asked.

"Ah, she's dead Sophie," Lake said. "Really fucking bad."

"Did they find her?" Sophie said, putting a hand over her face. No. Please. Concentrate. Focus on this now. Heartbreak is a luxury you can afford only later.

"She... an octopus bite. She killed herself with one of her pets. Sophie, are you there?" Lake asked.

"She read it. She read it, didn't she Lake?"

"Of course, she read it, Sophie."

Sophie clenched her fists so tight her palms bled. "Is it there? Is the whole thing there?"

"She said it was missing, but I should listen to you in the end."

"Yes! Listen to me Lake, can you be at Pioneer Square? 10 minutes?"

"Esme's gone Sophie, you bring me the cash and whatever car you have and I'm getting Ash tonight."

"Lake, is it complete?"

"My side is complete Sophie. When you're done here, the least you could do for Esme is take care of her fish and that snake." Lake's voice wavered as he insisted. "It's the least you could since she died for something you wanted."

Lake hung up. He dried his hands against the brick walls and concrete. He looked at the small, boring thing in his hands in the bad light and slowed his steps, running the spine of the Book across his palms.

He cracked his phone to pieces. He was a block away from Pioneer Square with time to spare. He wondered about the future. How to get the smell of the flames and the filth off? How to explain the stink and the whole long story to Asher?

He would apologize. He would be square and be straight and tell Asher he could do anything he wanted. He would tell him face-to-face. He'd have it all out. He'd let the fever run the course, but he'd keep Asher safe. He'd settle with Monty Boate soon after, working the details of some lure in his head followed by a rundown of forever-new names that would be easy to remember when he and Asher flew south of the equator.

He took a moment to catch his breath.

He opened the Book and his eyes went gold as he marveled at the shades of blue as he read. In the time it took to wait and wonder about the breeze, all the words from the Book of Blue Daggers crawled up to occupy his mind, to tell him that Sophie had lied, and his life would now be completely different forever.

# CHAPTER SEVENTEEN

*The Book of Blue Daggers Ch. 4, "The Burned Alliance"*

**EARLIER, IN THE BOOK OF BLUE DAGGERS**

The man in the shadows watched as his city burned.

Esper, the seer, died shivering in his arms at the bay side as she gave him the Book, just as The Hand of Light revealed their flames to the city streets.

A dark surge charged through Lux, a swelling tide cresting that told him to charge in, scatter their skulls, slash to bits anyone carrying a flame. And yet, Lux obeyed the blue and soothing voice that promised to keep him free from chains and cells forever. The voice of the indigo knife insisted, and he remained in the shadows. The dark blade asked, so he pressed himself to the brick well, his bloody leather jacket blending into the murk.

Lux's blue eyes, gray as the ocean after a storm, roved across the fires boiling in the central square of the city. The great statues and filigreed monuments of Motero Bay were falling, cracked, and shattered to the ground by the Hand of Light, and the thunderclap noise of history toppling boomed down the street like the steps of a monstrous beast awakened.

"Purity! Purity!" they bellowed, their voices morphing into a single monstrous roar. They drenched unbelievers, beggars, and passer-by alike in scented oils, the cries of these unwilling torches swallowed by the sweet, incense-heavy smoke. In the city's heart, beggars were strung from lampposts, their flesh branded under the jeers of the frothing crowd pulsating as a single white flock bathed in embers and grease.

Lux sensed the incessant clicks of his brass timepiece. Ash was late, an oddity for such a spry youth.

In anticipation of their flight path, Lux unfurled the map from his pocket, scrutinizing it. With Ash, they could fly straight through the marine layer, escaping the city's smoky grasp before dawn unveiled the sins of the bay. Even with a leisurely throttle, they could reach the jungle-rimmed Painted Islands by the time the sun dared to crest the sky.

Time gnawed away, each tick a reminder. A specter stirred behind him in the alley, and with a fluid grace, Lux drew the blue dagger. The weapon hummed; its faint glow splashed a winter aurora against the canted walls of the tropical city way alley.

No enemy awaited his blade, just Dr. Civest, master of potions and scientific wizardry, who stumbled, sprawled into Lux, his last breaths and heartbeats coming fast as he squeezed the hands of his old friend.

"Dr. C?"

"Selia... she betrayed us! Don't give her the Book!"

"Impossible. She's the one who asked me to do this. Why would she-"

"No, look there!" Dr C. motioned with his hand to the square, the flames unfurling like petals of a heliotrope at the new rays of the sun.

Lux strained to see the volcanic center of violence and rage at the crest of the crowd. He sifted through the tormented faces. Ash dangled from a lamppost, a sinister rope tight between his neck and the hot iron. He was filthy from the smoke and the blood and their handprints. The Hands of Light jostled him like a toy, pounding and blistering his open legs with their brands and torches.

But how? Selia. The name echoed through Lux's mind, drowning the riotous cries of the city. The thought of it bewildered Lux. Why? Not after all they had been through, and all he had just accomplished.

But a low drone in the base of Lux's mind made him believe. The Eucalyptus Queen must have gotten to Selia, and she, like a coward, led her right to him.

Of course, Esper tried to warn him. That the Book would destroy him, and that he would see her in the cave. Prophecies only rang true the more doomed you became, the logic resolving perfect, only when it was impossibly late to change it.

So, then it was true. She had betrayed him. He had lost Ash, but he still had the Book, and the Book was just the thing that Selia wanted. And now Lux would see to it that Selia now had nothing but a date with the blade.

Before Dr. C's last breath, he had pressed a bandolier of glassine stoppered tubes, each marked with an "H," into Lux's hands. Lux understood what it was: the last great work of his friend's masterpiece mind, a vial of compressed fluid to incapacitate his enemies.

"Thank you, friend," Lux said, sweeping Dr. C's eyelids closed.

Lux looked back towards the square, now filled with the bald and skin-bleached fire-worshippers. Selia bobbed shoulder-to-shoulder sideways through the cultists, her bloodshot eyes out-staring the firebrands. Looking for Lux. She was easy to see; her chopped white hair matched to the color of the smoke and her sickness worse, Selia stooped and her fever sweats shined in the flame.

A towering man, drooling as he bellowed, thrust a brand into Ash's disfigured face, branding him a traitor. Lux glimpsed the man's blonde hair and metal teeth. Merrick. The blue dagger ached to draw those teeth out, one by one.

Lux unbuckled the satchel, revealing the book. It seemed so mundane, and he wondered what secrets it held to warrant this foul murder and betrayal that would surely end in more lives lost.

Through the smoke, it was too hard to see. With a flash and a flex, Lux snapped his green-tinted goggles to his face and clicked them on. They buzzed like summer insects and his vision pierced through darkness and smoke, both with a vivid emerald hue. A suffocating serpent cut off his path to the seaport. No matter, Lux could brave the black beach's treacherous steps and take the long way around.

Lux stowed Dr. C's potions into his purple leather jacket pocket. The Hands of Light were shouting after him, running. The bodies in the square, Ash's included, were an inferno now.

Lux skipped through the shantytowns of Motero Bay, past rusty nail shacks teetering on sand dunes and mud flats. He could smell the sharp sting of eucalyptus as two of the queen's enforcers prowled around the steps to The Black Beach. One cradled a pistol in his hands, both of them straining against the smoke.

Lux stumbled onto the stairs, the rising sun casting his fleeing form in shadow. He sprinted along the black sand, aiming for the stone steps.

The Hermes, Lux's seaplane, bobbed peacefully in the water. He flung open the side door and slid into the cockpit as the first slips of morning light gleamed off the windows.

No. They'd gotten to it first.

He could smell the sour air of the eucalyptus wafting from a knotted garland they'd left on the floor. His hands frantically searched beneath the console, grazing snapped wires, popped fuses, and something else — thick, solid tubes with wires diving deep into the heart of the engines.

Quickly snatching the garland in his hand, Lux dove for the water and went deep into the black until his lungs went red as rust and screamed for him to surface. Above him, his precious Hermes burst into a thousand white-hot pieces, shots of brass rivets and wire lengths, and shattered strips of landing gear.

Lux surfaced, the air thick with fuel at the surface. One yellow wingtip tilted and saluted before sinking below the waves. He wrestled to the surface of the dark beach across a patch of saltwater vines.

Somehow, the Book was still dry. Even submerged in the deep, the saltwater and fuel poured off dry, just as he took it hours ago. He set it on the beach, the sand black and fine from thousands of years of tides sweeping it away from the volcanic stone.

There was no chance for the Northern Islands now. They would have known his route. Selia would have told the queen his destination.

A ragged group of fishers, beggars, and outcasts from the city were cooking a pitiful meal by the cliff side. They eyed Lux warily as he lay his purple wool-topped coat across a hulking piece of driftwood, gravitating towards their warmth. They were grim and hungry, too hungry to talk or ask questions.

Except one.

"Heading south?"

The man was blind. His eyes were crudely stitched with dark thread, and he lifted his nose to sniff at the oily garland Lux threaded about his fingers.

"I'm just trying to get warm."

"It's treacherous, going south. You need a guide."

"I won't take any of your food. The warmth is all I need."

The blind man shook his head. No one in the ragged group noticed or cared about their conversation. The blind man took a piece of paper from a notch on a driftwood log half buried in the black sand, presenting him with a labyrinth of drawing.

"Journey south is very dangerous, even for a salt-water thief like yourself. I can show you all the hidden paths."

The map was difficult to figure at first. It drew a passage Lux had never seen before, by either land or sea. It made no sense. It made even less coming from a man with no eyes.

"You don't need eyes to get where you are going. In fact, they can slow you down. Deceive you with their confidence," the blind man said.

Lux traced the map with his fingers, ignoring what his eyes saw. He felt the path more than he saw it. It dawned on him. Yes, the route was there. It was fast, quick, no one would ever expect it.

# CHAPTER EIGHTEEN

*The Raven End*

## KENMORE, WA – PIONEER SQUARE WA OCTOBER 28

It was almost almost almost hers.

The pages of Esme's false Book of Blue Daggers on the table nearby echoed with cerulean. The path to the doorway exit flurried ultramarine and blinked like fireflies. With just the corner of her eyes, she unlocked a hidden portion of the visible spectrum.

The frequency was just for her, just for the desire. The broadcast was strong and true on the wavelength of all things possible. A thin Egyptian gauze that only she could see. She reached out and touched the low nanometer gleam, a blue song that slipped through walls before echoing off to nothing.

She would have the Book if she could just bridge through this pain to make the journey.

The coils of the snake realigned something deep inside her, and Sophie could breathe normally only when she twisted her body over her hips. She had stopped the bleeding, but her leg was swollen candy red, soft as icing, and beaded sticky wet yellow when she tried to bend it. Her toenails had blown out from the pressure, and she had peeled open a medical cabinet in Esme's office looking for anything to chase it away.

She pulled Norco 10/300s from the shelves. Sophie chewed through two and did math when the pain kept pace. She took twenty plus of the white pills and went to the steel sink in Esme's workspace. She turned the water until it ran bracing cold. She rinsed out two glass jars and made three sheets of paper towels. With an empty jar, she pinned and rolled and crushed the pills between the paper towels. Pills, grit, dust. Then spread the powder out and rounded it over again against the glass to get it as fine as she could. She tapped the little mound into the empty jar. She measured two inches of water in the other jar, as cold as she could get it without ice, and slowly poured the cold water into the other, dissolving the mound and set the jar aside to stay cool.

Sophie stripped naked to the waist and dampened a towel from the steel sink to wipe the blood away, clear away the tape and cotton. The cool water ran down wound channels and the nerve-ends flashed with pain.

"God dammit!" Sophie shouted and punched her fist against the big steel sink.

Her whole body shook in pieces, and it took her two, three, four minutes to breathe normally and wipe her face cold and clean again and stop shaking. She stared at the ceiling and inhaled slowly, as her muscles unspooled bit by bit. She checked the time. She wondered if Lake had arrived. She wondered if he was having ideas while waiting.

Sophie drank a full cup of water. A lizard part of her brain smelled chocolate and sugar and bright food dyes in a desk drawer. It was agony to move. Her toes bled through bright red. She pressed it again and again at the knee and ankle and she could feel a gulf of fluid move and knots of muscle work lose. She bent it further and shouted again at the pain, but it could bend deeper now. She pressed hard as she could into the heel and arch of the foot and onto her toes until she thought she could walk on them.

She mentally ran her blood replacement count numbers. She was losing the battle like sandcastles in a high tide and not getting any back. She cross-referenced the grind of Paroxysmal nocturnal hemoglobinuria. She couldn't keep the rates solid. Doing math was like climbing a ladder of smoke. She had to eat.

First with her bare foot on the ground and then the whole weight of the leg. The first step a crescendo crackle of tendons and pops and gurgling. Her foot landed at an ankle going inwards, her big toe pointing towards the other, and after another step, she was able to stand upright and balanced. She took another popping step and stood with her arms outstretched before reaching the desk.

She pulled open a magnificent drawer of old Twix bars, dusty Snickers, wrapped hard candies, a delicious rainbow of gummies, beautiful soggy peanut butter cups, and sour gumballs in wax paper twists. Sophie gulped water. She unwrapped candy so sweet and moist, the smell of it made her dizzy. She dug in. She went lightheaded and nauseous from the sugar rush. She wasn't sure when she could eat next. She smothered soft chocolates, peanut butter cups and caramels together into a thick dark pancake with her brown and greased hands against the desk. She fed it to herself from between her fingers, holding the crumbs and sugary mess together with her palms. She wiped what she could from her face, licked the taste of it off her knuckles, and felt the corn syrup crust against her cheeks.

Ten minutes was enough for the separation process. Enough to keep the acetaminophen 300 from overdosing her liver. She held her prepared jars to the light and saw slippery clouds of water. Sophie took a rubber band and slipped another paper towel around the neck of the second jar. She swirled the water and poured it in, the white acetaminophen powder too thick for passage. The jar was empty, and she threw the paper towel with the slick wet mass of liver-ruining acetaminophen away.

The cold water was bitter from the dissolved hydrocodone, and it sent her to a place both bright-minded and slow. All troubles were resolved immediately, but putting thoughts into effect seemed bizarre and affectless.

Steady in the head, she ran the numbers. Her body carried a gallon and a half of blood, and hers was less formidable than most. Perhaps cups, a pint, was lost to the snake and on the floor. She wouldn't replace it in time. The solution was easy. Going to the hospital was impossible. Sophie had a couple weeks, that's it, unless she found the Book.

Sophie felt good. She felt good knowing something so certain. That the timeline was settled.

Her foot wasn't bleeding, but her shoes still wouldn't fit. She scissored her pants to ludicrous shorts just beneath tiny pointless pockets.

In the car, she pulled a jacket on and rolled down the windows all the way. The street-speed rain machined off the jacket and ran through her hair. The cool water felt good washing down her swollen leg and dripping toes. Sophie went through downtown Seattle exchanging to the night shift. Conspiracy panhandlers curled into triangles and heating pipe patches and tagged out the night watch. Night handlers so scarred and weeping from the wounds they could barely stand to be seen from the light of the moon.

Sophie parked on the street, heading the wrong way. She got out and limped barefoot under yellow lights to the park at Pioneer Square. She stood in the shadow of the red cedar totem Pole and shouted Lake's name. A shadow moved under the glass and wrought iron pergola at the south end, drying to a sky figurine in the breeze and the rain.

No Lake. No Book.

At the Raven End of the totem pole's shadow, a paint-spattered man picked through papers and cards and a pair of untied shoes. He fingered a pile of black sand that glittered blue as he heaped it around on the bricks. He leaned against a column of the delicate iron pergola and tested the new soles against his own. He shook his head and dumped the shoes onto the ground.

Sophie limped towards him, balancing herself, arms extended out and her head low. She moved fast on bare feet. The man was haggard and street-skinny and wearing three layers of plastic. She bounced a shoulder into him, and he stumbled and fell against the iron column of the Pergola stop.

"Crazy bitch!" he said.

Sophie moved between his punch and grabbed his thick whiskered face between her hands and bounced it against the wrought detail on one of the columns. His eyes went sideways and white, and Sophie didn't let go. She took his scabbed ears and passed his head against the detail again. He slid down. The column echoed out a low croon.

Sophie ran through his pockets and pulled a sheaf of high bills and a Mastercard that said MICHAEL WEATHER. Sophie grabbed a fistful of downspout rain against her mouth. Her legs hopped, her mouth dry, her body one step ahead and ready for the flight. She braced herself on the pole above his head and breathed deep. She asked about the shoes, the Book, the man who would have been there. She poured water on his face to get his eyes working again.

"You saw him! Did he read it?"

"Why are you both barefoot?"

"What happened to him?"

"He stripped down. He was barefoot just like you."

"Did he have a book?"

The man nodded. Sophie put half the cash in his pockets and said, "Tell me."

"His eyes went gold, and I thought he was doing street preaching. He was just talking to himself." The man pointed to the big river raven's beak at the base of the totem pole. "He was talking to the pole, right there. He said he knew she lied."

Sophie gave him the rest of the money. The card. She asked him what else.

"He had a knife. Blue glass knife, looked like glow in the dark. And he talked about blues, but not like the songs, like the color. He said he would get those who did him wrong. He just left. He just left his shoes and his shit."

"When?"

"Ten minutes ago. I didn't want him to see me."

She tipped black sand out of Lake's shoes. It was smooth and glossy, volcanic black, stolen from some faraway beach.

Sophie licked blood and rainwater from her lips. The storm and the streetlights helped her put the pieces together. She understood what Howard Cyone was trying to say, Oscar Koo, too. They had warned her about the Book. They had told her, and she just didn't listen.

The Book of Blue Daggers had seen her coming from a mile away. It knew what she wanted now, and it knew exactly why.

# CHAPTER NINETEEN

*The Book of Blue Daggers Ch. 6, "The Garland"*

## AROUND THE SAME TIME, IN THE BOOK OF BLUE DAGGERS

The inn stood at the junction of two rivers. Lux knew no questions would be asked, and no answers offered. The reputation of a place like this depended on the staff ignoring the bloodstains on a tired traveler's cuffs, or the contents of their strange and heavy bags they insisted on carrying themselves. The business was silent, and Lux was a well paying customer.

A wine-soaked cluster of sailors occupied the common room, their bloodshot eyes hovering over a half-drained jug. As Lux crossed the room, their gaze strayed from their liquor, sharp and calculating. His blade, Amnesia, thrummed with anticipation against his hip. With a cold, unflinching stare, Lux threw their curiosity back at them. The sailors didn't need more than the silent cue, and Amnesia settled back, dimming for another day.

The room at 337 was a shell of simplicity – a bare bulb, a precarious desk, a hard mattress. Lux nodded to himself. This was more than enough.

He opened the window of his room. He could hear the two rivers outside, mingling in the rain.

He made sure the door to the room was locked and examined the eucalyptus garland. It was cut fresh and knotted end to end. Even on the table Lux could draw the strong sharp scent reminiscent of honey, mint, and limes but all on its own. A lone assassin with a pistol would never dare wear these garlands on their own. No risk was so great.

It was true then. The Eucalyptus Queen was alive. Even after Lux had watched her die.

Lux put his hand outside the window. He pooled flakes of rain in his hand.

Thoughts of Ash flashed before him. All Ash ever wanted was an escape from the harsh city. That naivety and hope had led him to Zetco, then Selia, and then to a rope on fire. He'd sought Lux's aid and had been rewarded with a noose and a brand.

Lux used the water from his hands to slice the blood from Amnesia. The pink drops fell away from the hooked point of the blade before Lux wiped the blade and handle clean and dry with a thin leather cloth. He buffed it bright until he could see the room through the icy pane of the blade.

There were guttural whispers in the hallway. Amnesia stirred restlessly. It knew what was close. It could hear the cocked hammers of the revolvers and musk and smell the gun oil far quicker than Lux ever could.

The Book went back into the satchel, safely tucked away. Lux held Amnesia aloft, the comforting chill of its blue blade against his palm.

Quick whispers cut the silence. Lux cut the bulb. The skirt of slow footfalls in the hallway and snapped voices. He could hear two at least. They were figuring out the going of it just outside the door. Which side to take. Which one was coming in first. A clumsy and brutal play. They would be pressed together in the hall, bellies shuffling against the wall.

Amnesia hummed low in Lux's hand. Purring low as an animal, panting as Lux squeezed the blue dagger tight. He smoothed himself into the shadow, Lux feeling the blade echo in his hand as he stepped to the door and yanked the handle open.

Amnesia made a fierce popping noise, a pulse that echoed through all of Lux's joints as it slashed through the two men now darting into the room. A trigger clicked, and a slug drilled through the wall and buried into the next room. Lux could smell the eucalyptus oil on the assassin's breath and see it red in their eyes.

The gunman squeezed the trigger again, but Lux pressed his finger between the hammer and the action and twisted the other thumb into the eye of the triggerman. The man howled and bared his teeth like a trapped mongrel. He freed up the pistol, and they fumbled with it like children. Lux screwed the man's eye loose as the pistol blasted a shot that took one of Lux's fingers off at the base. Amidst the lingering echo, Lux could hear the faint thump of his lost finger hitting the floor.

Lux spun and traced Amnesia around the gunman's stomach. A swell of soft, pink tissue spilled out as the man stumbled forward, clutching his open gut. Lux's hand was slick and numbing, the missing finger a strange void in his clenched fist. He struggled to find which digit had been lost, his thumb fumbled clumsily against his remaining fingers.

With a fierce, blood-stained grip, Lux seized the wrist of the other man. He slipped him off his feet and pumped Amnesia again and again into his flesh until the blood poured out black from deep inside the organs. The room filled with the men's tortured cries and whispered prayers.

One of the men fumbled for a dagger, but two powerful kicks landed him at Lux's feet. He pinned their faces under his boot, driving Amnesia through their throats with calculated brutality.

Zetco. He could retrace his steps out from the man who was financing this whole sour affair. He'd introduce him to Amnesia, and their acquaintance would see to the next step of the way.

"I know," Lux said as he slipped out into the rain. "I know."

His footsteps quickened into a run, carrying him away from the confluence of the two rivers, disappearing into the dampened darkness.

# CHAPTER TWENTY

*The Finger*

## ABERDEEN WA OCTOBER 28

The birdsong pink dawn was just rising when Sophie met Nick Wyeth for the first time. He was dabbing blood spots off purple Japanese sneakers with a borrowed towel, and he had a human finger in his pocket.

Sophie had dug up shallow graves of receipts and transactions and shook herself stiff against starlight with coffee and sublingual Adderall IR. She had downloaded Lake's rental car GPS log by spoofing a corporate ID and waking up rental managers several states away.

Sophie followed. A predator of infinite persistence.

The log of the GPS still traced every mile, every trip, and every lookup he made in the memory cache. Lake had run the time and distance between Olympia and Aberdeen on the GPS. Trip to the coast, to Aberdeen, that was his plan B if he needed to pull the ripcord if he got crossed.

With the dawn at her back on Highway 8, her body went covered-in-ants then she felt nothing at all as she slid into a blackout. She blinked herself back and discovered herself in a filthy restroom with stained ceilings. She was peeing orange red into a toilet. Her hands were numb, and the blood looked worse.

"Are you alive in there?" an annoyed voice outside the restroom door asked.

"Yeah," Sophie said.

"I don't have any Narcan. You need to get the fuck out," the voice said.

"Yeah."

"I give you two minutes then and I'm coming in with a bucket of ice water. Hey, you hear me? I'm tired of this shit."

"I won't take two minutes."

Sophie flexed her hands and waved them up and down. She timed it out. She already had to pee again. It was bright, orange and foamy, like kids cream soda. Numbers were running backwards, her body tracking into the negative. Her fingers felt like she'd been punching a wasps' nest.

Sophie squeezed at the pinpoints of the snakebites underneath her bandages on her legs. The fluid ran out clear, thin. Sophie sighed. She wasn't infected. She tossed the bandages. She rolled a paper towel from the wall dispenser and doubled it up. She padded on top of the pale sticky fluid, collecting at the bites.

At the counter, a kid wearing headphones rolled his eyes as Sophie walked out crooked. He tapped a bucket full of water with his foot.

"Are you buying anything?" he asked.

Sophie enjoyed the cold feeling of a Gatorade bottle along her wrists and neck. She found salt packets, half-and-half, a box of donuts stuffed with cream, a tin of ghost-pepper almonds, and a box of off-brand bandages with penguins on the outside. She wrapped the items in a bright-green Seattle Seahawks sweatshirt with a storm-blue 12 on it marked HALF-OFF!!!

She ran on fumes and vapor and a scent that drew her Southwest. She got nausea full from Gatorade, donuts, and coffee creamer loaded with salt. She drew a picture on the back of the bag of donuts. See Sophie run. See Sophie steal. See Lake look bewildered as he looks for the Book, question marks bouncing above his head. Run, Sophie, run.

She drove with the windows down and didn't tempt the blackouts.

The sign outside Aberdeen nodded 'Come as You Are'. Sophie parked at a Walmart and walked through the low sun of the parking lot lights. It was dark along the rail tracks past an access way at a glass-splashed end of the lot. She traded the white light of the parking lot for the paint-stroke pastels rising up from morning light at the east end of the tracks.

Sophie could hear the Wishkah and Chehalis rivers sloping into each other, mingling before they washed into the sea. Somewhere she remembered they had dissolved Kurt Cobain's ashes into the Wishkah. She wondered if anything remained, or if they had all run into the junction of two rivers and run into the sea.

The Best Western smelled like bleach, and there was a pool somewhere down a hallway. Sophie walked past the desk and went to the first floor. She listened for voices, trying to divine the Book with her hands. She could feel the vibration, the frequency of it. She could hear the echo of the words read aloud or even just pass through someone's eyes. She pressed her fingertips to every door handle, like a fireman testing the knobs for a sign of heat.

Next to the big plastic ice machine on the third floor, she walked by a blonde man, squeaking a wet towel against his purple sneakers.

She could see it. A blue light, an electric blue, a glacial water blue. At 337, Sophie put her hand to the door and felt the waves. A crackling breeze came from the closed door, and Sophie realized she was standing in a stripe of blood. It had swollen against the door and leaked into the hallway.

The blonde man with the now-clean sneakers stood behind her.

"I have a gun," she lied.

Nick Wyeth was holding a towel dotted with blood and ice water and standing close. His purple sneakers were damp and had a white star on the side. His fingernails were black at the tips, and he angled his green eyes low to stare right into Sophie. He told her he didn't believe her.

"Lake isn't in there," he said.

Sophie pressed a hand to her side. She eyed an elevator. The long hallway behind her. The doorway beside her.

"Go in. Stay to the left," he said.

Wyeth lifted a plastic keycard out of his pocket. Sophie took a step and traced blood. She stamped it against the carpet as Wyeth unlocked the door.

"What about our shoes?" she asked.

"What?"

"Our shoes. The blood?"

Wyeth dropped the ice-chipped towel on the stripe of blood and heeled it flat and even. He swiped the card in the lock and leaned into the door. He said to stay to the left again, and to keep the light off.

Two men lay bunched up on a shower liner together at the entryway. The curtain and a bed sheet floated across them. They were dead, slashed, and the bed sheet and curtain were both soaked.

She took more steps into the room and pressed at the first switch she could see. Nick closed the door behind him.

"Grab that cup, would you?" Wyeth asked.

Sophie grabbed and held out a plastic coffee cup. Nick unfolded a foil coffee bag from his jacket and shook a human finger into the cup. The finger was gray and had a split nail dark with black sand. Sophie looked at the finger, then her own hand, and then back again. Even using a desk lamp, she didn't know what digit it was.

"I did the same thing," Wyeth said. "Not the thumb, but otherwise..." Wyeth shrugged.

Wyeth stood past the shower curtain in the entry and flipped the entry light on. Arterial jets looped from the ceiling to the far cheap drywall. Sophie could see blood on the windows behind her. Hard specks and dried grains like satellites all the way from the backswing of the knife into the entryway. What fucking force. What fucking character.

Sophie pointed to the hands and knees and crusted sparks of blood at the rim of the curtained pile. She held out the cup with the finger rattling inside.

"One of theirs?" she asked.

"All twenty." He held his hand to a black hole the size of a dime in the wall and put his left ring finger to it. He bent it down and back, down and back again. He pointed to a crescent of black and crimson on the wall, then the floor.

"Looks like it was three of them. They pulled the trigger one time, and it took off his finger. Is your name still Sophie?"

Sophie nodded.

"At first, I thought your name was Sophie O'Keefe. Then, for a very long time, I thought I figured it out that you were Sophie Sherman. That isn't correct though, is it?"

Sophie was dizzy. She had a feeling like ticks were latching on and feeding on all the guts beneath her stomach.

"You presented evidence against Lake at his trial. Why are you in Aberdeen?" she asked.

"Being that I had previous experience with Lake, the lawyers who hired him thought it was best to retain my services on the occasion that he didn't live up to their ideal. I'm Nick Wyeth."

"The lawyers? Who's behind the curtain, Nick?"

"The less details I know, the better. Zapata and Bontecue retained me to find Lake, who didn't complete what they contracted him for. Fair to say that's why I'm acquainting myself with you here as well?"

"Stop trying to be sly, Wyeth. You look like a Labrador trying to learn calculus."

"I'm trying to find where Lake is. If you can help me, I can help you."

"Are you the next man up to find the Book? Or are they trying to make sure Lake doesn't stab your employers to death?"

"I don't acquire anything, Sophie. My preference is to avoid anything present tense. I try to only manifest in information."

Sophie made note of the obvious.

"That's Lake's finger?"

"It is. It was."

"How did you know he came here?" she asked.

"I want to start at the beginning, so to speak."

Wyeth took a towel from the bathroom and lifted the shower curtain. The old man underneath it still had his steel-rimmed glasses on. He smelled like old sweat and hair tonic. The tache noir stripe had formed outwards from his blue eyes and his tongue lolled in the air, the same color as his teeth. Wyeth tugged down his collar.

He had old tattoos, the India Ink bleached green from years in the sun. A pinup girl in a sailor's cap. A Navy battleship with full rigging masts blown by strong wind and "FUCK COMMUNISM" in faux-zen brushstrokes.

Wyeth pointed to a handgun, an M&P with a garage-lathe silencer. The silencer was spray painted black and wobbled past the barrel. Sophie could see knobbed scars on his knuckles. The black gunpowder flakes sprayed into the webbing off his palms. The lost fingernails swallowed up by the distals after an abyss of violence.

The other man was much younger, and he'd been slashed much worse, the blood black from organ veins. Every button from his shirt had been ripped from the seam. He had a treasure box of drop shadow tattoos. Ornaments of alchemical metals, triangles worked by lines, horned circles, the full run of zodiac symbols across a young man's thin shoulders and pale chest. He wore a page of knowledge from his shoulders to stomach, bisected by a foot-long rip now settling into jelly dark bubbles.

Wyeth pulled on thin blue rubber gloves from a pocket in his jacket. He plucked a slotted card from the younger man's pocket. He tossed it to Sophie.

It was at her feet. A magnetic entry card with three light purple waves on it. There was a picture of the young man on it. "NOAH CATLOW" under that. He looked even younger in the bad light of the picture. He had a skinny neck stemmed in a lavender scarf above the words STAFF—RAINIER WIND SPA.

"To start, this is Noah Catlow," Wyeth said.

"To start, Lake had never killed anyone," Sophie said.

"He seems to have no trouble with it now..." Wyeth said. "Barbara Bontecue and Taylor Zapata are highly incentivized to find him. You should be just as incentivized."

"Noah was one of Dillinger's alchemy friends, I take it?"

"Noah Catlow made meth and MDMA in a dry lab for the Odin Warriors. AB and peckerwood white power gangs in Moses Lake. He tutored Dillinger in medieval witchcraft and sold him cold iron at a platinum price point," Wyeth said.

"And you just thought Noah would lead you to Lake and then the Book. Have you even told Bontecue and Zapata what kind of danger they are in?"

"You know, Sophie, there's this nasty rumor you ask about the Book like some little girl and her lost puppy."

Wyeth made a high voice, like a little girl. He raised his shoulders and opened his eyes wide and looked from wall-to-wall.

"Do you know where the Book is? Have you seen it? Can you tell me where the Book is?" He stopped with the voice but kept talking. "So, I know you and I want the same thing. More or less, yeah, the Book."

"I don't... the Book is..."

"It is unusual. They had the darkness, the gun, two against one." Wyeth made some steps and elbows. He imagined holding a knife with one hand or both. Sophie watched him imitate Lake there and then. Put his finger against the wall. The trigger pull. Nothing more than a few seconds. Deep cuts. A melee over in a few quick breaths. The black star lights would take them off their feet and Wyeth wondered if they would dream as they bled out. He shrugged and gave up. He couldn't understand it.

"They had the drop on him. Guns, too. All he had was a knife, and Lake had been in all but one real fight in his life. How did he survive?"

Turning on the bathroom light, Noah's pale little body was easier to see. She could read it and explain it now.

Noah Catlow had such slim shoulders and a dip in his sternum. His buck teeth bunched out over his lips, crooked and gray, like he'd grown up drinking bad well water. His tattoos were homemade, the shake and the buzz of the needle gun visible on the fuzzy lines and bad layering.

"Those tattoos are alchemical symbols. Mercury, sulfur, aqua regia. Circumspect Fire Earth and Air. Dillinger died when..." Sophie pointed to her collarbone. "He had a symbol here. It looks like an arrow, with a line flowing along. It means purity. Dillinger died trying to cure himself. Distill his body from the unnecessary. Noah taught him how to do it."

"Taught him how to die?" Wyeth asked.

"No. Noah tried to teach Dillinger how to... ascend maybe, but not in a spiritual sense. Or maybe Noah tricked him," Sophie said.

"Will you look at something?" Wyeth asked. "Catlow had this in his pocket. Give me the Sophie explanation of that, if you please?"

A big piece of sketch pad paper unfolded lots of new horizons. Sophie wondered if Catlow had any idea what he'd been doing. The drawing was good. He'd taken some time. The name "noah" sat all lowercase in the corner.

The characters in the drawing were easy to recognize. Noah from his teeth, his slim shoulders. He was joyfully alive. Grinning. Wearing a necklace of eucalyptus leaves. The older man was dressed the same. They stood in a similar narrow entry that Sophie stood now, looking at the picture of them standing in. However, there was only one body on the floor, and no carpet or liner. Catlow had drawn Lake, crumpled against the wall where Noah now lay. Bleeding from his hand, slashed at the neck, a dagger by his side.

In the drawing, Noah was holding a Book, pulled from a wide-mouthed satchel. The puzzle piece slammed into place like a boulder thrown from the sky. It made sense now, and Sophie could see who was pulling the strings.

The Book had been busy.

"Sophie... Sophie, why are you smiling?" Wyeth asked, and with some breezy practiced chuckle Wyeth put a hand towards Sophie's shoulder. She spun away and looped to grab a fist-sized coffee maker on a desk. She shattered it against the wall and aimed the ripped glass right at Wyeth's eyes.

"Don't....don't touch me, Wyeth. Don't ever touch fucking me."

"How did he know they were coming? How did Lake know they were coming to kill him and survive?"

"You've thought about it, Wyeth. Tell me."

Wyeth smiled at Sophie.

"The Book has some... code that can analyze probabilities. Some kind of seed algorithm. Through some pervasive unknown influence, Lake and the Book are able to transform that into real-world probability and use that to always make the best possible play."

"Some influence. Lake is absolutely making the correct decisions. Noah got tricked, and it killed him," Sophie said.

Wyeth looked at the bodies. "How could it trick him?"

"Noah got tricked by the Book. He did something... he read it, he got it wrong, just when he thought he would be the one and only."

The one and only. Sophie spun off her axis and wondered if the chapter and pages of the Book were just tricks for her, too. She held Noah's clever, doomed drawing in her hands. Noah would have had a moment so certain and sure, that he was on the precipice of total victory. Sophie wondered when he realized he had made the wrong play. Perhaps the dagger caught and dragged against his ribs? Or when he slumped against the doorway, listening to his own last breath drag out, wondering when the Book had planned to turn on him?

Sophie was certain he didn't have a doubt until the last moment. Just like her, never a doubt, not a single one. Until now.

# CHAPTER TWENTY-ONE

*A New Kind of Time*

## MOUNT RAINIER, WA OCTOBER 29

Sophie's headlights burned through a soft white tunnel of fog on the shade side of Mt. Rainier.

The car crested out at a thousand feet. Sophie drove into the clean sky from an ocean of mist, the peaks of the fir trees jutting like ragged masts. Sophie pulled to the side of the road and pushed the button for the emergency blinkers, eating a lineup of powdered donuts, strawberry milk, two cheese sausage egg sandwiches, a bag of dried sour cherries, and a liter of purified water.

Ahead, she could see a sentinel rock with three purple waves chiseled into it, next to a white wooden sign that read RAINIER WIND SPA. Sophie parked on the muddy shoulder and took out Noah's card that Wyeth found. The card was clean and dry but had the blood whiff from the hotel room. She rubbed it over with napkins, but the scent kept.

The big clock in her head slashed away second-by-second. A steel band choked the base of her skull, and she was peeing the color of a valentine rose every day now. She had stopped working the calendar and timeline in her head, the equation too inefficient to track the days. There was only the then, the now, and everything in between. The only time that mattered was here, today, right now, and the new kind of time was accomplishing, doing, being.

She said it again, "Don't change pace when you're in it. You're committed to this now." Now. Then. And the in-between.

Sophie chewed aspirin and chased it with the Norco dissolved in water. She crunched a thermal pack and wrapped it into a Velcro strap around her pelvis. She opened the car door and put her legs out, bent her knee and winced. She cranked it probably farther than it needed, but it kept her from walking sidewinder. She could feel where the pain would have been without the Norco and aspirin, her tendons pulled loose and angling her legs the wrong directions.

The Rainier Wind Spa lobby was done up to smell like balsam oil and bamboo over hot stones and tilled earth. The staff wore no makeup and walked in bare feet, all dressed in green from sage to fern.

A woman in a raincoat was talking too loudly. She was almost shouting. The spa staff in slacks behind a live-edge slab desk tried to answer her impossible questions. Yes, of course, yes, of course, but she told them, no, they weren't getting anywhere. She was definitely shouting now.

Next to the phone and a computer and a wooden oil diffuser were a list of staff names. Sophie checked for Noah.

The woman in the raincoat started saying she would make calls, yes, she would. She'd start making calls right now unless she got answers.

"We are not an inpatient facility, Ms. Mapp, we apologize, but we would prefer-"

The list showed Noah Catlow - IT/Networking with a room number and a mobile contact number. Sophie pulled the list from where it was taped.

Someone touched Ms. Mapp by the elbow, and she ran towards a corridor shouting, "Dad! Dad!" above the serene music and the sound of waterfalls.

Just through bamboo doors, the floors were slick with rock mist. Sophie could still hear her shouting. She was face to face with a bronze plaque the size of a television with a man's face, twice larger than life, cut into it read: "William Dillinger BenefactorPurveyorStudent"

The room aside was a storage closet with a computer cabled out to a Wi-Fi router jump and an ethernet box. Yellow muddy boots sat on the floor and a rainproof jacket was hooked on the wall.

In a lone framed picture on the desk, Noah Catlow stood next to William Dillinger and a woman much older than Bill Dillinger. She was seated, and she had a hibiscus flower pinned to her crane-print kimono. The three of them were smiling, laughing, their shoulders touching, the woman and Bill showing off the huge white apples in their hands, Noah was showing a good sketch of the three of them to the camera. Friends Forever. More clever, doomed drawings.

In a desk drawer, Sophie found a double set of magnetic RFID keys marked EMERALD TABLET. She found a spiral drawing pad thick with talent. Noah Catlow dated the pad two months ago.

He drew maps of rivers and coasts. Crowds of fire-worshippers with faces in the smoke. The schematics of seaplanes. Diagrams and labels of open wounds, some bleeding, some with bubbles and some with teeth.

Catlow sketched precognition on the last pages. He penciled how he looked moments before that violent death. He drew himself and the older man, both alive and vigorous. What an adventuring duo, a thin man and a bruiser. Catlow drew himself with perfect reflection, his uneven teeth and pocked-marked chin caught exact, along with the fiction of matching scarves, jeweled earrings, their boots cleated with mud from the rain.

In the picture, the older man pressed coins to an innkeeper as he motioned towards the stairs, the older man's mouth no doubt whispering some threat of silence. Sophie watched them slither in the hallway at the door to 337. Catlow quietly pulled the hammer back on a pistol. The thick silencer slipped and screwed on tight.

Rasps of a last torn-out page on the pad remained. Sophie unfolded the picture that Wyeth gave her in the hotel. The drama with Lake defeated and dead and underneath their boots.

The tufts of paper lined up. Noah had seen the future just perfectly, right up until it lied to him.

Sophie made faces to herself, imitating what Noah Catlow would have looked like when the dagger hooked him. She peeled her lips back and pulled her eyes real wide. She made twisted-up faces. Grimacing his shock, a sneer, a puckered wince.

"Oh, no!" she whispered, wondering if she was getting Noah's voice right.

Angry shouts, loud shouts, several voices, echoed down the hallway.

"Just tell me!" the Mapp woman shouted.

In the lobby, the woman in the raincoat had escalated past all serenity. She was throwing mail and ylang-ylang scented towels at employees. Someone insisted she please listen, just listen. Another threatened that they were recording this for evidence.

"Where is my father?" the Mapp woman in the raincoat said and shouted in a few various ways.

"Beth, please," a woman from the spa said. "Beth, it's ok. Beth, we understand how frustrated you are right now."

"Ms. Mapp, please, George signed himself out last night," the man said, holding a tablet in front of her. A smiling old man, a signature, and an answer that didn't calm anyone down.

"Then tell me where he went!"

"We understand your frustration, and we promise we are just as concerned as you are."

He pointed to a picture of her father on the check in screen. GEORGE MAPP wore steel-frame glasses, naval tattoos, a mint-colored robe tight up to his neck.

Beth Mapp fiddled with her raincoat buttons as a woman from the front desk opened the front door for her, promising that they would call her and that they had already put in a call to the Sheriff about her father. Beth buttoned up her coat up and tried to think of something to say but just shook her head to cry.

Beth sat in the parking lot with the door open. Her eyes were raccoon black from the makeup and the tears, and she sat in a cloud of vaporizer smoke.

Sophie worked it through front to back. There were questions and responses and a dialogue and an answer to what she wanted. It was as simple as a child's game, but she had no other way. She couldn't stand the game, the wasted time, the counterfeit effect.

She started in, easy.

"This place is so difficult. Before my great-uncle passed...." Sophie sighed, shrugged. "They're just impossible."

"I just want to know where he is. They can't give straight answers on anything." Beth said.

"I'm Sophie. If you're in recovery, this place is amazing, but..."

Beth exhaled "But if you're FAMILY..."

"Has your father ever worked with Noah?" Sophie asked. "Sometimes I think he's the only one here who knows what he's doing."

Beth raised her eyebrows. She looked around the parking lot and squeezed Sophie's hand.

"Noah can do magic. They didn't want to believe dad went into remission because of him, but he did. It's true."

"Remission?" Sophie asked.

There were secrets to be shared. Beth held Sophie's hands against a phone. She zoomed in on the hospital files, asking Sophie to wait, look, see.

"They had dad on a PICC line. Look at this, Sophie. A doctor showed me this and told me he had six weeks to live. Six. weeks." X-rays of MAPP, G. was a skeleton splashed with stage 4 bristles and tumorous rice. A lymphatic system of sprouting seeds and roots tangled in the bones.

"That was three years ago," she said. "That's one-hundred and fifty-six weeks."

Sophie nodded. The X-rays read out the death sentence. Weeks, days before the bloom and blossom of mortality. The George Mapp Sophie saw wrapped up in a shower curtain in the

Aberdeen Best Western was healthy, after a fashion. Alive. Something miraculous and marvelous had interceded in between. Sophie nodded and smiled at Beth. She agreed Noah could do things she could barely understand.

"Noah's medicine worked." Beth rubbed her eyes with her thumbs. "He could have been so rich, but he didn't care."

"I know. Don't think my uncle tried," Sophie said.

Beth narrowed her eyes on Sophie. "Was your uncle, I mean, your great-uncle..."

"Bill Dillinger." Sophie asked. "You can say whatever you want. I don't care what people think about him."

Beth laughed. She covered her mouth and apologized.

"Sorry, I shouldn't-"

"He had good intentions. I mean, he tried to have good intentions. So, your dad knew him through Noah?" Sophie asked.

Beth got close to Sophie before looking around, even though nobody was around. She talked in a low voice and Sophie didn't break eye contact even as Beth rubbed the tears away.

"So, can I ask, um, a question about him? It has to do with my dad," Beth asked.

"Of course. I don't do family secrets."

"Noah brought Bill over twice. He brought these old women with him. He said they were his special friends, but they... they weren't his girlfriends, were they? All they talked about was the Book and that...group they belonged to. The Herman group."

"The Hermetic Circle," Sophie said. "They were a really tight group. They went everywhere together."

"That's it. That's right. A couple times. Dillinger. He'd keep introducing people as his friends, but... they acted more like they all owed money to him."

"Bill, he didn't treat anyone like a friend. My grandmother told me once she had to call his secretary to schedule him for their anniversary."

"Bill kept saying he could pay, but Noah didn't want money."

"He wanted to just buy the cure from Noah?"

"Noah explained it to him. He explained it to the old ladies, too. He told them the cure lived at a verdant pool with sunshine inside. The cure was in there and Noah knew it. Why didn't he just... just..."

Sophie nodded. The whole day and night shifted as a whole new galaxy was born before her. Noah Catlow knew. No one knew. No one was aware. Only Sophie. But Noah Catlow knew.

"Noah was just as soft as a puppy, Beth. That's all," Sophie said.

"He could have just asked. Why didn't he just ask? He was too gentle and people like Bill Dillinger and his lady friend were just too greedy. I'm sorry, Sophie. I shouldn't be so negative. I made a promise I wouldn't be negative."

Beth fanned her eyes and sobbed. Sophie leaned to hug her, and Beth hugged her back. Sophie felt Beth's body catching on the breaths as she got herself steady again. Sophie worked to hold back a wince of pain while pulling out of the hug and smiling at Beth.

"I have to call my dad's brother. If you find Noah, will you call me, is... is that ok?"

"Of course, Beth. Of course."

"Noah will turn up. He'll know where dad is."

Sophie nodded. She agreed with Beth that they would turn up soon, and that Noah knew everything.

# CHAPTER TWENTY-TWO

*The Height of Perfection Of Mastery*

## TACOMA, WA OCTOBER 30

The dark room at Emerald Tablet hummed with bad news.

Noah's server room lay in a valley between the container ships that floated high as mountains and the towering silos of industrial solvents, liquid fuels, and millions of gallons of food additives and flavorings. The paper mills had shut down long ago, but the air at the port of Tacoma still smelled so stiff and strong you could see a shift in focus as the wind changed direction.

Backup diesel generators the size of school buses lined one side of the corrugated steel facility where HYADES DATA CENTER was painted on in yellow letters. There was a number and an email address, "FOR INQUIRIES" next to a keypad at the door.

Wyeth was standing next to a door lettered EMERALD TABLET in brass paint. He wore a leather jacket zipped tight to a white wool turtleneck. He stood in the doorway with reflective sunglasses still on indoors and turned his head sideways at Sophie.

"What are you doing here?" Sophie asked.

"How long have you been awake?" Wyeth asked.

It took her a moment. "Thirty... four hours. Why are you here?"

"A maid found those bodies at the hotel. They'll probably figure some meth deal bullshit, but after 48 hours, a detective is going to line up Noah's fingerprints to his business records, leading right to this doorway."

"So, we have a little bit of a head start?"

"Little bit."

The door was marked with a sun and moon, a bronze triangle. Wyeth pointed to them.

"I already took a peek, found this right inside," Wyeth said.

Wyeth handed Sophie an amber pharmacist's bottle, three-quarters full of liquid.

"Haldol, Noah Catlow..." Sophie said. "That's a big dose for a... little guy."

Haldol was a no-joke slug of a treatment plan at a 4mg daily sip. Sophie unwrapped the Haldol warning leaflet. It tumbled the length of her arm. It noted Haldol was prescribed for illnesses affecting thinking, feeling, behaving. For feeling aggressive. For seeing things that weren't there. For believing things that weren't true. For the snaps and tics and barks of Tourette's. For becoming unduly suspicious. For becoming hostile, impulsive, enthusiastic.

"Schizophrenia?" Sophie asked.

"Maybe. Schizoaffective. Drug-induced psychosis. Hard to know now..." Wyeth said.

Sophie eyed the harrowing black box warning. It cautioned that he should call his doctor IMMEDIATELY if he experienced sudden extrapyramidal side effects, their manifestations bullet-pointed in the leaflet as: severe problems controlling the limbs, jerking, trembling, movements, a facial expression that looked like a mask. If a tongue went numb. If it crawled around your mouth. If you started screaming and screaming and couldn't stop, but no noise came out at all. If you lost control of your body and it felt like something else took over and was flicking your tongue and contorting your face and shouting unknown words from some unknown plane.

The Emerald Tablet was bad inside. Noah packed the drywall with a tapestry of photographs, pen-and-ink drawings, city blueprints, topographical maps of highways and state parks. A path ran in straight lines and doubled back on itself. Aberdeen. Dillinger's house. Dead ends out past the mountains, both ways, THE VERDANT POOL a title, a destination, double X scribbled out.

"Look at this crazy motherfucker," Wyeth said.

"It made sense to him, Wyeth," Sophie said. She tried to find a path on the maps. "He thought he was getting really close."

Noah had unmistakable scenes of the Book drawn out. A dagger stabbed hilt-deep in the sand. A smooth-rock cave, full of succulents and ferns, drawing light from a second sun underneath a subterranean lake. A woman escaping to blue moonlight by moving through a skylight, the moonlight crooking her silhouette.

"Tell you what, this guy can draw." Wyeth smudged his fingers across the charcoal drawings. "You know, I read once, creative types, music, art in particular, have a higher rate of schizophrenia. Hey, you think this woman looks like you?"

Wyeth pointed to a subject who strode across all the walls and pictures. A patron of ink and charcoal. Her face and hair were thin and different, but Sophie knew herself too clearly. Noah caught her pale face, her thin eyebrows, the wrinkles around her eyes and forehead. Sophie watched herself bleed in the black ink.

She found a picture of herself in the cave amidst the ferns and vines. The long shadows drawing black ribbons against the walls and ceilings from the undersea sun, her knees wet against the laps of the mercury pool of burning light.

"How did this creature ever luck into finding Lake?" Wyeth asked.

Wyeth dug up archaeology in a trash can. Bandages in sediment layers. The papers and curled backings and the crusted fleshy loops of 3-inch bandages. The big kind you'd take some skin off with it, guaranteed. There were three boxes in the trash, along with the mess. A quarter-reel of gauze snaked black and stiff in there too.

A tiny voice whispered. Sophie picked up headphones and tapped at a keyboard. Noah's voice chattered a mile-a-minute. YouTube channel BlueCatEnantiomer looped through videos, endlessly repeating. Noah wore black t-shirts and 8-Bit foam whiskers and kitty-cat ears. He gave chronicles of hallucinogens and drug trials from the test subject himself, still shaking from the time spent in the Entheogen wilderness.

"BlueCat is baaaa-aaa-cckkk everyone. This is, this was the newest version I just made. A tour of the universe. I have to draw my dream for you..." Noah took a pen and blinked out of sync before setting it on paper "... before I forget what happens."

Noah gave first-hand test-subject reports of drugs he brewed up and then dosed himself on, the mirror-analogues to LSD, bromo-dragonfly, DMT, something that had the business end of PCP without the problems or aggression, the serotonin handshake of hallucinogens minus the onset time.

Noah caught seizures on digital. He fast-edited past blackouts. His eyes went bloodshot or his lids as thin as dime slots. He unstitched dreamland and received on all frequencies. He knew the mental realm was accepting of all keys and that some would open skeleton locks.

Noah giggled on-screen. He said everything tied back to the core text.

"It's called the Book of Blue Daggers now, but it wasn't always that way. In 1899 it was Lieutenants Tale and 1922 The Orphan in a Lavender Dress and 1937 Field Manual to Andalucian Wetlands. The words change, easy, easy, right? It's a universal set of themes and concepts and imagery and symbolism, properly decoded, that correctly identifies it. It's always there."

Sophie listened closely. Noah panted and purred as he explained on bad audio.

"It's not the shape of the book or the words inside that allow it to hide in plain sight. You see, it's going to feel the same and look the same and you can hold it the same. A book is a book is a book here. But there's something different about this, because no matter what, the colors, the symbols, where the story reaches the end are always the same."

Noah stood on the screen and peeled off a bandage from his hip. Showing a cup-sized wound, the black burns threaded through with silver.

"The Book led him all the way. It's easy to say radiation burns are a small price to... see.. see... the pages. These pages all the way and let him think he had won and then it tricked him."

Noah licked his lips and flicked two soft blue pills, dark as licorice, into his mouth and started to chew.

Sophie put the headphones down.

"I won't tell on you if you won't tell on me," Wyeth said, whistling.

Wyeth tucked away a lock pick set and smiled at the steel cabinet. Noah's experiments beyond time and space.

Just a first glance and Sophie caught Palmgren pill presses, a Sartorius balance, empty Gatorade bottles flushed and filled and marked 3,4-Methylenedioxyphenylpropan-2-one, Gamma-butyrolactone, and a mason jar with a screw-on lid marked Ergocristine in gold sharpie.

"Ergocristine?" Sophie said, staring at the bottle. "That's Summer of Love, Dead-head LSD. What else does he have?"

"Acetic anhydride, too. And, uh, Diethyl Ether. These are all schedule I, Schedule II chemicals. Care to guess?" Wyeth asked.

Sophie squinted her eyes. "He's trying to grow something from the Book here. But that's not... you can't-"

From the bottom shelf, Wyeth dealt out blue and white express envelopes sheathed with aluminum foil. He zipped one open and poured a slick golden dust that pooled into a thin grease on the steel drawer of the cabinet. Symbols teased on the return addresses: ♍,♊,♋.

"Wanna get high and be somebody?" Wyeth chuckled.

The babble pace from BlueCatEnantiomer went on and on, a sentence that described the keys to eternity and ran on just as long, rambling about how only your mind could achieve perfect mastery. Your body an impractical vessel to achieve total enlightenment with-

"How long have you been looking for the Book?" Wyeth asked.

"You're not the kind of person I would tell."

"Who would be the kind of person?"

"Sophie shrugged. She didn't know either.

She tapped a photo of Bill Dillinger. It was centered in a collage of his house, his hoards, the flooded basement where he died.

Dillinger was shirtless. His old muscles were like ropes taut across canvas and his skin was bruised green and deeply puckered in places, and in those places it was bleeding. Dillinger pressed his hands together and was soaked to his waist from the water that was glowing from within.

Wyeth took the picture down. "What kind of details can you give me about the Verdant Pool?"

"The last chapter of the Book. It's an underground river, a lake, where the shores grow with, um..."

Sophie closed her eyes. Oh! These words! She dared to let herself think of them again!

"I remember the words from the Book. What grows there. Listen to me, Wyeth."

"Sure."

He wasn't.

"No, listen."

Wyeth looked at her. He was, finally.

"Where shores grow flora with roots that draw from the water celestial." Sophie said Words she'd imagined every single day but never, ever said out loud before.

In the picture, a blue light from under the water dazzled and broke the surface in shards across Bill Dillinger's face. It rippled across the ceiling and walls that Sophie recognized as the place he died.

"You don't mean this as a metaphor. You're talking literally, as we stand here," Wyeth said.

"It isn't symbolism, no. No. It's all real." Sophie was draining away.

"Right from the pages of the Book. They thought they could grow whatever grew-" Sophie pointed to the picture, tapping her finger at water foaming around Dillinger's calves. "-At the shoreline of water enlightened."

Sophie pointed to the blue in the water, the points on the map. She was flooded now. She was bleeding inside. She realized it now. Now, yes, now.

"You don't care about the Book. Or Lake," Sophie said. "You think Noah found something better."

"Exactly right," Wyeth said. He was almost laughing.

Wyeth held up an envelope filled with the dandelion-colored dust between two fingers. "Noah found a cure. A cure for everything if we're right."

Sophie dodged the noose, but it still took her by surprise. Wyeth let her hang there as she stood dizzy. He snapped his fingers and pinched her shoulder.

"Hey, Sophie, wake up!" Wyeth clapped at her and smiled. "You just realized why I'm in this?"

He chuckled when he realized how alone she'd always been. There was Wyeth, and the lawyers, and the old lady. They were all looking at her, just waiting for her to catch on. Wyeth had a proud look on his face, like he was glad he didn't have to spell things out for Sophie.

Sophie shoved Wyeth hard, and she screamed at him. The top of her vision went gray as she said, "FUCK YOU." She put her hands out to catch herself, but they got in the way. "Fuck you, Wyeth. You hypocrite!"

"I can tell you're pretty bad, but you shouldn't be. I don't have to explain it step-by-step to you. That's always such a chore," Wyeth said.

"Who is the old lady?"

Wyeth laughed. "The Queen Bee who writes the checks? I'd never tell you her name in a million years."

"Lake's going to murder her, and Taylor Zapata and Barbara Bontecue. You know he can find them. You know he's going to kill them," Sophie said.

"Tick-tock, tick-tock, then help me find Lake and the Book, Sophie." Wyeth said.

"The Hermetic Circle hired you to keep tabs on Noah Catlow?"

Wyeth flicked his eyebrows and nodded. "After Dillinger died, they needed to find the cure from Noah. They call Zapata and Bontecue, Zapata and Bontecue call me. They refuse to explain, but motivation isn't hard to figure out. Being a secret society doesn't mean you are good at keeping secrets."

"And Lake?"

Sophie didn't get up. Wyeth sat down beside her.

"Noah thought he would end up with the Book post-Bill Dillinger DOA, not accounting on Howard Cyone's mania throwing everything to the wind. Like you, Noah is a classic paranoid, and refuses to directly get or ask for what he wants."

"And The Hermetic Circle thought they could lure Noah into getting the Book and making the cure for them. Dangling Lake as the bait," Sophie said.

"I recommended Lake for the manual aspects. I will admit fault and take responsibility for not accounting for your presence," Lake said.

"You're like watching a robot being told to apologize. You didn't expect that the Book would... figure it out? That it wouldn't see through what you were doing? That you could draw Noah out, but the Book wouldn't kill him?" Sophie said.

"Sophie, I'd rather ask for help than continue apologizing."

"I lied to Lake, Wyeth. I lied to him about being able to save his son, and save our friend, and for that, he's going to cut me and everyone else involved into tiny little pieces."

"I know you won't let this prospect of certain doom alter your behavior in any real way, Sophie. My benefactor just wants the cure. She doesn't care about the Book, per se. I think you'll find she'll be more than pleased to share any knowledge gained."

"Share it with who?"

"Who do you think these people are? They're not evil people, and they're not cruel. They're just like Dillinger, people of means and money who are serious about surviving imminent death that modern medicine says cannot be cured. They have a common motivation in that they think a universal cure is at hand. You share, um, similar interests, in that your bodies are winding down." Wyeth made a spiraling motion with fingers, like a leaf looping down.

"What?"

"Your condition? I can't pronounce your condition, uh, your bad blood."

"Fuck you, fuck YOU Wyeth!"

"Do you think it's a wonder I don't ask you every ten minutes if you need to lie down? If you should be sweating like that in a cold room? If your eyes should look that shade? It's pretty impressive that you keep standing."

But she wasn't. Finally, nothing worked and Sophie landed in pieces. The breeze in the room could have jostled her around. She was going to ask Wyeth to brush the ants and beetles off her arms and legs, but remembered the feeling would go away on its own. She jammed her numb fists into her armpits and squeezed as hard as she imagined she could go.

"How did Noah find the cure?"

"He found a path through the Book. Can you show me the path, Sophie?"

Sophie nodded.

"The Book will find out, just after telling us what it told Noah," Sophie said. "And the Book will show Lake exactly how to kill us."

# CHAPTER TWENTY-THREE

*Then By That Desire*

## ENUMCLAW, WA, HALLOWEEN

Sophie told Beth Mapp that Noah and her father George were still alive, and that she could find them. Sophie was going to row Beth into a riptide ocean of lies to get the answers she needed, and then leave Beth stranded as a dot in infinite blue.

On a fast-food bag smudged with fry oil, Sophie drew to remind herself that she was the one and only and that Wyeth and the others were wrong, so wrong. She allowed herself to finally draw the Verdant Pool, to allow herself to admit that it wouldn't jinx her. She asked without any fear of repercussion from a universe of atoms wound up to smash her just when she got what she wanted.

She allowed herself to imagine it. Her tears dotted the bag and her face in ink, on the shore of the wild-growing cave that would cure her, fix her, resolve her of all disease and frailty. Her image was soaking, her knees half-sunk, her palms turned up and scooping the water still lit from the sun beneath its surface. She held the bag and begged for it to come true, please, please let me have this, she said, please, before crumpling it and throwing it away.

It was sundown on Halloween, and Beth wore a bandanna and a foam cowboy hat. She gave Sophie a cheap satin cape and white fangs. Join in the fun. They handed out packets of candy from a laundry basket. Beth had filled it all the way up and googly-eyed kids scooped handfuls. A crowd of dogs clacked and panted and whined behind closed doors. Beth said they were desperate about all the new smells. Beth called them all her babies, at least three, but probably more. She had a glass jar rattling on her neck with their puppy teeth inside. Beth said she had tried to train them as puppies and give them away but just couldn't bear to see them go.

"I need to tell you the truth, Beth."

"Do you know where my dad is?"

Sophie imagined it fast-forward. The maid finding the bodies. The police untangling, then, body bags. The morgue routine. Ink stains on fingers stiff as marble statues. Two bodies with blanks next to the intake name field. They'd cross match Noah on guilty fingerprints, George Mapp on the serial numbers of knee implants, hernia mesh patches, Veterans Administration details. They wouldn't need to check dental records. They wouldn't need to check DNA.

"Not yet. But I need you to listen, Beth. I'm sorry I didn't tell you this before."

"What is it?"

"My name isn't Sophie. I'm Nicole Wyeth, and I do corporate investigations. Mallinckrodt Pharmaceutical believes something illegal is happening at Rainier Wind Spa, and that your father, and Noah Catlow, are aware of it."

"Oh, my god," Beth said.

"Your father will not be in any legal trouble. Right now, the legal authorities are barely aware of what is going on. But Noah, and I believe your father, saw, or took, something important."

Beth turned off the lights at the front. Kids out front yelled. Beth pulled at her fingernails until they curled like the ends of a fresh twig.

"Noah? And, and my father?"

"Noah has a complicated past. He was arrested for fraud in Palo Alto but served no time. He was charged with distribution of narcotics in San Francisco, which is pending. The police believe he's a dangerous man. Beth, it's important you tell me everything you know, because Noah knows where your father is."

This last part was only a lie in the way Beth understood the timeline.

Sophie would have to row fast. A morgue would connect the dots and a sheriff's car would roll out and someone with an apologetic but serious voice would house call Beth Mapp and blow Sophie's story to smithereens. There was only one way to get moving, and Beth had to believe there was someone alive at the other end to make it happen.

"What did your father do with Noah?"

"He trusts Noah. Noah saved his life."

"And he would do anything for Noah?"

"I don't like what you're implying. A beautiful soul like Noah wouldn't hurt him. Noah is, is, a beautiful soul," Beth said. "He didn't call himself a doctor, but me and dad saw him heal people and save lives, and I don't mean with medicine."

Beth showed Sophie hospital bills, a packet of medical sheets she took everywhere for her dad. Foot screws, replaced knees, weeks in hospitals from sepsis, and accidents with handsaws. Swollen lymph nodes and dubious test results.

"If you can help me, find Noah." Sophie said. "I can find your father."

Beth licked her lips and talked in a soft voice that almost drifted away.

"I thought it might be you. Noah said if someone asked, I shouldn't be afraid to tell them."

"Tell them what?"

"Noah told me someone would ask about this exactly. He said he read a book of secrets and that he and my father were going to take it from them."

"From The Hermetic Circle?"

Beth nodded.

Beth whispered so low and soft Sophie had to get close enough to feel the warm breath of her words. "Noah said the spaces between the words and sentences were a path to see and take. Dad showed me how they could grab something they needed and never get caught."

"What did they take?" Sophie asked.

Beth licked her lips again. She closed her eyes. She wouldn't say.

"They had a plan," she whispered. "It worked."

Sophie drove. Beth talked and stripped her fingernails to curls as she directed Sophie down side streets. She gave directions to a house Noah rented. Beth told Sophie about how she bought duct tape, garbage bags, these big box fans. How she had to go to three different hardware stores to get the different fans. How she got talked into buying sets of power strips so the big box fans didn't burst the fuses at Noah's place. How Noah gave her cash to pay for everything. How he told her she had to get the instructions perfect, but she wrote it down anyway after he left her hands. Beth mimed it with her pink fingers. Cover the windows with bags. Dark as a cave, check it in daylight. Run the fans at high speed. Towards the doors. Double tape everything.

"Sorry Nicole, I pick when I'm nervous," she said and wiped her leaking fingertips on the Halloween bandanna. "You can park here."

The neighborhood was packed tight, the houses small, bunched and wood rotted.

"Noah read the Book. He was. Um. He didn't tell me that was..."

Beth talked in a voice that was between a whisper and silence.

"That he was what? That he was scared?"

Beth shook her head. "Noah said he had to be careful with it. He said he didn't want to get tricked."

Beth climbed underneath the tilted mossy wreck of Noah's porch and scrounged a key hidden somewhere from a Tupperware box. She had the cowgirl hat laced up under her chin, dangling and wet now from the moss and moisture of Noah's house. She handed the key to Sophie but said she wouldn't go inside.

"I promised I wouldn't after I locked up."

"Will you show me around?"

Beth shook her head. "I promised." She put the cowboy hat back on and crossed her arms.

A breeze came from under the backdoor and a drone from within.

With the flashlight on her phone, she could see steel fans churning in the darkness. Dots of black mold patterned every wall, and braille text ran knee high up from the floor. The slick dark words and numbers read out something, but Sophie couldn't assemble it.

In the kitchen, she could smell the refrigerator unplugged. Another mold explosion even as she stepped between another fan in the doorway. A line of white-pink mushroom bulbs swelled from the floorboards, and something flapped underneath the buzz of unseen fans.

The fans circled the humid air in dark waves. Something bumped. Sophie went to her knees on the swollen, wet floorboards. Her knees sagged into the wet pink mulch of the kitchen floor as she crept into the darkness. She slid her fingers to the slick wall and rolled her body alongside.

Sophie pressed her ear to the warm, moist floor. Underneath; voices, scrapes, a crackling noise. Sophie stayed in the darkness and slithered to a door jamb. She probed her hands into the darkness. A carpet. She slid along her belly across the hallway, inching with her feet. She could hear the noises closer as she felt a wooden stair in her hand.

Sophie barely spared a breath for the time it took. Her body ached, and she shook at trying to control it. She moved to the stairs, her jaw wrenched tight and her legs cramping against the knee, bracing as she stepped down. No voices rose from the black. She waited there for the foot splash to spray against her face and something to clamp against her ankle and elbows between the open stair slats and begin to drag her through.

"Closer down," it murmured. There was a yell as thin as the sound of children on the horizon.

There was a splash at the bottom and Sophie waited. She held tight to the railing and counted steps. She could smell water at the bottom. Burning wood and plastic. Sophie broke a flashlight to the darkness.

Water flooded in from a violent crack in the foundation. A clutch of frogs chirped as papers and pill bottles swirled in the muck. The floor beams were black and scalloped from the heat and the soot covered the ceiling like a layer of frost, and she saw the treasure that they had taken.

A huge steel container, flat gray and thick and shaped like an enormous battery, stood in the middle of the basement. It was charred and the burnt scent filled her nostrils. Its insides had been peeled open and tools, welding supplies, lay submerged nearby.

The inside looked like a honeycomb. Sophie could see the layers of it peeling around black-and-yellow CAUTION DANGER radiation trefoils noting DANGER CAUTION. Etched into the steel itself read US DEPARTMENT OF ENERGY HANFORD SITE.

Metal coils from the drilled-out locks along with piles of welders confetti bobbled at the water around the base of it.

A duct lay empty at the heart of it, bubbled white from the heat. The egg crate's insides bare all the way up and down. Sophie knew they contained uranium rods. Dragon's ribs and boiling bones. The fuel from reactors and nuclear power across the nation. The radioactive lengths of metal inside raced away by Noah and George. The basement was still warm from the touch of a half-life a million-years long.

Sophie gasped.

She slowly moved her hands across her body. Were the gamma rays cutting through her now? Was there light-speed radiation unspooling loose strands at the tips of a DNA helix as she stood knee deep in the water? Would an impending death make a noise, a heat, of any kind of sign at all?

She breathed herself back in and rubbed her eyes. Her vision was alright. Her eyes worked just fine. A heat that ran faster than light had lit the fuse on her body from deep inside.

A page of yellow paper fluttered in the updraft. It was aloft in the stream of air, flapping like a lost bird in the gloom until Sophie caught it with a ringing smack against the container. She held the paper folded out with one hand and her flashlight with the other.

Noah's style was clear enough. Just a quick sketch. Even in the basement, it was easy to see.

A woman in a cape stood in water, perhaps in a cave. She stood in front of a huge, stark obelisk. With her hand she traced notches carved into the face of the obelisk as jagged arrows, black magic auras, a loathsome potence radiated outwards from the obelisk and lanced the woman through and through.

Sophie recognized the here and now, touching the container, watching herself, as Noah had seen it happen. They had only met when his body was dead, but Noah knew she would be in this half-life room still hot from the uranium rods, wide eyed, putting together pieces while holding a picture of herself.

Sophie smiled. Noah thought this would be some kind of puzzle, didn't he? He stole radioactive rods to create the glow under the shore, and he killed Dillinger with a false Verdant Pool. The Book wasn't just steps ahead; it was the whole story, and Noah thought he'd be laughing at this from somewhere else, not as a corpse getting tagged out with no one left to ID the body.

Maybe the Book of Blue Daggers had a sense of humor, because Noah wasn't going to be laughing from beyond the grave at this.

In this basement of frog chirps and radiation burns, Sophie, at last, grasped the dark methodology.

The energy burst through her, and her laughter echoed into the wet and filthy basement. The malign intelligence in the air. The weapons were out, and Sophie could see e-v-e-r-y-t-h-i-n-g. The Book didn't work with a brutal club or knife. It relied on greed and superstition. The turn of a cruel coincidence. The book would lead you from one thing to another, in links of savage causality. Like a killer's return to the cooling murder scene, the Book of Blue Daggers was covering its tracks. It was burning off those who touched it, seen it, had read those holy letters and divine characters.

The Book loathed those who were clear in their longing. Noah, Mapp, and Dillinger had been too obvious, too open in their love. Wagner Koo and his son as well. Lake, the lawyers, Esme. Their plans came with nothing close to cutting. Their attempts to play suitor to the Book got them cast into a deathtrap of their design. Sophie saw the trap laid perfectly clear now.

The Book gave them desire, and then by desire it destroyed them.

# CHAPTER TWENTY-FOUR

*The Book of Blue Daggers Ch. 11, "Shadow Walk"*

**EARLIER, IN THE BOOK OF BLUE DAGGERS**

Underneath the cruel city, Lux was hunting.

Lux entered the sewer just as the golden sunset dipped level to the mouth of the tunnel, bathing it in a full half-mile of flickering glow. He jogged under the city into a conduit that appeared red and freshly forged, broken only by the speedy passage of the lengthy shadow.

As the twilight grew, the tunnel glow dimmed, and Lux tightened his goggles about his face. He flicked the aluminum switch on the bridge of the thick leather strap and glass lenses and the circuitry hummed the tunnel into a visible nightlife in firefly green.

He navigated west, then north, towards the Crestbloom District, where the heavy fragrance of star blossom blooms permeated the underground. Echoes of casual conversations from well-to-do citizens and the innocent banter of children playing in the twilight reached his ears from the grates above him. He mentally noted the maintenance grates marking his path to Zetco's mansion - three, five, seven.

Suddenly, the goggles burst white with an oncoming rush of water. Lux could hear the deluge coming from a shattered pipe. Zetco's magnificent fountains were leaking from underneath, the smell clean and metallic here in the fresh masonry of the city tunnels.

Through the thick spray, Lux found passage up from the tunnel into the Crestbloom, finding his path on a childlike metal ladder built for the Rufflethroats that first laid brick to this district.

Lux ascended the ladder, each rung a battle against the force of the water. He anchored himself, balancing precariously with one foot on a lower rung while looping an elbow through another, heaving himself upward to the next slick metal bar in a rhythmic repetition. His missing finger and the phantom ache forced Lux to double-check every grip he made was true. Amnesia hummed, buzzing to escape its sheath as he climbed higher. He stilled the blade, whispering promises of impending action — steady now, you'll have your time, steady now.

Gripping the narrow rungs tightly, Lux strained against a grate above him, held fast by bolts under the pink gas lamp glow from the pristine grounds above. His feet stood trapeze steady against the tiny ladder, his hands searching for a lock along the cruel grate along the fountain drain.

Amnesia twitched as Lux prodded and pried. He was close. Locating the ends of the bolts and their fittings, Amnesia scrambled and burst an electric-white light as it sprang through the fittings of the grate.

Zetco's manor exuded an even more exclusive charm behind its gates. Luminescent wings of nocturnal tranquil moths dotted the tendrils of Twilight Vines. Zetco had adorned his winding pathways with the intoxicating aromas of the celestial blooms and amaryllis petals, while crushed iridescent seashells crunched beneath Lux's boots.

Stepping off the shell-studded trail, Lux ventured towards the estate's rear galley entrance. Amnesia cast off electric blue sparks, its vibrations as fierce as a rabid dog, as Lux used it to slice his way in through the rear door.

In a dark hallway, a tall man with two black lengths of hair across his shoulders stood and delicately twisted a small brass key against the dials of a tower clock. He shifted a bronze-and-silver dial wheel to the proper chronology. He rubbed his fingers clean against an oilcloth he had tucked into a breast pocket.

The man saw a reflection. Perhaps the blue pulse.

Lux could see the sunlight passion of the dagger, Amnesia reflecting against the man's face as it approached with the buzz of a mad swarm of vermin.

Amnesia danced three wheeling swipes, each closer than the last. Amnesia clicked his defensive fingers away, then his hand and forearm, then dug deep into his ribs. There was no resistance or breeze from Amnesia as it carved against the meat. Just a deep, deeper, deepest shade of blue as it dug in.

The tall man's face froze in astonishment. Amnesia clicked like beetles in heat and then whooshed like leaves in the wind as Lux grabbed the man's shirt and settled him onto the wooden floor.

Amnesia dimmed, pale and slim in the darkness.

Lux heard a plinking noise. *Tink.* Something irregular. *Tink-tink.* Like an unworked clock straining and failing to rework its gears back towards proper hours. *Tink.* The dagger in his hand made enough noise. Now it was grunting.

Zetco lounged in a common room. He wore slippers and a thin silk robe and leaned far back on a chaise. One by one he took, and then considered, dark and ripe cherries from a tall glass. He split them with the front of his teeth, holding the pit between his cheek while chewing and considering his next choice, spitting the black pits into a polished steel cup. *Tink.* He reached to pluck another. *Tink.*

He held a box, a bow, and a ribbon in front of him. *Tink.* A beautiful dried yellow flower he gently sniffed and then set inside the box. *Tink.*

A long and expertly bound ledger lay on the table in front of Zetco. In between bites of cherry, he would slowly write and compare the columns and entries to one another. Zetco put a finger to his lips and let a moment of accounting work behind his eyes, before blinking and removing his finger to pick up the pen again and tally notes and figures.

"I was warned, you know," Zetco said. "It appears they were right."

"About what?" Lux asked.

"About your prowess. Shall we talk about destiny, Lux?"

Destiny indeed. Amnesia flickered blue as a flame of aviation fuel; the smokeless fire barely visible in the shadows of the room.

Zetco held the ledger up between them. A flower marked next to each name.

"These are the members of the Eucalyptus Grove itself, Lux. And the powdered remains of these blooms…" Zetco waved to the waxed sheaf of yellow petals, "Are the grasp that the Queen holds them with."

"The source has run dry," Lux said. "That's why she wants the Book, isn't it?"

"The Book you hold is the gardener's guide. The map to Verdant Pool, the shoreline of infinite life."

"Where is the queen?"

"I don't know, Lux."

"You're lying. Tell me or I'll kill you." Lux let Amnesia hiss and spark at Zetco's face, the blade aching for a chance to cut him layer from layer.

"You're going to kill me either way. I'm neither stalk nor petal of the Eucalyptus Grove. I facilitate their panacea, but I don't know their sanctuary. But if it will save my life, I can help you."

"You can't help me."

Zetco held one of the yellow fruiting bodies to him.

"Let me show you what the queen can offer."

Lux held the Blue Dagger to Zetco, and it keened with dark anticipation.

Zetco put the crushed yellow flower petals in a saucer and then set it alight, soon watching it smoke and smolder. Zetco gathered thick strands of smoke in his hands and breathed them deep into his mouth as though he was sipping water from his palm. The edges of his eyes sparkled with golden notches, and he offered a hand of smoke to Lux.

The smell sent his mind twisting. It was a mountain valley wind filled with the smell of throttling fuel. It made his head swim. His fingers went numb. His missing finger ached as the scars there cracked open.

The wound on his hand peeled back and roped out and the bone knitted forth joint-to-joint. Lux's arm felt golden daylight and his finger flashed from nothing to flesh again. He immediately touched it, to be sure it wasn't a trick or a false light or confusion. He felt it, was sure of it. He bit against it and could taste it and make pain to it. His lost finger was coming back from nothing more than the breath of a golden flower.

"That was the last of it?" Lux asked.

"The queen's garden has gone fallow. The Grove will die unless they can find the way to The Verdant Pool."

Zetco eyed Lux's satchel. He calmly laid a hand against it. He didn't reach for the pages inside. He stared at Lux with the fresh eyes of a younger, newer man.

"Where shores grow flora with roots that draw from the water celestial."

"With the Book?" Lux asked. "You want to show me the way?"

"I have surmised that the Book wants to return to the shores of The Verdant Pool. With you being in possession of it, and the queen being in such need of it, one may also presume that you, Lux, have the upper hand in this endeavor."

Zetco took the Book from the satchel. His eyes grew wide, twinkling golden as he smoothed his hands across the cover.

"You see, Lux, I can take you there, for I know how to divine the secret words and codes in these pages."

"And in return?"

Zetco licked his lips, brushing his hands across the pages as he fingered the edges and slipped his hands inside, speaking softly as he opened the Book to a chapter of beauty and wonder and delight.

"She'll follow us there, and you can have-"

Amnesia was the one reading and guiding now. Lux grabbed the mumbling man and slid his body along the knife, scouring him full across the length of the blade. The cup of cherry pits burst and spilled across the floor, the drupes cascading across the room, as Lux held Amnesia angled prone and lifted Zetco to his feet with his free hand against the point of the grinning blue blade. Zetco and his lengthy and varied interiors tumbled across the table in front of him, staining the ledger and soaking the chosen chapters of the Book.

Zetco's lips moved. He was still able, after a fashion, before his eyes dimmed and the organs that lay across the table, yet still connected, clenched once and turned pale.

Lux picked up the ledgers that Zetco had been working on. Even stained, Lux could read the names and certain addresses, those with and without flowers. Places and names. Times and dates. Deliveries. The path of flowers and buds and seeds. The processes of sorting.

The ledger was just a skeleton of things. But given flesh by hours of deduction, until the gore of Zetco ran cold, dark and stiff as the withered cherry pits, he was able to know two things.

Zetco thought he understood what Lux had wanted. He knew that he could lure the Eucalyptus Queen to him at any time. With the Book by his side, that much was a given. But now, he and Amnesia knew something much more valuable. Where the yellow flowers were being processed, and who would be most desperate for the cure.

Amnesia thrummed at the thought of knowing where Selia was. Of realizing she would be sleeping quietly, behind some thin lock or flimsy door.

"Soon friend. Soon," Lux said, rubbing the knife to a soothing tone. "We'll find Selia soon."

# CHAPTER TWENTY-FIVE

*Make a Path, Mark a Way*

## TACOMA, WASHINGTON NOVEMBER 1

Sophie was burning inside.

Wyeth kept asking something insipid while she sifted through Noah's lab bottles for a prescription she knew he had. She shook the RADIOGARDASE bottle for CATLOW, NOAH. The pills were as blue as panther-fur and shifted like beetles in her palm.

"How long will it take them to, uh, connect the fingerprints of Noah and George Mapp's bodies to who they are?" Sophie asked Wyeth.

"They have yet to do so," Wyeth said.

Sophie put the pills in her mouth dry. She was dying, and there were embers inside of her.

"Do you know who has the bodies?" Sophie asked.

Sophie looked for water. Something to drink. Anything.

"The morgue in Aberdeen," Wyeth said.

"When they do the autopsy, they're going to find out that Noah has radiation poisoning. Cesium-137," Sophie said.

"What's in your mouth, Sophie?" Wyeth asked.

Sophie leaned her head back. She swallowed hard and couldn't help but chew. A pill burst and the blue paint taste burst at the back of her throat. She got most of it, but it ran across her tongue. Esme was right, precisely right. No matter what, she'd be running forever from the flames inside of her. The closer she came to saving her life, the more scared she was, and she wanted to ask Esme if it would ever stop, could ever stop, but Sophie already knew the answer.

"If they cremate him, they'll spread the radiation in his body."

Her body was terrain for invisible wounds. The radiation wounds from invisible bullets an atom wide, gunned over and over her body. She stood there in the wet and heat of the basement and took the rifle line without even knowing. Without even a blindfold and a cigarette.

"Your lips are blue, Sophie. You look like a Picasso."

The Book had a hand down her throat. She could taste the color of it on her lips and the smell of it at the back of her throat. The peel-away on the prescription bottle said not to worry if her urine was blue or teal when she pissed the cesium-137 bonded molecules away. It had a cartoon graphic to remind you to flush three times, be sure to do it with the lid down.

"It's going to help remove cesium that, uh, that I might have poisoned myself with in George Mapp's basement. He and Noah stole spent nuclear fuel rods for Dillinger."

Wyeth shook his head. "Sorry, the only place they could do that would be the Hanford Site, and they would have been filled with enough bullets to use them as anchors before they got anywhere close to the storage casks."

Sophie shook her head. "The Book mapped it out. It would have known the exact time and place to avoid being seen. They looted a coffin for the cooling rods. Silly me, they didn't put the stake back in the vampire when they were done. The same way they almost got Lake."

It came to her, it dawned all around her, she understood in a beautiful, wonderful relaxing flow the answers to so many questions. The wax seal. Why Noah was so confident he and Mapp could find and kill Lake even though he didn't have the Book in hand.

"Call your employer, Wyeth."

"Excuse me?"

"I have what she wants, and she has what I want."

Wyeth slimmed his eyes, still playing coy at the whole thing, but Sophie was miles ahead.

"What are you doing? Trying to join the club?"

"Noah found Lake after the auction, didn't he?"

"Yes, so?"

"He couldn't have done it without the Book. Noah wouldn't have even attempted it without it."

"He didn't have it. Lake had it. That's why you're here, isn't it?"

"Not all of it. Before Howard Cyone lost it, Noah expurgated pages from the Book, just as it would have asked him to."

"That's... that's a pretty good guess there, Sophie."

"Call her."

"Are you making me an offer?" Wyeth asked.

Sophie pressed her hands against her spinning, burning head and clenched her jaw. A chance at it.

"What does she want for the pages?" Sophie asked.

"You tell me?" Wyeth said.

"Tell them they won't die," Sophie said. "Tell them I know how to create in the lab what died with Noah."

"I'll call Taylor right now, and you can have the pages tonight," Wyeth said. "How can I be sure?"

"Because I'm the only other person who has read the Book and is still left alive and in one piece," Sophie said. "Because I can give them what the Book tells them they need."

"You're closer than you've ever been in your life. Show me proof." Wyeth shook the phone. "Show them you're not just another Noah Catlow."

"You fucking goblin, Wyeth. You fucking infection merchant."

Wyeth nodded, smiled, licking his perfect white teeth clean. "Sure, get angry, Sophie, it's a motivating emotion."

Sophie penciled the code of horoscopes and alchemy sketches of the sun and moon inked onto the drywall of the Emerald Tablet server room. She hypothesized Noah's process through a labyrinth of glass pipes, alembics, a sand bath, a nest of crucibles, hand-bellows, a maze or borosilicate tubes and cups, a mortar and pestle still dusted from the coming and going.

The experiment gained and deposited essential elements along the way as it crawled from solid to gas to liquid and back again as she stepped on Noah's shoulders to see further horizons than his fried-out eyes could ever reach. Sophie shoved Wyeth's face into the cracks she made in Noah's code. A moment of silence for our departed Psychedelic King Supreme.

Wyeth was right about alchemy. Noah was going to use radiation to change lead into gold for The Hermetic Circle.

"Do you see how you discern one form into another?" Sophie pointed Wyeth to a thick round dish marked with a curved and styled '♍' "This marks when a spirit is made corporeal."

Tiny crystals blossomed from the bed of the dish. Tufts of chick-fur. Blonde sprouts. The cure was taking root but hadn't yet fruited. The medicine came in the form of daffodil fronds that turned liquid in the heat of her hand.

She lifted the yellow to Wyeth's eyes.

"Mercury ♉ ,, here. Cinnabar, there. Magnesium ✸ , Platinum ☽☉, Aqua Fortis. Noah didn't use chemistry alone. He used alchemy, and radiation to make the cure. It doesn't matter how, he found it and did it."

"One to another?" Wyeth asked.

"Transformation," Sophie said. "Lead into gold. Weak to strong. Naïve to wise. Dying to alive. The symbolism was meant to train you to see things as metaphors, variables, one thing standing in for another. If you know the clues, you can read the guide."

"You can do this anytime?" Wyeth asked.

"I want the pages. Tonight."

He made the call.

"Just don't show my face," she said, Wyeth nodding as he put the call to Taylor Zapata on speaker. It went straight through to voicemail. Wyeth licked his lips and texted. He cleared his throat and called back to voicemail again.

"Zapata always answers, let me just..."

"Wyeth dialed another number, but Sophie could see it dawn on him before he would admit it. A call right to voicemail "If this is an emergency you can call my partner Taylor Zapata at..." Wyeth was still in enough denial to leave voicemails. Sophie watched Wyeth lick his lips and stare at his phone with an unsteady hand, Sophie nearly ready to burst into laughter.

Wyeth looked at her.

Sophie shook her head. She drew a finger across her neck and stuck her tongue out.

"More than just one step ahead, you dumb fuck." Sophie laughed.

"We don't know precisely what-" Sophie grabbed Wyeth's phone away from his fingers and flung it against the server room wall. Wyeth got so close she could smell the anger on his breath, but his shouts seemed like a dim, dim echo. The Book was rubbing off on her.

She took another beautiful midnight blue Radiogardase pellet and crushed it in the palm of her hand.

"It marks the path, and it guides the way."

Spitting into her hand, Sophie smoothed the ultramarine pigment between her palms, squeezing great waves and starry nights across the floor before slapping her hands to Noah's pictures on the wall. She left whorls and fingerprints thick with indigo and cobalt against the shimmering foam glow deep in the frames of The Verdant Pool, smearing the cave with the deepest shade of mushroom blue.

"Lake knows where he's going, and knows where he's going to be, doesn't he, Esme?" Sophie said.

Sophie could see the end now, exactly where it would happen. She grabbed the picture of herself at the edge of The Verdant pool and held it inches from her face. She licked the Prussian Blue from her knuckles and spit a mass of blue against the paper; the color filling the peacock water on the page.

Sophie held the page above her face, the shoreline of The Verdant Pool overflowing onto her nose and cheeks and chin. It flowed into her eyes and back into her mouth and she was burning, and she was bleeding and she was dying inside more than ever.

She was closer now to the Book than Noah or Dillinger or anyone ever would be.

"Making a path. Marking a way," Sophie said. Her hands bled with ink, and she could see the end, and the trail leading backwards from the gleaming pool, and all she knew was that she would find the way.

# CHAPTER TWENTY-SIX

*The Book of Blue Daggers. Ch. 13, "The Viridian Waves"*

**JUST THEN, IN THE BOOK OF BLUE DAGGERS**

The seer died in his arms.

Esper's hair was still wet from the viridian waves that ebbed back to the sea, leaving behind only skeleton-foamed tide pools. She was beautiful, and he still couldn't understand her riddles.

Lux had returned to where it began, where Esper gave him the Book, where she told him it would destroy him, where she died in his arms, and where he saw the ocean recede.

The numbers and figures in Zetco's ledger of yellow-flower deals yielded fallow fields. A blue-and-cream topographic map unfolded at the back of the ledger keyed to the addresses, but they revealed nothing but decayed businesses, rotted storefronts, and damp warehouses silent as tombs with just as much life inside. The ledger had revealed nothing and his only chance at getting revenge for those that had killed his friends was dissolving in the sea breezes.

Amnesia sulked in the sheath as Lux calculated at the sea, looking back and trying to remember.

It began with The Omen. The waters of the bay had peeled back and never pushed forth again, and the wet basalt plain sparkled new and fresh for miles beyond the beach. There were tidal pools where the deepest clefts remained, a million-year groove in the ocean floor where Polychaete worms as ancient as the sea itself dined on the bones of things just as elder.

Lux wandered the once-drowned ocean floor, gauging by the sea life where he had met Esper the seer. Orange and purple stars clung to slick tidal rocks, their edges sharp and silver in the sunset. He found the overhang boulder where Esper had died, the thick, dripping shelf above her housed a ceiling of thousands of frilled anemones, limply swaying in the ocean winds.

Esper was sap-mouthed and sweet breathed, talking jagged rhymes about drinking from a vine at the bottom of the sea. Lux had heard stories of the Motero Bay seers, how they could see the future and lived backwards into the past by gleaning visions from intoxicating vines and fruits. He heard of darker rumors too, that they at times drank too deeply to know when to temper themselves and could see only their future oblivion.

Esper had gone too far, her visions too extraordinary to contain. Her breath was sweet and her tongue sticky with colorful sap. She called Lux by different names, and handed him the Book, only to tell Lux that it would destroy him.

"You'll find her in the cave. Listen to her Lake, listen to Sophie at the end," Esper said.

Riddles amongst the ocean rocks.

Lux kneeled to the pool where she died and tried to decipher. Who was Lake, and who was Sophie? How could something so simple as a Book he held in a pouch at his side destroy him?

Lux watched as twilight dissolved into a clear and moonlit night. As he wandered the soft ground between moon polished rocks, Lux began to understand.

The figures in the ledgers must have meant something, but the times and places that Zetco wrote down meant nothing, led to nothing, created nothing.

He examined the ledger again in the silver darkness.

These dates and times couldn't possibly work. Sudden days, bursts of activity, then blank marks of silence for months, the mastermind scheme less predictable than any wave break or sudden squall.

The waves.

The riddles.

Suddenly he understood.

Of course. Lake. Sophie. Esper was telling him that something that appeared to be one thing wasn't, that it was another. The riddles were mirrors, and Lux began to understand now. The book wouldn't destroy him, it would destroy Selia, just so long as she met him at the cave.

How simple. Esper could indeed see far into the future.

Lux drew his finger across the pen-marks on the ledger. Zetco wasn't using dates and times of day, he was using locations on a map, the landing points of where the yellow flowers would be dropped and delivered.

The bursts of coordinates made sense now, and Lux untwisted the riddle. One day in November was used time and time again, the coordinates mapped to a flat field on a grid point far north of the city. A place where all the flowers flowed from.

The coordinates on the ledger map exposed the location to him: Rosenquist Field, far north of the city. A flat and grassy airstrip perfect for these plans.

The queen may have found a way to come back from the dead, but she never found a way to change her old schemes.

~ ~ ~

At Rosenquist Field, the black airship hummed off the greasy ocean plain like a malevolent cloud, scattering the brush and debris in the propeller wash. The front of the huge gondola was an enormous stateroom bound in crystal, and Lux knew the queen was somewhere inside.

Lux dodged behind the airframe of a dilapidated biplane, watching men anchor the airship with taut cables and ropes, fighting the weather and movement of the massive ship like an animal bucking and shuffling at a collar.

Men in caps and eucalyptus garlands clutched at linen parcels dropped from the windows as the blimp hovered and buzzed above the airfield. At the window, Lux saw Merrick, the man who murdered Ash, shouting commands unheard.

The airship buzzed into gear and began to drift away, as the men with garlands gathered the last of the wrapped parcels and quickly moved to their assignments.

As the clouds wrapped the moon, Lux sprinted and darted and grasped an errant tow rope as the airship infected the sky. Stranded amongst the low clouds, Lux hoisted himself along the cold rope, Amnesia encouraging him upwards, further upwards, towards the belly of the vast, humming machine.

It was frigid in the cold night air as Lux found purchase on a steel catwalk beneath the dark envelope of the airship. He slipped Amnesia from the sheath, a brilliant azure splashing blue across the catwalk and illuminating a hatch below, into the gondola itself.

Lux flipped the collar of his jacket up against the wind and the blue and moonlight, listening at the skylight hatch for voices inside.

Lux knew the way now. He didn't need to find the grove, now that he knew where to find the queen herself.

# CHAPTER TWENTY-SEVEN

*So Easy to See*

## GIG HARBOR, WASHINGTON NOVEMBER 3

Her face was still streaked and lined with the Prussian Blue.

Wyeth had left sometime in the shouting match as Sophie's face mapped the path from the leaks off the picture. A blue surveyance ran from forehead to neck in Qing Dynasty scales and rivers.

Sophie ransacked and packed Noah's illicits. The Haloperidol and the Radiogardase. The yellow powder, slick in the foil. The drawings of dead men and cliffs and the quest to a burning cave. She filled a daypack to bursting. Sophie limped out of the server room at Emerald Tablet on a black morning and left the door wide open.

An ache ground away at her. Her anxiety birthed a lodestone at the nest of her brain and it spun and milled and wound away until she angled her body and plotted a path towards the faraway thunder. The lodestone settled in vibrato and leaked hot chalk into her throat.

The neighborhood was quick off Highway 16 and Sophie came in as morning commuters rolled out. She put on a black headband. She looked all around in the car's mirror. Not quite an upstanding citizen, but she didn't think that she would warrant an immediate phone call.

It was past dawn, and the gray sky was pebbled with blue. She was everything, all of it. Sophie parked six houses down and got out. She bunched her fists in a joggers' stance and used a long stride in the new boots to get to Taylor's house.

The lodestone smoothed out. She was in a perfect groove now. The side door with a Yale touchless keypad was left open. Just inside the door, she found a dog collar, unclipped. The blue dog-bone tag said "Boone." A white tag had a number for Green Fields Veterinary, and the rabies vax date from six months ago.

Sophie was in between now; it was so easy to see. Lake had been here, and she could see the traces.

A wind of light stippled across the door jambs and knobs, the phosphorescent algae fog left from the presence of the Book, burning away in the morning light.

In a step-down living room, at the foot of a white-iron Bornholm clock, Roy Parwanni floated pale. The step-down was a bamboo floored tub, and all of Roy had emptied into it. He had been slashed, his fingers, hand, and forearm excised in separate swipes.

Shallow slaps of red dusted the walls and ceiling. Hardening to twists. The stir in the air from the knife hadn't settled all the way to the floor, and the echo of the screams was still bouncing off the walls.

Taylor was on the couch. Everything had been taken out but his eyes and teeth. Lake had drained him from the belly. Lake had held him there and worked the cuts and made him watch. There were pages next to him, stapled together. There were muddy handprints on the pages. A color photo of the Book was on his lap.

"No," Sophie said.

Sophie looked at the prints and creases. Half-whorls left in blood and sticky grease. Sophie looked at her hands and compared them. She lined up her fingers on the pages. In the divots and on the stains that surrounded the signature of someone named, "Hannah Motsenbocker."

Lake's ring fingers were there on both hands. His lizard's tail regrown. Sophie popped her fingernail against the paper. She looked at the death grip on Taylor's face. The fingers there, too. Lake had all ten fingers again.

She stood and held the pages inches to Tyler's withered eyes. Dowsing for the Book. Was there a reflection of it left there in the wrinkling gloss? Was there a fading imprint on his iris of Lake taunting him, steering open his wounds?

Oh? See here, she imagined Lake goading, his sneer reflected into the killing blade.

Sophie wondered if she would receive a similar taunt as the dagger pushed inside, or if this slow bleeding death and taunt was part of the Book's plan already.

At the edge of his hand lay an envelope spilling with foil packets. Filled with quilled yellow powder from Noah's lab, now corroding the fabric of the couch. Sophie found a drawing of herself from a distant land folded alongside the packets.

On the back, Nick Wyeth wrote: "The last good batch."-NW

A wireless printer clicked in another room, slapping a reel of address stickers beyond empty. A gummed heap of stickers ran to the same address. PO BOX 262 Pullman, WA 99163. There were more envelopes, fresh ones, batted with the foil and never sealed, in a cardboard box, beside it, and a machine for measuring postage.

She called Wyeth. She could see the water and the reflection from the sky from where she stood.

"Sophie, are you still alive?" Wyeth asked.

"They haven't invented a phone that does that yet," Sophie said.

"Alright. What about Taylor Zapata?"

"Only in the memory of others."

"Are you certain that you're correct? About the choices you're making?"

"You need to tell Hannah Motsenbocker that Lake knows her name now. I can save her but I need what she has."

"I'm sorry I kept up such a facade, but you can talk to me directly about what you mean."

"There's a death warrant for you, for me, and for Hannah. Get me the chapters that Noah had and I can save us."

"When the police find these bodies, I'll make sure to direct them to the DNA you've no doubt left around. You know how to make the cure, Sophie. Show-and-tell first."

Wyeth hung up.

PO boxes way out east. Pullman. Sophie looked up close at the yellow tufted crystals Noah created. Tiny yellow feathers. The last of the good batch for the whole of The Hermetic Circle.

Sophie pressed her face to the printed picture of the Book. They thought the printed lies would save them and they still didn't get it. Wyeth and Hannah thought they had the upper hand on something that had read all the way to the end.

They thought the Book was one thing, but no. It was another thing, complete in its creation and manifestation.

Sophie walked out of the house the same way she came in. She had bloodstains on her elbows and cuffs, but at least wasn't trailing it on her sneakers. She was sure she had been seen. She was sure she left fingerprints. She was sure someone had seen a woman who had been crying blue ink.

But who cared about being seen? She'd be dead before a trial even started.

From the rearview, Sophie saw the whole neighborhood tense up. Police spooled yellow tape around mailbox posts to block off the whole street in front of Taylor's house. Neighbors in quilted jackets and collared shirts watched with their hands tucked in. Detectives swaggered out and gave everyone the brush off.

A fire truck blipped red on the swing around, blocking the view to the driveway where EMT workers clacked the sheeted-up bodies into the back of an ambulance. The detective got names, shared pens, took pictures, took notes as a jogger waves fingers just in front of her face to explain a woman she saw with blue ink all over.

A gorgeous Irish Setter with no collar lolled against a neighbor and someone waved a detective over, ready to crack the case. A policeman knelt down, raising the dog collar from inside at a neighbor who nodded yes, yes, that's his, that's his, that's Boone. A bored paramedic rubbed Boone's face, and the neighbors shouted and scanned the streets, but by then Sophie was long gone.

# CHAPTER TWENTY-EIGHT

*Interdiction*

## AUBURN, WASHINGTON NOVEMBER 4

Taylor's house was already pinned on TikTok for high-line murder and crime addicts. Horrifying. Shocking. Mangled. Mutilated. Sentence fragments screeched out loud. Brutal slayings. Unknown intruder. Body with the mark of torture. There was a woman with a blue face. Online detectives connected it to Osiris. No, someone else said Mercury, no, it was clear it never happened. The Blue Woman was real, but the murders weren't.

Sophie snapped the SIM card between her teeth and flexed the phone in half, and watched it sink into the Puyallup river. She parked her car, maybe forever, at the Muckleshoot casino parking garage and got a cab downtown from the stand at the front.

At the Wal-Mart garden center, a girl named Izzy waved to Sophie with both hands when she got out of the cab. Izzy had dyed white bangs and a black velvet hat and a scarf as long as she was tall. Sophie and Izzy shook hands, and they talked about Izzy's 2001 Subaru wagon for sale and Sophie ran it around the parking lot.

Sophie said, "Feels good enough." And Izzy kept talking about the bad air conditioning and how the car first belonged to her mom.

Sophie limped and put out money on the dashboard in three slots. Hundred-dollar bills. Izzy had a blue plastic folder that had the title and some printed sheets and smudged printouts from Jiffy Lube.

"Can I see your driver's license, Sophie? I'm supposed to keep track of everything for my taxes," she said.

"We can write a receipt for it. All you need is a name for the buyer."

Izzy chewed on her lips and said, "Um, the DMV might give me a hard time, won't it be better if I have your number and address?"

"No." Sophie laid out more money. "It won't be better."

Sophie held the keys and stacked the money into a straight flat stack and handed it to Izzy and when she took it, she said, "I don't have an address. I'm just going to buy this in cash."

"I'm just trying to do this right, so I don't get in trouble. With my credit, or..."

"Izzy, I'm not going to put my name on anything. I'll give you an extra two hundred cash for the trouble, and you can work it out any way you see it. But something is looking for me, and it can find me if I write my name down on paper."

Sophie put her bag in the back and looked at Izzy, who folded the crisp bills and read over the papers with only her own name on them.

At a gas station, Sophie filled the tank and paid extra for the full wash. She went to an auto parts store on Highway 18 and bought a multi-tool and a lightbulb set for the rear lamps. Sophie used the screwdriver to move the cover in the rear, and then the pliers to unhook the bulb assembly from the collar. She plucked the burned-out bulb with a Kleenex and set it on the mat. She took the new bulb out and held it in the Kleenex so her hands wouldn't oil the glass. She pressed the bulb into the slot and rotated the assembly back into the collar. She moved the cover back on and tossed the old bulb. She checked the new lights and compared the glow. She went back inside and bought another pair to replace both sides.

The mist and rain went sssssss against the concrete dividers and corridor of fir trees. Sophie was going northeast along Tiger Mountain State Forest and heading to meet I-90 East. The traffic would slow, and Sophie wondered how far Lake would be behind her. Would he be here in the forest, the Book wrapped in a filthy satchel as he slinked his way across the state? Lake could cloud-walk, the Book advising him of the driest nights, the warmest walls, a rapid way across via rivers and timber-scrambles. Sophie took the interchange to the big interstate heading east and decided she was the one catching up.

It took hours, and she noticed it was warm and the sun was out. She was off of 90 and onto state roads. Just huge flat racer straightaways. Yellow and green farmlands. The fields spooled with dials of hay; the landscape planed by some single enormous tool peeling in random time. A child leaving mud-chalked John Deeres haphazard and some with tires sunk to the axle in bean fields. Watering tools, a quarter mile pipe on wheels, left out there in the field for someone to pick it up as the beanstalks snuck up against tire treads. The hills here foggy and smoked with a layer of wheat-dust as the combines and big Gleaner S9s rumbled and clipped the hillsides up and down the gradients.

Sophie blinked away from the Palouse hills and check down roads that led to Pullman. Trees here and there. She was close to a college town, the wide trucks and haulers tagged out for hybrids and compacts and German convertibles.

She turned off near the Postal Service building by the trailer park. Sunburned kids played on big wheels in sight of couples drinking tallboys in a square of lawn chairs and tractor tire sandpits. Sophie followed a sign with adhesive letters that said INQUIRIES?

Mickey had a pompadour, black tattoos of panthers, pinup girls, snake eyes dice on his arms. He wore a blue denim work shirt tucked in and buttoned all the way and was in the shade working the cats and anchors into an engine block when Sophie asked him about rent for space at the trailer park.

"You the lady that called?"

Sophie nodded. Mickey unloaded a quarter-bottle of orange liquid up to both elbows and worked in a shop towel. "You gotta come back tomorrow."

"But I just got here," Sophie said.

Mickey shook his head and nodded off to a mint-green-and-white trailer. It still had a 'RENT ME' sign in the front window.

"The waterman isn't quick, so no water. Electricity isn't ready to be switched over." Mickey littered a pile of towels at his feet, wringing the greasy orange liquid from his knuckles. "Still haven't switched the locks out, like I said."

"I don't care about the water, and I don't need any light. I'll be fine."

Mickey shook his head.

"I have money. I just need a place to sleep tonight."

"Naw."

"What if I just stay on the lot?" Sophie pointed towards her car.

Mickey shrugged. "Waterman should be here tomorrow. Electricity too. Until then…" Mickey shrugged again.

With the back seats laid down all the way and a blanket spread across, Sophie laid down. Her leg was bent from the road and pressed her body at all angles. She hadn't slept, had she? There was a sunset in Seattle and a sunrise again and it was turning to night. She had seen the whole clip of day and night, all the way up and down.

There was her path, and then Lake's, unseen. They would cross. She knew it. She felt it. It was written. The lines would converge at a savage point, and Sophie's twisted leg ached at the thought of it.

She took an envelope addressed to PO BOX 262. She flicked at it in her vibrating hands and decided nothing good was worth sleeping on. Nothing was worth sleeping on when the time was exactly right.

Sophie bound the canary-down powder into a tight foil square the size of a quarter. She cut the packing tape between her teeth and wrapped it up inside an envelope. She left it unmarked, untraced, and stamped it. Her leg was crooked as hell from the road, and she leaned against the mailbox to drop it in. She read the pickup times. There were dim hours left before the morning grab to see who would dangle at the end of her lure.

The binoculars from the pharmacy gave her a wide view of the parking lot and a good view of the entrance. While keeping an eye on it, she used store-brand sensitive skin wipes across her whole body. They came off smudged black and brown and orange, and on them she could smell the constant fear, doubt, hope, desire, and the tornado expectation burning that extruded from her body through every pore.

She couldn't stand the smell anymore, of herself, of anything. She tied the bag off and dumped it outside the window. She pulled her clothes off, all of it, and sat naked in the car as the night came on, pulling a wool blanket from behind the seats tight across her shoulders.

It was just her. It was only ever her.

Listening to the wind, Sophie stared at the mailbox to see who would come calling. She would wait for the flat blaze of the sunset to rise in her eyes, and then she would move by nothing more or less than nature.

# CHAPTER TWENTY-NINE

*The Book of Blue Daggers, Ch. 16, "Above a City on Fire"*

**A LITTLE PAST THAT IN THE BOOK OF BLUE DAGGERS**

Even as iron manacles bit into his flesh, even as pain lanced through his shattered teeth, Lux remained enthralled by the grandeur of the view.

At three thousand feet, the view from the airship's stateroom was a grand way to take in the full sweep of Motero Bay. Even through crashing waves of pain, the beauty of the sunset laying foils of gold across the jungle and the sprawl of the city struck Lux as nothing less than miraculous.

The stateroom of the Eucalyptus Queen was a cruel aerial Eden. A tropical inferno encased in thick crystal panels, heated by the steam emissions from the wicked engines. The place teemed with an intoxicating array of verdant vines, their suction-cupped tendrils clinging to each surface. The room was a carnivorous garden under glass, seductively perfumed and broiling under the green thumb of the reborn Queen.

"You can barely hear the engines, can you?" The Eucalyptus Queen said. She was the one person who never drew sweat in a room tilting past a hundred degrees. The Eucalyptus Queen worked the control wheels and dialed the airship towards the sunset. The whole room burst with an eye-watering gold as the sun against the bay painted the stateroom in full.

For someone who escaped death, the Eucalyptus Queen appeared startlingly youthful. Lux surmised she had regained her bloom, akin to a fruit ripening or a flower unfurling its radiant petals. The disheartening stoop had vanished from her posture, and her teeth, earlier dulled by age, now gleamed sharp and white as a leopard.

Her eyes, however, a dark and unchanging pool of enigmatic blue, remained ever the same.

"I'll never tell you where The Verdant Pool is. You'll run out of flowers, and you'll never find the source," Lux said.

"It's knowledge that brings power, Lux. Not damage or the ability to inflict. Knowledge. You caught up. That's a wonderful lesson for you," the Queen said.

The Eucalyptus Queen snorted and spit into her palm. She held it out to the vines and tickled out a blue-furred spider. It glinted metallic and its bright blue fur shook as it sucked the spit from her palm.

"If you only had the time to put that knowledge into practice, Lux. There's nothing more tragic than a lesson learned too late," the Queen said.

The Queen twitched her thumb and gently rotated her hand to let the huge spider acrobat across her wrist. The arthropod scrambled as smooth as liquid and perched at her shoulder.

Merrick soon stepped into the stateroom. He could say no words, his lips scarred to white slots, slim and pressed flat against his teeth. His face was taut and pink, and he had no hair left at all, his defining features replaced by worm-thick scars.

The blue spider grew bright and bristled as Merrick approached the Queen. Merrick eyed the black-eyed arachnid warily. His large disfigured hands trembled as he stepped close to the Eucalyptus Queen, his eyes always flicking close as the spider tested the air with its pink paws.

Lux's fingers discreetly traced the outline of the hidden vial of the H compound that the Queen'shenchmen had overlooked. Safely ensconced against his ankle, strapped to his boot, it was his unseen lifeline. His tongue prodded the ersatz tooth lodged firmly in his cheek, his features contorting into an unpleasant grimace.

Lux manipulated his grimace into an expression of raw fear and profound torment. The Queen reveled in this display, smiling and circling him like an avaricious cat, her cruel satisfaction palpable. Her rasping voice regaled him with tales of her uncanny ability to command beasts and insects, her pride particularly fixated on this example's distinct coloration.

"The Azure *Poecilotheria*. Much like me, long presumed dead. Much like me, incorrectly so."

The blue spider perched on a vine and curled there, unblinking. "The seer's worship these, as you know. Perhaps you have heard of their particular method for distilling a vision from their venom? No?"

The Queen approached the Poecilotheria and dangled a single tantalizing finger above it.

"They have them attack much-ripened fruit, then the seers drink the fermented juices. The Cowl Shamans say it is an exquisite journey, provided you survive it. The venom has the curious property of making time dilate, so that a single minute takes an hour to experience, an hour takes a day. If one has the understanding, one can explore the inner mind as never before, as the debilitating pain provides such focus."

"What an opportunity for enlightenment," Lux said.

The Queen smiled.

"I encourage you to survive, Lux. Our conversations afterwards would be most fascinating."

"I very much doubt that."

With a soft precision, Lux bore down on the artificial tooth. Unlatching the metal hook hidden inside, Lux spit the metal tool between his fingers and began working on the lock of the cuff with supreme dexterity.

The Queen's breath drew ragged, and she pressed a hand to her throat. Already Lux could see wrinkles and dark spots fighting to appear. Lux fought back a smile, realizing the Queen maybe had crawled back from the grave, but the grave hadn't given up the battle.

"You must excuse me, Lux, I have concerns that must be... attended to. Merrick, do as you please with him."

The Queen lay a frond at Lux's feet, quickly turning and shuffling out of the atrium as the spider grasped his leg in a delicate embrace. Lux felt the small pink padded feet and claws examining every nervous inch of his exposed flesh, curious as to which part to begin feasting on.

Merrick stood far back and smiled between his nothingness lips. Lux clicked the forked edge of the tool against the spring and the catch of the hand locks, swinging the chains free to the floor with a clatter as Merrick gawked at him with a confused and blank stare.

Faster than Merrick's eyes could follow, Lux snatched the vial at his ankle. The Poecilotheria skittered across the chains, raising its pink feet high and flashing its body the color of sapphires in warning.

Merrick advanced towards Lux, his nail-less hands lunging to clutch at Lux's throat. Lux wedged the vial of H compound between them and popped the lid free. The compressed contents within the sealed vial erupted with a shrill hiss. The acrid green vapors contorted Lux's vision as the sunset-drenched stateroom wobbled and sagged before his eyes.

The dewy gas swirled around Merrick's waxy face as he snarled and pawed at the air in desperate retaliation. He choked and swallowed gulps of the noxious fumes, swinging wildly at Lux with his scarred and ragged fists. It took mere heartbeats before the room spun out of control, sending them both crashing to the floor, a heady dizziness sweeping over them.

The spider crawled between them, even more ferocious in color, a lightning-storm crashing from its thorax to its fat pink paws. Lux tilted the furious arthropod up into the frond, steadying himself against the floor with his one free hand.

He held the spider above Merrick, its body ringing with lightning-strike pulses. Merrick's white wriggling eyelids watered as he saw, inches away, the sunset reflected in eight points of pitiless light from the spider's eyes.

Merrick started to beg as the spider steepled two thin pedipalps towards the warm air coming from his mouth.

"Please, Lux, please!"

"Did Ash beg you too?"

"I'm sorry, the Queen, she..."

"Did she give you no choice?"

The spider hovered in Merrick's warm breath and dabbed a pink pad into the sweat of Merrick's thin lips.

"Of course not!"

"Where is Grove? Tell me, where is the gathering?"

"At her orchards! Please, Lux, I can show you the way! At a mansion in the woods!"

"Beg for me!"

"Please, Lux, please!"

Merrick's body shook uncontrollably. Lux smiled and said, "Alright then."

He rattled the frond above his face and watched the blue spider clutch onto Merrick's withered nose. The blue insect sparkled all manner of the sky and sea breezes before choosing to dine on Merricks soft and featureless face. Merrick's screams tapered into feeble whimpers, as his perception of time slowed and slipped to a black and infinite flow of venom.

Pulling his boots back on, Lux concentrated on hearing the vibration of the Amnesia.

Even above the noise of the engines and the pitiful long squeals of Merrick, Lux detected the exact location of Amnesia, and knew it would soon find a way into his hands, then find a way into so much more.

# CHAPTER THIRTY

*You Are So Close*

## PULLMAN, WASHINGTON NOVEMBER 5

Sleep never worked out. She saw the blue burn the black from the sky from up above the trailer park. She listened with the windows down.

Sophie's eyes were strained and seeing double from the binoculars. She was dizzy from the cheap focus ring, leaning to see the letters, poster tubes, envelopes in hands as post office regulars made the morning rounds.

She sat far in the passenger side to cork her bad leg out straight. She drank a caffeine shot that had a hornet on the bottle. Swallowing felt like breaking new ground. Every blink felt like ripping at a fresh scab. Every breath was like sucking through a filtration mask.

Sophie twisted off the flexible incontinence underwear and put it into the garbage bag on the floor of the passenger side.

She had hit the timeline. The color was black as volcanic glass in streaks. She was bleeding out black. She tied the bag off. She put on a new pair of heavy leakage underwear, that had a gusset of material finger thick that made no noise at all when she scooted around. They were impossible to make out under her Huskies sweatpants. She would go for hours like this.

Sophie was never taking her eyes off the door. She had to catch one moment that would happen gravity fast. She could spare no chance of missing it. The envelope and the cure inside would move as fast as desire would take it, and she had to be faster.

She took a fat black marker and wrote "YOU ARE SO CLOSE" on her hand and then across her wrist. She had to stop getting confused. Mystified. Doubting. She kept things concrete, physical. Never a thought in her mind about a thing she couldn't see or touch or smell.

Sophie caught the envelope she made mid-flight. Bulky with Noah's cure of yellow quills passing out the door. She made the handwriting through her binoculars. It was in a man's hands. Then his pocket. He had a beard. Duck boots. Badly dressed, like an imitation of someone he'd admired and failed to be. He had transition lenses spoiling purple in the morning sunlight.

Sophie lifted her body to the driver's side and swung her feet to the pedals. She watched him fiddle with it in his front sweat, close enough to whiff a lanyard with a UNIVERSITY STAFF card tucked into a shirt pocket.

The professor slipped the envelope open at the corner. She could hear him frustrated with the tape. He worked the envelope in his teeth while he pecked at his phone and waited. He spoke. She couldn't read lips. He spoke and spoke and answered something. He shook his head and jammed the envelope under his shirt.

Sophie parked near the professor. He dodged students running past in crimson shirts and sandals. He walked towards a glass building marked "Chemistry - Motsenbocker Annex." Sophie followed. Sophie watched him hold his arms folded tight to his jacket, pressing like an amateur magician.

Sophie walked through a hallway painted with oceans, starbursts, amoeba, nebula, painted gossamer thin and stretched the whole length. The short blind strokes of Oscar Koo. A vision statement near the door reminded students and staff and visitors one and all of the commitment to diversity of visions, thought, experiences, all of them brought forth by the generous Motsenbocker largesse.

A man grabbed the professor and cornered him against a nebula of the painting. His voice cracked and he couldn't control his volume and he had two bald O's visible across his scalp, pink soda can rims, the patches raised where hair didn't grow from the brain surgery corings.

"Dr. Berkowski, why is it doing this to us?" the scarred man asked and shouted.

"It's just the way it is written," Dr. Berkowski said.

"Hannah promised us," the scarred man said.

"Is that why we are here? Because we believe in Hannah Motsenbocker?" the Doctor answered.

"No."

"Then tell me why."

"Because we believe the Book has the path to what we seek."

"Then why do you doubt it?"

The man with the scars wiped tears from his eyes. He reached for Dr. Berkowski. He grabbed him softly and told him he was scared.

"Lorenzo is here. He's at the airstrip. He came here early to discuss this exact thing," Dr. Berkowski said. The man with the scars nodded. They walked outside, and Sophie followed.

The professor and the man with scars on his brain broke through the crowds headed north. There weren't many airstrips around, and she could keep a good distance.

They were into the ribbon hills of the Palouse. They pulled into an airstrip and parked in a hanger full of seed bags stacked high to the ceiling.

Dr. Berkowski and the man with scars stood outside the doors to the seed warehouse. A meeting commenced. A woman on a crutch and an air cast, a couple with matching oxygen tanks. A black Mercedes driven by a spectrally thin man allowed the group to hug and hold hands before going inside the warehouse.

Sophie used a door marked EMPLOYEES ONLY on the other side. The place reeked of rubber and seed dust. It was echoing the whine of prop-engines on the breeze of the big indoor hangers.

Seed haulers in overalls and work boots set up a leather chaise, lamps, and three air purifiers on high. They hustled an extension cord between two rows of two cabin sized red Case-IH leveling combines. Sophie lifted herself into one of the big tire rims and pulled her bad leg in beside her. Berkowski led a woman with a scarf on her bare head to a couch and held her oxygen tank in her lap. He hugged another man, whose hands tremored nonstop and whose eyes never blinked.

Sophie could smell their bad breath and menthol drops and chemo odor from across the wall of grain.

The slim man from the Mercedes put a hand to his throat. The group grew quiet, and he spoke in a forced whisper.

"Hannah told us she was having the Book delivered," the whispering man said.

"That is true, Lorenzo," Berkowski said.

"Then what happened to our cure?" Lorenzo asked.

"When we have the entire Book," Berkowski said.

"Cargile, some of us cannot wait that long," Lorenzo said.

"She will have the whole thing at the gathering of the grove. Our dreams will be delivered," the scarred man said.

"We've heard rumors about another alchemist. A woman. Is it true they found someone to replace Noah?" the woman with the silk scarf asked.

Dr. Cargile Berkowski looked at the ground. It was obvious. It was clear.

"My god. My god!" Lorenzo croaked.

"Hannah's plan will see us to the grave," the woman said.

"She won't even survive the night, Dr. Berkowski!" the scarred man said.

"The time for doubts was at the beginning. Not now, not at the end," Berkowski said.

"We should explore every other opportunity available," Lorenzo said.

"We believe in what the Book says. Hannah does not control the Book. It will go just how it was written," Berskowski said.

"We should expand any path open to us," Lorenzo said.

"Yes. Someone else. Dillinger's plan," the woman said.

"Why are you here then, Allison? Lorenzo? Why are any of us here? Because we believe in the word and the page and the color. Because we believe that Hannah can read it and translate it better than we can. Allison, Paul, Lorenzo, we are all, on this day, surviving, because of what has been created from the words of the Book. Because of Hannah. Do you remember where you were two years ago? Do you remember when you had weeks to live? This is just another moment when we will look back and realize that time was not nearly as short and pressed as it seemed," Berkowski said.

"Correct, correct, correct," the man with scars said.

"That's just what Dillinger thought. Look at the example the Book made of him," Lorenzo said.

"Hannah Motsenbocker is the Queen of our little grove, and we need to treat her as such," Berkowski said. "Hannah knows how to not get tricked, and soon, we will have a new alchemist."

"But who?" Lorenzo asked.

"Does it matter? The Book will bring her to us, and she will bring the cure to us, and she will join us. It's written. When has it ever lied to us?"

# CHAPTER THIRTY-ONE

*Building a Signal*

## PULLMAN, WASHINGTON NOVEMBER 5

Sophie drank everything she had. She was dizzy. She had to pee. She had to throw up. She didn't have time. Nothing resembling time at all. She didn't even have time to put the marker down after drawing a cartoon on the side of a carton of orange juice. She drew her future plans in detailed hopes and dreams with a fine point sharpie.

A picture of a queen on a throne, the Book laying on the throne's arm. An old lady surrounded by supplicants and boy did they love what she was passing out from a Santa Claus sack. The rickety crowd was too busy passing around smoking envelopes to notice Sophie sneaking around the back of the throne. The queen tossed envelopes full of the cure into the air, her subjects swiping at the air to grab what they thought was the winning number. The queen looking puzzled at the Book, question marks bouncing around her head—last panel, Sophie, Sophie, sneaking out a skylight with the Book held tight as can be.

The plan. The perfect picture. A thousand words that Sophie would make happen.

Sophie was with Berkowski step-for-step. She nailed his heartbeat, the pat of those boots against the pavement. Sophie could feel the magnet pull deep in her skull. She was connected to him, elemental, like a bird following an invisible migration path across a whole wide ocean. She would never lose him now.

He never once checked behind him. He was back on campus. He opened a set of double doors next to a ghastly plaque. Two vampire brass faces welcomed you to the Motsenbocker Chemistry Annex. Hannah and Gene, wishing to allow the continued sawmill fortunes to glean future discoveries. This lab was built on fortunes derived from charcoal and sawdust, the building constructed on a lakebed of pine tar, turpentine, and formaldehyde cooked and distilled from countless miles of silver-barked trees.

Sophie watched him walk into a museum of ancient glasswork tubes and flasks and behind a door marked "C. Berkowski, Inorganic Chemistry."

Peering in through the doorway Sophie took in a panorama of bookshelves lined and dusted and dripping with resin toads, statues, mortars, iron weights. Two boxes of books from a university press collecting dust as a doorstop: <u>"Newton, the Green Lyon, and the Bridge between Magic and Fact"</u>, by Cargile Berkowski."

Stooped and sweating over metal pans and spring baking weights, Cargile opened the foil packets that Sophie mailed to him. His hands worked fast and steady as a man at a concert piano. He scooped the yellow insides of the packet into a glass dish, before separating them into lines with a miniature metal spatula.

His phone rang. He pushed the office door bolts tight, and Sophie followed.

The Transit van's mechanical ramp whirred and set Hannah Motsenbocker into the way of the sun. She puckered her lips against the glare. Hannah was in a fine padded wheelchair, and her driver came quickly by to grip the handles of it.

Hannah wore black orthopedic shoes, and her knees bunched uselessly against one another. Her hair was thinning, streaked with gray and white. She had it pulled back above a daybreak purple muslin scarf and a sage green caftan wrap. Her body was ancient, but her smile slashed white in the sun, and her voice rang loud and distinct as a winter crow.

Hannah's enormous, clean-faced driver leaned at the handles behind her, the cuffs of his pants tucked into rubber boots chalked with gravel and loam.

Sophie watched Hannah's deep blue eyes track the action. Hannah snatched the envelope from Berkowski the moment it appeared from his pocket. She put her nose inside where it was torn open and took a long addict's whiff. She closed her eyes and settled and eased back into her chair. She touched and squeezed the hand of her driver. With a buffed and lacquered nail pointing at him, she told Berkowski something important, something critical, something with a timeline.

"I need more time, or more hands, Mrs. Motsenbocker," he said.

"Professor Berkowski, I've given you everything that money can buy. A tick of the clock is the only thing that cannot be purchased."

"What about the woman? Wyeth said she broke the code on Noah Catlow's process."

"She'll be here soon, professor. Robert, please, get me out of the sun."

From the dark inside the van, Hannah hooked the yellow dust out into her lap. Berkowski looked around, frantic, grimace-faced, as Robert turned the big V8 engine over and Hannah lit a flame and laid a wreath of smoke around Berkowski's hair. Hannah cackled as the professor waved it away, as she inhaled and blew it into his face again, pressed a button that slid the van doors shut and ordered Robert to take her away.

Sophie returned to Cargile's faculty to exhume the documentation. Familiar stages, a recounting, a recipe. A wild deliberation of plant hearts and boiled barks, a cooled distillate of fictional liquids and ersatz waters. Someplace without true north. Cargile had notes on blue-lined paper. Translating the Book of Blue Daggers. He was hopeless compared to Noah. Compared to her.

Writing names, explaining theory, getting his equations down. ♏ ♄ π ♋♂ He was building a signal.

Cargile was writing his own death warrant. He had no idea the words and theory were oscillating tumultuous on one frequency so far off the band that it would beckon the single listener to it from anywhere across the planet.

Cargile's notes were leaving blood in the water and Lake would be circling the prey, the scent total amidst the radio noise. Sophie reviewed Cargile's fucked up theories that came close enough to get him killed and said, "It's close enough." And then she saw him staring directly at her.

Professor Cargile Berkowski stood there in the doorway with a candy bar and looked like a shocked cartoon owl. He yelped as Sophie pulled him through the doorway on his way to the tile floor.

He tripped over his boots, and pressed a hand to his bloody nose as Sophie straddled him awkwardly between her knees, leaning and holding a fuming bottle of aqua regia from the cabinet just above his face.

The liquid corroded in the air, and Cargile let out a high-pitched yowl and he begged.

"Do you know what that is?" he whimpered.

"Hydrochloric and nitric acid. Get out your phone," Sophie said.

"She'll pay you anything. She owns the whole building. Please, please, put that down. I'll call and you'll have whatever price in fifteen minutes-"

The smell was something like butane and sandalwood, maybe almond and ammonia. It jumped off Cargile Berkowski as he squirmed beneath her.

"How much does she pay you?" Sophie asked.

"She doesn't. I don't want money," Cargile said.

"How much of the Book have you read?" Sophie asked Cargile. He looked at her and breathed slower. Easier now.

"Please just... please put that down? Don't... don't hurt me, you can just ask," Cargile said. Sophie shut the door behind her and locked it.

"How long can she go without a full dose?" Sophie mimed smoking a cigarette." Without a full long drag of it?"

"A day. Maybe less. It's the only thing keeping her alive."

"Does she know who has the Book now?"

"The Book tricked Dillinger. She knows that. The Book tricked Dillinger, but Hannah Motsenbocker isn't that stupid. She can read between the lines. You're the one who figured out Noah's process, aren't you?" Cargile asked.

"Does she know who I am?" Sophie asked.

Cargile shook his head. "Just that you were female. And that you know how to create the cure from flowers at The Verdant Pool," Cargile said.

"Did you ever work with Dillinger?"

Cargile nodded. "He thought he could beat it. Hannah told me the Book didn't play fair with either of them. She can beat it. She knows how to stay one step ahead. I mean, she said you would be here and just look!"

"Noah thought he could beat it too," Sophie said.

Sophie punched the number by memory into Cargile's phone.

"Is Hannah alright?" Wyeth asked from several hundred miles away.

"I can put her back together again, Wyeth."

"Sophie, you know the police-"

"I can make it here and now, Wyeth. Ready to finally make the smart play?"

A pause at the other end. Even after all this time, Wyeth still had to consider the angles when the math was clear as could be.

"What's the offer, Sophie?"

"I'll give her the cure for the chapters she has. Want to tell Hannah Motsenbocker her dreams can come true?"

# CHAPTER THIRTY-TWO

*The Golden Lion*

## PULLMAN, WASHINGTON NOVEMBER 7

Sophie snapped on rubber-lined gardening gloves to protect her hands from burns. She cranked the hair dryer to its maximum setting and popped off six green caps from half-liter water bottles. With an infant ear aspirator, she sipped a little water from each of the six bottles, making sure the water level reached just below the label.

She extracted clear, potent drops from Noah Catlow's liquid haloperidol prescription and introduced it drop by drop to a test batch of water. As she added the Haloperidol to the water, she observed it spiral down. It dissolved well in, with claw-like tendrils, disappearing completely as she tilted the bottles back and forth.

Sophie couldn't smell anything. The mineral water boasted taste from rock fed natural springs. It would cover up whatever might be there. Sophie drew twelve milliliter rods into the liquid syringe and replaced the missing water with huge jolts of Haldol. Pushing in emergency room dosages for the dispersal of schizophrenics, werewolves, those in the midst of an acute psychotic episode.

The bottle caps had cooled and shrunk. Sophie re-heated them against the gardening gloves. She set them onto the bottle necks, cooling until they narrowed in place against the tight plastic threads. She shook the bottles and turned them upside down. Everything was cooled and nothing leaked.

It was night. Sophie walked crooked. She was coasting. She was so close. It was barely enough.

Cargile Berkowski let her into the Motsenbocker annex. Sophie had the spiked water and a hard box case of Noah Catlow's psychedelic feathered crystals in a cheap aquamarine backpack. Sophie jumped onto a laboratory counter and wrapped the backpack onto her lap.

Cargile turned on the lab equipment. He opened the fume hoods. Sophie asked that he turn the fans on, keep the processed air running. Anything to keep the moisture out. Anything as best he could to keep it dry. Cargile locked the doors behind them and turned the hallway lights off. He said it was the weekend and they should have the annex entirely to themselves.

Cargile chewed his lips and shrugged. His nose was red and bruised, and he looked at Sophie as he touched it. He pushed the blowers as high as they could go. Sophie put her wrist to the flat dry air pouring out.

"You're certain there is no one else here?" Sophie asked.

Cargile coughed at the dry air.

"I'm the only one with a keycard to the annex on weekend hours," Cargile said.

"Is there a refrigerator here?" Sophie held the package of mineral water up.

"What is the temperature it needs to remain at?"

"Cold."

Cargile used a mag card to unlock a sample refrigerator. "This goes from 2C to 8C. What does it need to be?"

"Just keep it cold," Sophie said.

Cargile clicked the red counters to 5C. Wyeth called Sophie on Cargile's phone. He said he needed to meet both of them.

He was sitting in front of a Jeep all-wheel drive. It had fingers of mud traced from the fender to the window. Wyeth shook Cargile's hand and gritted his teeth as he did it.

 Wyeth nodded.

Wyeth pointed at the doorway and walked inside. Cargile shook his head the whole way down.

"When will you make the call?" Sophie asked.

"Dr. Berkowski, if the cure is real, you'll know?" Wyeth asked.

Cargile nodded yes.

"When he confirms, I can call Mike Wace at Gig Harbor PD. Get you off that hook at least," Wyeth Said.

"That's not enough," Sophie said.

"Your fingerprints are at the scene of a double-homicide in a rich white neighborhood. This is a platinum-tier offer you're getting."

"Get me the pages. Noah had pages from the Book. That's the only thing that matters. Even with the cure, Lake is still going to kill me, and you, and Hannah if I don't get the pages and if the Book doesn't tell me how to stop him first."

"Hannah Motsenbocker is not afraid of Lake."

"She thinks she can do it all?" Sophie pointed to Cargile. "I can talk to her. Let me convince her."

"You're a replacement for Noah. She won't believe you."

Sophie played it. She had Cargile set the dials and weights and worked the heat lamps on. She told Wyeth that many hands made light work. They all had gloves on, white smocks with pockets. Sophie turned the heat up. Everyone's faces got red and sweaty.

They had to talk in shouts, short sentences above the yawn of the fume hood. Sophie and Cargile roll-called alchemy, elements, and essential metals. Sophie asked Cargile if the refrigerator was unlocked. He nodded, and she took the mineral water out. She pointed at the others and took out two more. Everyone took one. Everyone drank from one. Everyone got the fix in.

Sophie envisioned a countdown and hoped not to lose track. There was a Haloperidol fuse burning.

Wyeth put a hand above the flasks buried to their necks in the searing sand bath. He drew it back.

"Hot sand?"

"Heated silica," Cargile shouted. "For an even conduction." He sculpted his hands around an invisible glass masterwork.

It was heat and colored smoke. The fume hood inhaled cotton strands of it, caterpillar black columns of it, a blue and pink dancer flickering off roasted antimony. Sophie and Cargile choked an alembic's neck full of knobby red crystals under whiskers of smoke. She could feel something unspooling inside the back of her neck. The haloperidol was landing. She watched her hands. She watched theirs. She compared every second to every previous one. Gravity started playing games with her teeth and tongue.

Wyeth scraped the crystals into red pyramids and dripped sulphuric acid onto them. Cargile corrected him, assuring him that there was a difference between it and oil of vitriol. The crimson pyramids gummed, turned sugar pink, dissolved into swirling pools. It was the process above all. Sophie distilled a corn of gold five times exactly, cooking it to a powder and steam and fixing it back to a grain of purity. Cargile boiled alkalis and whisked the bubbles off the lips of the sand-flasks. They cut the powders into a thick wet puck. Sophie opened a divot and tiptoed through. Open it. Set the grain. Leave it open to air and light.

They took a moment to watch a netting of roots brace against a caked spectrum of soils. Wyeth was the first one to see. Look at it go, and they did. The first green tongue of the plant tasted air and light. The heat broiled dry off the Pyrex glass and made their faces flush and their hands itch. The green succulent stretched to what it thought was the sun and Cargile pulled at his lips and mumbled. Wyeth asked for mineral water and Sophie drank and watched Wyeth drink in the breeze between the door and the fume hood.

"This is where it comes from?" Wyeth asked.

"Where shores grow flora with roots that draw from the water celestial. Bringing The Verdant Pool right to our doorstep," Sophie lied.

"That's right. You grow it, just like the Book has written it." Berkowski grinned.

"The Book tells you how to do this?" Wyeth asked.

"If you understand how to read it, you can put it into practice," Sophie said.

Sophie looked Wyeth in the eyes and drank. She felt a wave of superglue pass between the blood-brain barrier. It tugged, teased, plucked at her muscles, and she felt a wave of gloss go over all. The Haloperidol countdown hit zero, and her body ticked a full second behind her brain. She reminded herself of the plan. She nailed it right there.

Cargile waved them over. Wyeth rubbed his lips and drank more water, and Sophie did too. She was slowing down. Getting glued to the ticks of the clock. Cargile tapped on the glass and onto the growing plant beyond. He tapped, and his taps were long and sloppy.

"I've only ever made the flower. Never the pollen. Never the fruit," Cargile said, grinning like a child.

"The pollen and the fruit?" Wyeth asked. He kept licking his lips and biting at the air, and Sophie wasn't even sure he knew he was doing it. He wiped on a layer of menthol ChapStick. He dropped it on the floor before putting it into his pocket. "What kind of fruit is this?"

"The fauna of The Verdant Pool. Oh my god, this is it. We've done it!" Berkowski said. "We brought it to life from the water celestial. Oh, my god."

The plant sapped the powder cake's moisture. Wyeth stared and never blinked as a peacock green shade of honey beaded on the skin of the blossomed fruit. Sophie used a wooden paddle to sweep the honey off. She tapped it into a plastic dish, the color barely hinted as it dried slick in the heat. Sophie couldn't keep up with the production. Cargile joined her. Cargile was falling to pieces.

Cargile took a device from a drawer and held it to the fruit and the honey. It was smaller than a phone. It was cheap plastic, white, had rubber buttons, and a vague pale screen. He waved it around the base of it.

"What's that?"

"A Radex 1503."

The Radex pinged and clicked. The screen read numbers and signs. It morsed one final pronouncement and Wyeth nodded.

"It's fucking radioactive?" Wyeth asked.

"Yes! Goddamit, I knew it!" Cargile said.

Cargile put on a magnifying lens and ring light and focused. He smiled, slurred. His hands rattled. Sophie had fallen off the tightrope. She had to think the steps through one, two, three. She had to build it back from the beginning. She had to make sure she had a step on Wyeth.

"Is it much?" Sophie asked.

Wyeth showed her the screen. Signs and numbers. It chirped again at its final thesis. The numbers looked low. Wyeth moved his face close to it.

"It's the real thing. Oh, my god. You did it, Sophie, you made it..." he said. He blithely dropped the Radex to the floor.

The yellow feathers, the wings, the fractal sunspots knitted out as they dried in sequence. Hard lines in an octagon pattern as the molecules multiplied up and out.

Sophie watched Wyeth. Wyeth licked his lips. He put on menthol ChapStick. He coughed and finished the water. Watched the first feather drop bundles curl out into the air beneath the lens.

Wyeth said, "That's amazing. That's incredible."

Sophie watched him rub his mouth and lick his teeth. He dropped the menthol tube at his feet. He looked at his hands, utterly confused.

Wyeth asked, "What is a regular dose?" but his mouth kept mouthing the question after he stopped. An animatronic trapped in the cycle.

"What is a regular dose? What is a regular dose? What is a regular dose?" His mouth kept asking it well after his mind stopped telling it to.

Wyeth didn't know why Sophie was looking at him like that. His mouth never stopped opening and almost-closing. Sophie saw Wyeth's eyes go haywire and his hand pinch his lips shut when he realized it.

He took a step towards Sophie. He saw Cargile curled, wet-mouthed, his hands and eyes fluttering open and closed.

Wyeth's mouth held open, and he drooled badly and moaned like a trapped animal. An invisible giant gripped his open mouth and flexed it to his shoulder, pressing his ear to his back. His lips cracked gray, and his mouth clicked dry as he begged.

He landed at Sophie's legs. She fell with him, and he stared at her, his eyes swiveling back almost fully white.

Sophie pulled the pin on it. The stopwatch started.

Out there, far beyond the horizon, a demon named Lux put his face to the dirt and drew in the scent. He breathed steam and howled against the starlit sky.

Sophie was wearing welder's gloves on frostbitten hands. She dragged Wyeth. She kept forgetting why. She kept asking for his keys, his phone. She couldn't remember. She was smaller than her body. She was a miniature within it. She was a marionette. She was dragging Wyeth. She remembered. She used two hands to pull through his pockets. Keys and phone.

She remembered. She closed her eyes and marionette armed and legged her way to the plant. She touched the honey. The crystals. She had two good fingers for this and pinched them into her pockets, safe and sound. She cut the puppet strings.

"Where does Hannah Motsenbocker live? Where's the party?" Sophie asked.

Wyeth was still bowled over. Still had that look in his eye and kept clicking.

Sophie sat down next to him. She put his phone in his hand.

"I can hurt you, Wyeth. I don't want to. I dosed you with Haldol. Me too. Real heavy. It's so you would listen. Do you understand?"

Sophie put a hand on Wyeth's head. "Yes," he said, or something like it. His breathing went somewhere manageable.

"Listen now. Lake is on his way. He's going to kill Hannah unless I find her first."

Wyeth shook his hand and tried to stand. His bones weighed ten thousand pounds each. He said no. He disagreed. Sophie put his head on the floor and pushed the phone into his hand. She shook the keys in front of his face.

"You know her address. You can tell me her address."

A blue light stirred up in the active molecules. Her hands were numb, and she slurred.

She saw it again. In the air she moved through and the trace of a handprint against Wyeth's face. Sophie's sweat and breath and the static in her hair smeared bioluminescent. A paint spatter flickered a cobalt sky against Wyeth as he quivered.

Wyeth typed an address. Sophie tugged away and pulled herself out.

Sophie ran in a world adhesive and saw a column of magnificent azure light crystalize from the earth halfway to the moon out ahead of her. She sprinted towards it on a twisted leg, finally unstuck from everything, all at once.

# CHAPTER THIRTY-THREE

*Party Crasher*

## SOMEWHERE WA, NOVEMBER 8

Sophie crash landed Wyeth's four-wheel drive into a wooden sign painted with green apples and twin red cherries that read MOTSENBOCKER FARMS before walking herself filthy into the hills.

The hills were cut into burial drifts, scraped pale by the moonlight. Sheep and lambs made the bulk of the mounds, the wool and lanolin curing the landscape to waves of wax. Sophie lopped across the landscape, her hands whiskered to the edges of the darkness in front of her, feeling her way to the blue on the horizon.

She stumbled onto a blacktop road that lay unlit and freshly paved. The uncured tar reflected black through the cedar forest like a river of smoke.

Music drifted over the stiff cold air, and Sophie slowed down with her head bent over and her shoes snapping from the cold air on the new asphalt. Carole King and Carly Simon. Paul Simon. Let the Sunshine In, the beginning popping, and the endings dragged off, the needle on the vinyl bouncing off the shadow.

A dozen cars were parked haphazardly on the side of the mansion. Sophie walked towards the music and stayed in the darkness. A party echoed from a glass atrium as big as the trees, the room as big as the forest and opened the whole outdoors, the music and conversation filtering into the sycamores and cedars and fir trees.

She could make out the in-crowd. They were dressed for an event supreme. Jewels and scarf layers and fresh shoes. The atrium was a glass skeleton barely containing a mountainside of tropical tendrils, vines and fenestrated leaves as thick as the trees were wide. Hired nurses offered handkerchiefs to dab the brows, the atrium broiling from brass steam heaters at the base of the windows.

The rest of the flock was convalescent. They took baby steps. They held their arms out. They needed the assistance of canes and walkers. They wrapped chemo scarves around their heads in a dozen different knots, ties, and satin wraps. They jangled with medical assistance bracelets, Vuitton-wrapped oxygen tanks, necklaces picked to compliment a braid of cancer scars. The conversation: strictly hospitals, renal functions, the sub-definitions of neoplasm and the employment of radiation fields.

They'd run extension cords from the open lower-floor doors onto the open side of the glass atrium. Cream canvas tents stretched and fought with the wet branches at the edges of the bubble of light. A woman in a caftan at the center of the patio put her hand to the vinyl and said "Lorenzo is here, ah, excuse me everyone, Lorenzo has arrived! Lorenzo is here!"

Lorenzo was wearing a skipper's hat, a blazer with brass buttons, and arrived to applause. He handed out printed sheets with instructions, with a silver envelope given to each and every one. The party crowd grew red eyed, welled up, and drew close.

"Don't get ahead of yourselves!" he said.

The crowd sprinkled crystal feathers from the envelopes.

"You have to wait!" Lorenzo said. "There's a ritual to this!"

The woman in the caftan said, "Lorenzo is right, Hannah isn't even here, everyone wait!"

Lorenzo lit a row of candles that Sophie could smell where she knelt at the forest line. The skipper used the same match on a clay pipe, while some of the goers used flat electric heaters and vaporizer pens. Three old ladies pinched a hot stone on a silver hookah.

"Let's start, anyway. In whatever way we choose to give a moment, let's all take a thought, a silence, a time for personal significance for Bill Dillinger. The original dreamer! The one who found our salvation at The Verdant Pool. He solved the words, he figured out the formula, and it took his all. Here's to you, Bill, so that we can be here today, tomorrow, and..."

Lorenzo winked and raised his eyebrows and laughed and said, "You know I was worried about jinxing this. I know we've all heard the rumors that this may be the last time we are able to do this for some period. But I can assure you, tonight, right as we speak..."

Lorenzo raised his eyebrows at the expectant crowd. He closed his eyes and pressed his palms together and said, "... a new alchemist has reached into the mirror and found the key. And this will not be the last time, but the first of many, many new times."

He slid and unfolded pages from a long leather case. He counted the pages and turned the ink better to see against the light. Sophie could smell the sandalwood, the tonka bean, the sage oil and tea tree. Lorenzo turned and pressed a hand down to quiet the crowd. He cleared his throat and started to read in the murmuring light.

He started at the beginning.

"I remember a monastery with perspiring stones in the early spring. The dimmest blue glow and lip smack puff of rushlight. The smell of wet fur across shoulders..."

"No. Oh no," Sophie whispered.

The party crowd was hare to the fox, though they sat, reclined, and braced themselves upright. They were a whitetail flicking on the hunting trail. They were a bloodied fin rolling under the waves before dire and pitiless teeth. The candlelight burned in the darkness of the forest and Sophie wasn't the only one who was watching, smelling, burning.

Sophie watched the blackness, adjusting her eyes to the trees. He was coming. She tried to find the shadows moving. He was here. Surely Lux would be leaping tree stumps and lacing through branches and logs.

Lorenzo kept speaking. "We thought our love would last. That we could bide our time before the flame and disease and hooves turned all blue skies and meadows gray. As though nothing could be worse. As though the blade and smoke-death was the worst way to die."

He would arrive, hunting the words spoken out loud. They would have summoned him as you would summon a bear with beer and a campfire grill, the bear not borne from a cub, but from moss and decaying leaves and the shadows of the trees and drawn to your campground trove, his bloody paws and muzzle smelling like sour milk as he mauls you to keep what is his, the very things that drew him to you.

From the driveway, Sophie watched as Hannah's driver, Robert, pushed red shells into a shotgun and smoothed a wool cap low against his eyes. He lowered himself into a covered UTV, small and nimble enough to move through the trees, dimming the orange lights as it puttered into the forest and then onto an unseen road.

The sound of beating wings and screams burst from the atrium. Sophie turned and saw Lake, bloody, bent, owl-eyed, and whirling as he moved and murdered. She held a hand across her eyes, shielding them from the welding spark blast of the dagger and the violent shadows it cast.

The words superimposed. A reeling tale of tattoos spun off his body in a thousand texts. A narration box burst off of Lake's body. Lux's form. The words "dagger", "bright", "spark" pulsing, dragging, spinning as Lux cascaded into reality.

Lorenzo stared as the pages fluttered from his hands. Lake knifed by with a passing stroke as Lorenzo read the golden text out loud, Lake peeling the skin from his hairline straight down, leaving Lorenzo's eyes in full red shock as his face dangled from his chin.

Lake turned and told them their time had come. Their shadows coned out against the trees behind as Lake held a cutting torch of cerulean flame above his head and bellowed to the blade.

The knife moved faster than the words pulling off Lake could describe. It speared the pages in the air and Lake bunched them with his free hand and set them to kindling in the flame. Lake spun the dagger inside the woman's caftan and rotated it, turning the knife like all hours of a clock.

Lorenzo put a blind hand out and the other members screamed. Lake caught a man at the shoulder with the blade and pressed him through the thick atrium glass, severing his fingers as he did so. He tortured the rest. They bent slowly forward or rocked themselves to a standing position from their soft seats as Lake moved through them, past them, yanking their hair back and punching the dagger through their windpipes, working the arctic flash into and out of bellies and fast across sagging chins.

Lake crushed their trembling and spotted wrists, his boots disintegrating skulls. They were pathetic in their attempts to get away. His fingers broke their paper-thin skin as he slammed them against each other, breaking their bodies into shards, cutting them savagely as he dumped them to the broken glass and vine. Their knees gave out, and they set aching on hands and crumbling feet or holding still on the fat leather couch, staring again and again at their open wounds and as they tried to sweep the blood back in.

Lux used their bodies to savage the mansion itself. He was aware of the limits that they could take, and he used this knowledge with clarity. He grabbed hair and waistlines and made battering rams of skulls and shoulders. The enormous atrium fell in a crescendo of bodies thrown through glass. Lake sawed drywall and joists with barbed ends of compound fractures. They mewled and sobbed, and he used their clothing as wicks and the lard that manifested from their greedy bodies as the wax to the flame.

Sophie ran to the forest and away from the screams. She listened for the puttering sound of the UTV and the glimmering orange running lights, like a lantern's flame.

Behind her, the smell grew black and plastic as the howls and sobs slowed. The mansion went ablaze and the cloud of smoke went visible, a darkness that bloomed blacker than a night full of stars. The forest took to the flames just as the furnace blew. A sweep of air and pressure knocked Sophie to the leaves and muck before the thunderclap hit her ears.

She was dizzy in the forest and losing her way in the smell of burning flesh and carpets, the combusted house now just thick smoke and haze, and the burning glow orange against the under canopy of the forest.

Sophie followed UTV tracks, crushed ferns, and sprayed mud. She couldn't hear anything but the ringing in her ears. She found a stream at the edge of the burial mounds, tufts of cattails, and tall grass. The stream gurgled almost invisible just at her feet.

Hannah sat above the orange lights of a vehicle as it idled. A racing harness braced Hannah deep into her seat. A thick plastic binder with loose-leaf pages stapled together in it was hole-punched and zip-tied to the harness. She held a thick plastic searchlight in one hand and a break-away shotgun across the other. Moths and ash chased through the tunnel of the searchlight beam.

"Robert, it's there! Do you see it?" she shouted. "I told you he wouldn't risk it!"

Robert waved the light closer. Hannah held the huge searchlight to him, here, closer, here, to here, at the rocks near a curve of the stream. He was center stage, kneeling on the flat rocks just steps away.

"Ma'am, it's here, it's here, ma'am," he said, holding a forearm to shade his eyes from the light.

He held The Book of Blue Daggers in his hand. Never scratched or wet or hazed from the sun or nature. Cut pure and white. Nature or violence or time wouldn't dare mark it. Sophie could read the title, daylight perfect, even through the darkness. Hannah set the gun across the driver's seat and fumbled against the harness latch. She jerked and tried lifting herself out and waved Robert closer.

"It isn't even wet, ma'am."

"Bring it here, Robert, here Robert now…" Hannah squeezed both arthritic thumbs against the clasps.

"Oh…. yes…" Robert said.

Robert took two steps as Hannah unclicked a latch. She squirmed sideways from the harness, angling her knees, pushing herself up from the seat. Robert's eyes glamoured fully blue from top to bottom. The words of the first page stitched a golden line that glowed across his pupils.

"No, no!" Hannah slithered from the seat.

Robert's lips mumbled silently as he read along, his big face gilded. Hannah unlocked the final latch and put a foot on the soft ground and limped breathlessly towards him.

Just feet away, Sophie clapped the hammer of the shotgun back. Hannah looked back with her lips pinched and her eyes filled with absolute confusion as Sophie kicked Hannah off her feet and onto the wet rocks.

Robert looked up from the Book, his cat eyes dazzling with golden words. Sophie had him. Sophie shook.

Sophie realized she was exactly here and now and she shouted, "The Book!" And in one burning move she pulled the trigger and then swept the Book clean from the air as he dropped it as his eyes dimmed gold to gray.

# CHAPTER THIRTY-FOUR

*The Cold Game*

## MEDICAL LAKE, WASHINGTON NOVEMBER 10

Sophie took time to breathe in the visitor's lobby of Eastern State Psychiatric Hospital.

She took the time to pour herself into someone else for the time being. For just time enough to get what she needed. Hiding her wrecked, limping leg. Hiding her bloodshot eyes behind sunglasses inside. She ignored her own scent, trailing burning rubber, scorched meat, and mold.

She had enough magic left to work a fake ID and a name on the visitor's registration. She had it straight and true that Oscar's Koo's assistant would be on his father's visitors list.

Of course, the Book was with her. She wore a white stripe off the edge of the pages from rubbing it so much. Her hand was blue, and the veins webbed at the surface from holding the squirming thing close and tight. The Book shifted like a cat trying to jump out of her grasp, rattling as it bucked in her hands.

The name tag read Marina, here for WAGNER KOO, and had a blue plastic backing that said Washington State Department of Health and Social Services. She swore to it she didn't bring in any alcohol, drugs, dangerous weapons of any kind. She swore to it she would take no pictures, that she understood that medical confidentiality was a patient's sacrosanct right. She put her initials on forms. She signed that she wouldn't hold the state responsible even if grievous harm came to her body.

An attendant swept a wand across her and declared her "ready to go." Sophie put her phone and keys into a plastic box. She wrote a name that wasn't hers onto the name tag sticker and smoothed onto the label. The attendant put the box into a gated cabinet and locked it shut.

The doorways clicked, beeped in a soothing way. A male nurse in dawn colored scrubs with a black mustache and steel-rimmed glasses from the hallway beyond waved Sophie over. Behind him, Sophie could see patients wandering in blankets, with curling toenails, whispering to their hands, their volume always wrong. It was bright through the windows on patients so pale and scant and it felt like they would evaporate in the sun.

"I'm Nurse Kienholz. I can lock that book up for you," the nurse said.

Sophie held tight. She would never let it go. Kienholz put a hand out. "No gifts."

"It's not a gift. There's information in here I need to discuss with him," Sophie said. For once, she wasn't lying.

Kienholz rolled his eyes. He pointed at another building through a window. "This patient is in another building. We have to walk to Geropsychiatric. Please follow me."

"When did he get transferred to Geropsychiatric?"

Kienholz sighed and walked ahead of Sophie. "Not enough beds in forensic. Wagner is over 50 so...Gero."

They walked outside onto a paved path connecting the buildings.

"Is Mr. Koo no longer considered a danger?"

"Mr. Koo's just fine, just dandy. Normal NGRI patient here," Kienholz said.

"Normal?"

Kienholz rolled his eyes again and counted off syllables on his fingers. "Not. Guilty. Reason. Insanity. Some set of people think they are just clever enough to think they can beat the system by claiming mental issues. Sometimes they are clever enough to slip by and drop out here."

At the other end of the sunny-day path, Kienholz opened another door. They entered.

"When you go to prison, you know when you are getting out. You get a sentence with an end date," he said.

Kienholz handed a card to another nurse, pointed to Sophie, and said, "We have a guest for Wagner Koo."

A woman stood at the wall, her skin and hair and clothes all flowing into precisely one gray shade. She was still-eyed and calm as a statue against the wall.

"You don't get a sentence here?"

"Never found guilty by a court of law. But they can only process out when they aren't quote-unquote insane," Kienholz said. He nodded to the other nurse.

They presented Sophie to a small visitor's room. The patients strayed away from the sunlight here as well. None of them sat at the tables or white plastic chairs. A collage was tacked to one wall next to a vending machine, letters cut from magazines, construction paper, glue-stuck along with yawning lions and giraffes and sea turtles that asked, "How am I FEELING today?"

"How often does that happen?" Sophie asked.

Kienholz shrugged. "I'll be honest, I actually saw it happen one time." Kienholz laughed and pointed past Sophie and said, "Hope he enjoys what you brought him."

Wagner Koo's black hair was an off-center starfish around his head and latticed with pink scars. He walked unsteadily and maneuvered his legs over and around invisible boxes. He clapped, shook and stuffed invisible items into his pocketless clothes.

Sophie watched his lobotomized head vibrate in a circle as he whistled, and tics pinched his cheeks. He caught Sophie in his steady green eyes and reeled to her.

Wagner sat on a plastic chair across from Sophie. The soft legs of it tapped "thak-thak-thak," against the floor as Wagner's flabby body cycled side-to-side. He kept his eyes on Sophie while he took things that didn't exist off the table and put them into his body.

"Wagner. I want to talk to you about your son," Sophie said.

"Lives... were saved." Wagner slowed down on the words he lost before remembering the rest, then spilling them out as fast as he could say it.

"You're the only one who survived," Sophie asked. "Where's The Verdant Pool?"

Wagner forked his fingers and pointed them at the bridge of his nose. "Tried it... here first." He shook his head away from the tremor. He jammed fingers onto the scars above his neck. "Then here, here... and here. Ruined... my speech, but I know... exactly what to say."

"Did the Book do this? Did it make you hurt your son and carve your brain to pieces?"

"Pure Alexia means you... can't read again. It took... time to scuttle that island... from the... map of the mind." Wagner rubbed a wild hand against the back of his head. "Made it invisible in the... occipital lobe, the... posterior cerebral artery. It... takes time... and effort to make... it so you can never see words again. Collateral. Damage."

"Do you remember what you did to Oscar?"

Wagner held his flickering hands out for Sophie to see and trapped her in his eyes so she could see his revolving face. "We... escaped the trap. Oscar went.... direct. Decided his eyes... better than his brain. You have to weigh the... risk."

"You both did it. You both read it. You both..."

"The... Book was so beautiful and real! I thought I wouldn't get tricked, but Oscar saved my life. We found a way... out." Wagner smiled. Beamed. If only his son could see him now.

"It wasn't your idea. It was Oscar's because you were too deep inside of it."

Wagner nodded and grinned sideways. He turned and pointed to the scars above his neck.

"Do you think I could... hold the knife here? I could never hold it and do it... myself. We saved each other."

Wagner mimed forks and knives. He and Oscar had slashed his neurons into dim sparks of meat, just to escape the Book.

"You put a knife in your brain to save your life, and all this time, I thought the Book was the one holding your hand."

Wagner made a motion with both hands. Sophie took the Book out and set it on one end of the table. Wagner kept his watery eyes steady with Sophie now even as she slid the Book across. Wagner took it in his hands and felt around the edges of it and put his fingers on the pages. Sophie kept staring, ready to reach out, ready to take it away.

He smiled and licked his lips and laughed at the Book. He turned the pages and couldn't see a thing. It reflected nothing against his limp green eyes.

"Where does the map end, Wagner? Where's The Verdant Pool?"

Wagner burped out the name. "Hanford Site. Radiation... Underground!"

Sophie watched him open the Book and mock the pages.

"I... tricked you. I got... away!" Wagner tremored, and giggled above the pages of the Book. He was looking at it, but he had prevented himself from seeing it.

"Underground? Is that the water celestial, Wagner?" Sophie asked, but Wagner didn't answer. He was staring at the door.

"Aren't you the popular one today?" Kienholz said. "No one in four years and now two in the same day."

Oscar Koo smiled beside Kienholz and swayed a red-and-white striped cane towards his father's low chuckle.

"I don't suppose you'll tell me your real name?" Oscar asked her.

"Sophie Hopper," Sophie finally admitted.

"You should know, Sophie, that as my father's legal guardian, I am called to approve any visitation."

Oscar sat next to Sophie and took off his dark sunglasses. He smiled and took her hands in his. His iridescent eyes had the look of a heat wave. Sophie could see a reflection of herself in both of them, a distant mirage.

"You would have never made it," Oscar said.

"To The Verdant Pool? I would have left from here."

"The Water... Celestial," Wagner said.

Oscar went on and on about the blue conspiracy and the journey and map. How the toxic wasteland at the Hanford Site was the only place the Book could come to an end.

"The Book will ask you to destroy it, but of course, who can kill their one true love?" Oscar laughed.

Wagner had taken the looped end of the cane and scooted the chair close to her. Oscar quickly grabbed both of Sophie's wrists, tight, and held them against the arms of the chair.

With a sharp pop, Wagner snapped the striped cane in two, gripping a foot-long spike while Oscar held Sophie prone and whispered, "Now dad, now!"

Sophie wriggled against Oscar as Wagner steadied her head with a thick, strong hand and pushed the spike towards her eye. The spike wobbled and slashed apart her eyebrow as Oscar said do it again, again, and Wagner put a thumb against her nose ridge to steady himself this time.

Sophie could hear her blood falling onto the floor and the thwacks of the chair and Wagner's yelps as he grooved her eyelid apart. Sophie pushed back, and they all fell to the ground, the plastic chair bursting from the weight as Sophie growled as Kienholz shouted and slapped a big red button on the wall.

Oscar fumbled for Sophie's hair and shouted, "Both her eyes! Quick!"

Kienholz lifted and spun Wagner by the shoulders. Wagner chopped the spike three times at the base of his throat and Kienholz's eyes went sideways, and he made a noise like a balloon fluttering out. Oscar set upon him and swiped at his waist to grab the keycard.

"Dad, go to The Hanford Caves. Get the Book and take it to the pool!" Oscar shouted.

Wagner turned with his arm out and fumbled for the Book on the ground. Sophie grabbed his wrist with both hands and drove the full length of the spike into Wagner, just below his belly. He grunted and curled over as he bled out red and bile-green. Oscar held the keycard and shouted.

"You got her! Now take it to the pool and drown it! Kill it!" he said. He didn't know.

The alarm had kicked up another tone. Sophie ran Oscar up against the wall and she could see her face in bloody stripes from the reflections in his eyes. Oscar shook all over and Sophie laughed out loud about the long con the Book had played on the both of them. How they butchered themselves for this. What a cold game. What a trick, indeed.

Wagner stretched out and died on his back, right there on the floor, as Oscar begged for answers. Nurses and a security team came too late for Kienholz, and Sophie took Oscar by the throat.

"You thought you would save me? You thought I wouldn't know what to do?" she asked.

"You'll give in just like everyone else!" Oscar said. "You love it too much!"

Sophie didn't have to beg them to believe her any longer. The Geropsychiatric unit erupted cataclysmic. A security team knocked Oscar down in zip-ties. They zipped Wagner's cooling ankles to his wrists and set him bleeding out on his belly. Someone kneeled and pressed their fingers through the mess on Kienholz's neck and shook their head. The patients sobbed and begged for Kienholz to come back. A bald man with no fingers and no teeth talked about fresh meat, good meat, mm-mm, the best cooking around.

The Book of Blue Daggers was belted in spatters across the pages, and someone offered to take it from her again. They'd seen it on the security cameras, and it wasn't Sophie who was doing the begging anymore.

Sophie couldn't see but wouldn't say it. A doctor put in stitches, and it was going to hurt, but nothing would hurt her this time, not this time, not again, and not anymore.

# CHAPTER THIRTY-FIVE

*The Verdant Pool*

## THE HANFORD SITE, WA AT THE END

There was no guilt, just radiation in the cooked plain.

Sophie looped the Radex detector around her neck on a nylon belt. She clicked the test button every half-minute. It pinged, and she kept her footing on the rutted path. The drifts lay in stiff angles in the air.

She taped a space blanket across her shoulders, her ears ringing with the noise of distant beaches. The gauze patch over one eye had her moving in wide loops across the split plain like a drunk silver insect never quite releasing its wings.

The shrub-steppe was dusted silver-blue in the moonlight here. The dirt polished to permanent wave crests in the moonlight so that Sophie barely needed a flashlight to see the trail way ahead. She didn't need a flashlight to see the whipsnakes in the cups of the trail way. She didn't need a light to see a clutch of google-eyed burrowing owls peering out towards her, quailing and bobbing at themselves from inside a rusted water pipe.

A sign scored by rust said, "US DEPARTMENT OF ENERGY – ALL ENTRY SUBJECT TO SEARCH."

The detector clicked and beeped. Sophie walked onto the foundation rubble of a vast Cold War infrastructure. A stairway plumed hot air into the breeze as she walked down, a half step at a time. The detector screen strobed and the noise of it echoed like a field of summer frogs. The tunnel below was arched and soundless and huge. Halfway down the stairs, she turned the detector off. There was a moonlight box of night sky behind her, smaller than her hand at arm's length, and just between her fingers as she saw more footprints gathered. She followed the prints leading away into the silent dry darkness off past the bottom of the stairs.

The underground was supported by numerated radioactive waste tombs, marking I, II, III, Sophie walking further and marking XLI, LI.

The titanic concrete masts were warm to the touch and wide as redwoods so she couldn't see one past another. Signs carved from one weightless piece of Garolite were fixed just below each numeral. Black letters exclaimed, " *What is here was dangerous and repulsive to us. This message is a warning about danger!*" and below that, the letters said:

"*The danger is still present, in your time, as it was in ours.*"

"*The danger is to the body, and it can kill.*"

"*The form of the danger is an emanation of energy.*"

The Book of Blue Daggers warped senses up by proximity. It was utterly different here. It changed everything.

In the dark Sophie could reach on to feel the grit and soft moss of the cavern mouth as she descended, listening to her footsteps echo off the pendulites wet with rockmilk, finally viewing the dip leading to the great curtained and phosphorescent dome. She could smell the packed clay, feel the tangle-ends of roots, and hear the crush of moths and blind cave-beetles under her feet. Lake was here. Lux was here.

She saw him, wet from the glow and standing at the radioactive edge of The Verdant Pool. He wore a purple leather jacket and glass-and-leather goggles dangled from his neck. He was thickly muscled and beautiful and terrible, gripping the dagger tight as it steamed in the air, water rushing off its indigo length.

The pool's bottom was a morning sun so bright she couldn't see to the bottom. The water burned softly, a ghost light from the radioactive spears burning at its floor. So blue. So beautiful. She was surrounded by fruit blossoming thick on emerald vines, and stepped across bulging citrus of amber yellow, and melon green vines striped with lilac and blush that laced every inch of the water-lapped ledge. Here the shores grew flora with roots that drew from a water celestial.

"Such a perfect blue," Lux said, and it was.

"Esme was right. She knew you would be here," Sophie said.

"The seer knew it would end here. You're right where she knew you would be, Selia. Her riddles were right. The Book would destroy you after all."

"We can leave together, Lake. We can end it here and survive. Esme was right, can't you see that?"

"You betrayed me. You betrayed me and you saw to it that Ash died."

"I was too late, Lake. I tried. I was selfish. I am so sorry."

"Your penalty is death," Lux declared.

"I'm not scared anymore, Lake. I don't need it anymore. I'm alive right now."

The blue dagger growled and glowed hot in Lux's hand as he stepped from the shore of the pool towards Sophie. Turning towards her, Sophie could see where the radiation had begun unraveling him, the hand holding the dagger peeled back to the bones in his grip.

"I told you it would save my life," Sophie said. "I was just wrong about when."

"After I kill you, I get to live forever."

"No one lives forever, Lake. We deserve what we have left."

The dagger moved as fast as it wanted, but there wasn't any chance. Lux was still catching up to her and even this wounded, she moved sideways and held him at the shore.

Sophie took the knife from Lux's melting hands. The dagger burned white-hot and withered her fingers to a black lizard-skin against the bones. Lux gasped as Sophie pressed the dagger deep into his chest.

Lux's wound steamed oily black. His arms coiled inwards and he writhed and the smoke spun from his body and he wandered into the pool. The black smoke gurgled off even as he sank into the light and disintegrated into the burning. He disintegrated, the layering of Lux stripped away, and he regained whatever left of Lake he had, as Sophie watched him reach out to her as he fell into the orbit of the underwater sun.

Sophie held the Book with her one live hand and pressed it beneath the surface. She held tight until the light and radiation played games with whatever was holding The Book of Blue Daggers together. Sophie could see the thing rustle, the pages rewriting themselves beneath the water's surface.

It wrote itself endlessly into the electric waters. In the soft tide of ink all the words fell out and they came to Sophie's fingers, and they wrote against them: thank you, thank you, thank you. Against the light and the reflection of the cavern's high walls topaz like the midday sky, thank you, Sophie, thank you.

They never guessed what they were really reading, no one, not for hundreds of years. They never pondered or understood this plea to release it. All who read the pages took their hand where it led them into their own permanent bonfire, until the end, where Sophie finally led it to its own. Thank you, Sophie, oh thank you, thank you.

It let them think it was a guide to perfection. It let them think it was a path to ever golden steppes, to wondrous things, secret dark and hidden things. At that moment, it was Sophie's completely, and even in the dim light where Sophie drowned the Book in the twisting flames, they had nothing but love for each other.

Sophie was just above the wreckage when she returned to the bottom of the stairs. The Verdant Pool disappeared behind her and there was little left but the graveyard of radiation as she slowly looked to the stairs and glimpsed at her life, one with nothing left to chase and untroubled by a single fault or fear at all.

A soft dawn cut by a band of the moon resolved the night sky at the stairwell's portal out. It came full circle to her in the wind. Nothing tricked her, and she survived from here, and she would survive as long as it would take.

It was just blue moonlight when she escaped by the skylight.

# Acknowledgements

Creating a novel is never a solitary endeavor. Behind every page, every chapter, and every idea, there are the echoes of the voices of those who've supported, inspired, and believed in the journey.

Sara McSpadden, Larry McSpadden, Charles Dragoo, and Deb Estabrook, your unwavering faith and love have been pivotal throughout this process.

For the invaluable feedback, brainstorming, and creative encouragement, immense gratitude goes to Phil Kijak, Rob Lancaster, Tyson Mueller, and John Welch.

Emily Beebe, Adam Gabriel Smith, Amy Retartha and Jen Halsey, a special acknowledgement for being there from the outset, consistently supporting and encouraging this novel's inception and evolution.

To John Tynes, Dennis Detwiler, Sabrina Bingham, and Alan Moore. Influences.

To Cody Sharp, Andrew Brynildson, Rebecca Quate, Liz McDonald, Brent Woodall, Susan Hurst, Lauren Hurst, Lucy Ainsworth, Mike Sebeckis, Jeremy Mitchell, Adam Norris, Jen Rhodes- your incredible support and encouragement have been instrumental.

In this novel's journey, each strand of encouragement, advice, and belief from Paige Mills, Scott Gorsky, Liz McDonald, Alex Rosenberger, Rob Lancaster, Susan Hurst, Lauren Hurst, Scott Schulte, Abram Genser, Judy Weber, Brad Rosenthal, Stan, Taylor, Belinda Short,, Casey Gray, Austin Hoffey, Ashley Gordon, David Voigt,, Jesse Gallagher, Jessica Richardson, Anna Wolf, Jeremiah, Russell, Ally Inglis, Sean Mayberry, Andrew Weber, David Goodwin, Steph Cooper, Cameron Oehler, Susan Crankshaw, Bethany Tomerlin Prince, Gage Troy, Jeff Chandler, Libby Bulloff, Adam Norris, Jenni Wissel, Matt Loman, Jessica Baldanzi, Kyle Reeser, Mike Manetta, Kristin Kiefer Fuller, Vincent Bryant, Matthew Plank, Philip Ramge, Sherry Mock, Kris Dougherty, John Scott Tynes, Khadija Hussain, Devin Barry, Stephen Kotowych, Adam Cole, Capaneus, Blaine, Buz Fennell, Cameron Reel, Nick Foster, Patrick Berg, Stephanie Hales, Emlynn Lynn, Amenze Oronsaye, John Miyasato, Elizabeth Martin, has contributed more than you will know.

Thank you to Carter and Emerson for their unique perspectives and boundless enthusiasm towards this.

And of course, Chrissy, my here and now. Without you, without your everything, this book wouldn't be anything.

# Bonus Material

## Four Blue Tales

*our Blue Tales are four semi-fictional tales about people I know, and who deeply cared about this project. In return for their incredible support and encouragement, I wrote about them encountering The Book of Blue Daggers in one form or another, and meeting a fairly terrible end because of it. So, thank you so much, John, Lucy, Brent, and Tyson. I will never forget your support and friendship, so in return, I wrote a story about something horrible that happens to a fictionalized version of you.*

It isn't the words on the cover that make it The Book of Blue Daggers, it is the intent of the expressions inside. That intent finds many forms, and many followers willing to listen, take the hand, and follow that intention well past a point of good reason, allowing it to walk them, step-by-step, into their own doom.

# John

## *The Ultraviolet*

To think, he even got it for free.

The music store was half-rate, primarily bruised and battered equipment from the road, but more full of stories and autographed photos of famous musicians holding guitars, playing synths, and shooting the devil horns than actually containing anything of value.

"Nothing in the shipment looked too nice, but I know how hands on you are." Francisco, the store owner, said.

"Have to check every detail. Never know what you can find."

You never know. John was right. People just trashed things without a second thought. John did the legwork. The research. He had the knowledge, and if other people didn't know what treasure they had, well, it wasn't his responsibility to tell them. It wasn't his responsibility to let a flea market stall know they were selling an acoustic Masaki Sakurai six-string for a hundred bucks cash. Or that a church basement sale was literally giving away Hammond Novachord for anyone who could get it up the stairs and out the same day. There was a lot of trash out there, but John always made sure to find the treasure.

While writing down serial numbers, John's fingers brushed against an accordion file, crushed and wedged between two tube-driven Peavey amps. He slowly worked to knead the file out between the weight of the stack, unaware that what was inside would change his life forever.

The paper manual inside was as thick as a dictionary and smelled like decades of weed smoke and tobacco.

"Hey, what does this go to?" John asked Francisco.

Francisco shrugged. "Guy came in, left it with those old tube amps. Any autographs on it?"

"Nah."

"Yours if you want it. You can keep the file, too." Francisco winked.

The whole thing looked to be typed up and smudged out on graph paper. The front page proclaimed ULTRAVIOLET SYNTHESIZER ASSEMBLY INSTRUCTIONS AND MANUAL FOR USE above a diagram of a constellation making up a grand piano.

To the world, it was old paper and faded ink. But like pulling a sword from granite stone, when John opened the manual he could see the circuit graphs, relays, and envelope moderators that offered something truly striking. To John, the intricate designs were just a howling labyrinth of unparalleled sonic power, begging to be set free.

It was like assembling a Frankenstein. The manual was specific though. Don't cut corners, don't get anything new. John found pre-1988 vacuum tubes. Spent good money ordering ancient Sony stereo parts, and in his first piece of criminal artistry, performed an organ heist on a Medusa pinball machine, peeling the circuit board, wires, and brain from a retro beer arcade downtown. The manual even told him what kind of screwdriver to use on the pinball machine.

His collection grew, a medley of the outdated and improbable, the pieces of the Ultraviolent spanning upstairs and down, the wire diagrams and relay organization flickering from his waking hours well into his dreams.

His apartment blazed with light to see every detail, every serial number, every stroke of the key smashed onto the manual that never left his side. Amidst the sharp tang of soldering metal and the erratic dance of shadows, John birthed "The Ultraviolet".

Despite the manual looking like nothing more than a lazy sheaf, it created a sleek and powerful looking-machine. The manual calculated a perfect harmonic shell for itself, an aluminum shell that John made from two Jaguar E-type fenders welded together. The final product, once birthed, a totally unique thing into the world before John had even set the thing to power.

And oh, when he did. The allure. The potential. The total capability at even the lowest setting.

Word spread like wildfire in the city's underground music realm, each whisper promising an experience, a sound that touched the very soul. With every performance, venues, hidden in graffiti-splashed alleyways, brimmed with eager souls. And as John's fingers danced over The Ultraviolet's unique 33 keys, the audience swayed, each beat drawing them deeper, wanting deeper, dreaming wider.

But this...this was too easy. The audience was begging to be entranced. They wanted it. But John knew there was more. Pouring over the manual again and again, he searched for something he knew must be there. He knew he must be missing something.

The audiences were in the palm of his hand. Breathing, dancing, swaying, their emotions his at the push of a key, but he knew it could go further.

There was a secret, he knew it. The full potential of the Ultraviolet couldn't just be in the production of the sound, the power of the emotion it could bring. Deep in the manual, he found it. Barely stated, but clear to one who had spent years studying it, a theoretical schematic explained how to nudge truer, clearer, more anointed frequencies from the heart of the Ultraviolet.

John yearned for it, dreamed of it, begged to vibrate with the pulse that crackled at the beginning and end of the universe itself. And one fateful evening, under the hazy glow of makeshift lights in a particularly exclusive venue, John decided he would share.

A frequency, hauntingly ethereal, unfurled from The Ultraviolet. A noise so beautiful to everyone came, and softly now, everyone came to a stop. The sound was quiet, though growing and familiar. It rose and rose and rose and the air grew thick around the Ultraviolent as the audience wept in rapture. The beautiful shockwave rippled through the venue, faces contorting in pain, and then... silence. An unsettling, complete silence.

The aftermath was chaos. People stumbled out, their faces etched with confusion and fear. They shouted, or at least they thought they did, for no sound reached their ears. They were deaf, every single one of them, struck down by the beautiful sound of the Ultraviolet.

Amid the mayhem, the police seized John, the manual, and The Ultraviolet. Detectives, in a bid to decipher the night's events, cracked open the manual in an effort to make sure John hadn't left any booby traps inside; what they found, however, was something far more unsettling.

Childish doodles, stick figures, and boxy machines with smiling faces stared back at them from hundreds of pages. John screamed at them to return the design, demanding that they could never understand its complicated grandeur.

In jail, John became a specter. He stood deaf in his cell, eyes distant, his hands and head swaying softly to a melody that none could hear. It was as if The Ultraviolet's final note had ensnared him, imprisoning him in a loop from which there was no escape.

But he wasn't the only one. Quietly, peacefully, so many other deaf victims of that night lined the streets across from the police station, swaying in time to the same tune as John. The police found other victims too, formerly upstanding members of society, in parks, street corners, underneath bridges, deafened but dancing slowly, gently, and always in tune with John, still in his cell, all of him still able to hear the same forever echo of the Ultraviolet.

# Azul

## *Lucy*

Lucy had a smoldering beauty and a confidence that came from striding through countless foreign streets alone. Her cosmopolitan life was tracked by a passport thick with exotic entry stamps and visa stickers. And yet, amidst the catalog of global travels, she sought something further, more authentic, and ever more exotic.

Whether it was the streets of Paris, the temples of Kyoto, or the hills of Rome, she still felt she was treading in the footsteps of others. More than a novel experience, she craved an essence lost in time. Lucy craved authenticity, and to be in a place unsullied by the whims of tourists, and the pervasive influence of foreign cash.

Lucy immersed herself in culture, food, and above all, languages. The personal communications of the people in anyplace she wandered. Lucy didn't just learn languages; she devoured them. She was astonished to learn people had to "try" to learn other languages, and still came up short. All that effort and they could barely order off a menu, even with the words printed in front of them!

Lucy had never been caught flat-footed abroad, always making sure to find someone local and fluent to read books with, make jokes with, even fake argue with, to make sure her accent wouldn't slip in a stressful situation. It was a point of pride, although one she would never brag about, that she had been mistaken for a local in Quebec, Munich, and Amsterdam, to note just a few.

Thus, in the travel section of a used bookstore, Lucy found what she had been looking for. As the sunset draped the sky pink and orange through the window outside, she paged through the dog-eared and well-creased culture and language book of a place she had never been, and never even heard of.

The guidebook told of islands well off the coast of Europe, small mountainous spits inhabited by ancient peoples pre-dating their Portuguese colonizers who simply called them "The Azul". The guide jocularly hinted at their provenance: that they were the last exiles from sunken Atlantis, that the bizarre Azul language was their key to remaining uncolonized by corrupting influences, that the Islands were the last redoubt of the Knights Templar.

Lucy was entranced. The Culture and Language of the Azul painted the picture of a mostly untouched land, and a dialect so puzzling only a few could decipher. It wasn't just a challenge; to Lucy, it was a dare.

And one she gladly accepted. The guide was her only chance at the language, and she tore into it like any other. With no one to practice with, and hardly a mention of the place anywhere online, Lucy had to make do, but felt her heart race as the challenge sharpened her wits, the language unlocking enchanting rhythm as she learned the intricate back and forth of conversational Azul.

Mere weeks later, with directions from the guidebook and the certainty of a convert, Lucy planned her route. From her first stop at Lisbon, she booked a Cessna Citation to the Azul islands, assuring the agent at the other end that yes, indeed, the small airport in Azul was a real place.

As the silver plane cut through the Atlantic clouds, Lucy immersed herself in the guide, each word and phrase a key to unlock the land's untapped mysteries.

The long descent across the ocean and the sea-battered shoreline revealed a tapestry of colors, and an uncharted landscape miraculously untouched by industrialization. The hues of green orchards sprawled as far as the eye could see, interspersed with curves of cerulean from serene streams, against a backdrop of white gypsum cliffs, a bulwark against the sea.

Upon landing, Lucy, armed with the guide's language, confidently engaged with the locals. Their reactions, however, puzzled her. Instead of appreciation, she was met with blank stares, their eyes devoid of recognition. In her pride, Lucy assumed they simply failed to understand the depth of their heritage. Perhaps her pride had gotten ahead of her. She would have to take it slow.

At the amiable hotel, her hypothesis was proven correct. After providing Luucy with a customary basket of small pears, oranges, and exceptionally strong chocolate, the concierge walked her to an exclusive club for heritage and discussion just off the town square, nestled at the foot of an ancient stone lookout tower.

Here, Lucy found herself amongst the elders, all adept in the ancient language she had worked tirelessly to master. Night after night, she reveled in the echoing conversations, basking in the shared enlightenment. Other travelers join in, certainly other readers of the guidebook, although fortunately just as adept at the Azu language as Lucy. News of the travelers grew, and what was once just a small twilight gathering grew to many in number, new members bringing sweets, garden herbs, berries they had picked that very day.

Yet, beneath the perceived profundity of her interactions within the club, Lucy began to feel an undercurrent of discord. The conversations she once thought deep and meaningful now felt off-kilter, as if she was missing a crucial piece of the puzzle. Some mornings, a shiver would course through her, deep to her bones, as though her body was trying to shake her to remember something, but she couldn't begin to guess at what it might be.

The club grew more popular and busy, inside and out. Family members of attendees stood outside, their faces long and their eyes red, waiting for the exit of fathers, sons, mothers, daughters from nights of conviviality and enjoyment in the culture. Lucy stared into their faces to understand why. Their look wasn't one of anger, but one closer to grievance, or pity.

Once, while wandering to the pear orchards outside of the town, Lucy caught bits of conversation between the locals, in between their sad and sympathetic glances. They were speaking at her, if not to her, and somehow she didn't understand.

That evening, after another intense session of heritage discussion at the club, Lucy decided to explore the oldest of the city streets. As she meandered through the cobblestone streets, she caught snippets of hushed conversations between the locals. They whispered of "the club of the lost" and refused to speak a word to her when approached, covering their mouths as they quickly, but politely, exited away.

Confused, Lucy approached the concierge from the hotel. The concierge's face twisted in confusion as Lucy asked why there was such fear. Asking again and again, the concierge mimed not being able to understand. In Azul, English, Portuguese, Spanish, French, Lucy attempted, garnering shrugs, confusion, until a look of frantic horror rose to the face of the concierge.

The concierge wrote her a note. Before Lucy's eyes, the words and letters were impossible to read. Upside down, mixed together. Lucy tried to write back, her lettering just as jumbled. She was as useless as a baby, her hands simply refusing to write what her mind had set out to do.

A cold grip squeezed Lucy's stomach. Memories of her interactions at the club played back, the once-clear conversations now sounding like senseless babble. She realized, with a nauseating horror, that her elite sanctuary was nothing more than a madhouse of her own making.

She rushed back to the club, hoping to confront the reality head-on. But as she entered, she found its members deep in conversation, their faces alight with the glow of brilliant discussions on heritage, culture, and the arts. To them, their dialogues were still profound, insightful exchanges, and Lucy's warnings fell on deaf ears.

Outside, the townspeople looked on with a mix of pity and sorrow. They held each other back, insisting that this place must take its course, that these people could not be helped now.

Then they watched as Lucy circled from person to person, gripping their shoulders and shouting babble at them until it was all too much, and she sat down and joined their conversations again, speaking Azul, fluent and perfect as any native, until the language became entirely her own.

# A Groove so Blue

*Brent*

All Brent had been told was that the hard grind would eventually pay off, but for now, the only things getting paid were his bills.   He'd at least escaped the dreadful stripclub, popup, and fly-by-night audio setups where if you didn't get paid up-front, and in cash, you weren't getting paid at all, and worked his way into a steady job.

Steady. Steady stiff black uniform, steady soundboard checks, steady wiring setups, steady lugging sound equipment around in the heat, steady setting up whatever the talent wanted for the day, steady the millionaire boss addressing him "my man", "brother", "chat". He was one step up from the swamp, but he couldn't hold onto the ladder forever.

At least the job was with Charles Ceru, yeah, of C-Note Productions. Even though his empire was built on royalties on tracks he produced with Cher, the Eagles and other bands that made it big with the Boomer generation, Ceru still had more than enough connections and flex to put someone in the center of the map.

Charles Ceru hadn't been a hot name in over a decade, but the first time Brent saw his house off Mulholland Drive in the hills above Los Angeles, he realized he was as relevant to the scene as ever. He even dared to ask Ceru a question about working with Dr.

Dre, before Ceru called him Brian, and faked a phone call to excuse himself.

But running wires, boards, and setting up acoustics at Ceru's parties was crucial when Brent's days eased into nights, when sunshine, pools, and canyon roads tagged out for neon rooms, frantic dancefloors, and pulsating beats.

Brent was an up-and-comer. And it was here, at the real grind of laying out beats in dark rooms sparkling with blue and pink neon, that Brent put the knowledge of the grind to use, blasting out tracks of his own creation to live crowds. Sometimes his own lyrics, sometimes guest vocals, but it was always his own beats and incredible soundscapes getting him noticed.

Brent had a secret, one he was stunned that no one else employed. While everyone else was looking forward, a million hands all snatching at the same trends, Brent zagged and found success looking backward.

Searching out ancient vinyl stores for fresh samples and interplanetary grooves, Brent found a paperback vinyl guide from the early 80s - "A Groove so Blue", that traced the seductive history of 70s and 80s LA free jazz, funk, and proto-hip hop. The tattered guide clued him into unknown artists and untouched sounds, samples, and drum breaks that hardly anyone else even knew existed.

And lately, it had been one artist in particular, the cult free jazz fusion outfit King Chaz. Brent had found ways to utilize and remix the blistering yet in-pocket drumming of Jackie Love and the otherworldly horns of Louie Love in ways that no one else began to conceive.

The sound was so fresh, so new. Vocalists started seeking him out, this guy who paid respect to the past and had a sound like no one else. Brent saw a way to grab the next rung up the ladder.

It ate at him though. The Love brothers had died years back, after some shit went down inside the band, the titular vocalist King Chaz leaving the brothers high and dry, and with the song rights in his hand.

So, it was quite the surprise when Brent scoped a picture of King Chaz himself in a spread of the outfit in a Groove So Blue picture spread. The singer, howling into the mic, had a groovy mustache and aviator shades on, but it was him, dead to rights. King Chaz, the man who left the Love Brothers to die poor, bereft, and without a song title to their name, was Charles Ceru.

Ceru. Of course. You don't get to a mansion in the hills, Brent thought, without stepping on a few backs, and now Brent knew exactly those backs belonged to.

Digging deep into his collection, it didn't take Brent long to set up an epic track, a 6-minute rocket launch called "Echoes" that brought Jackie Love into the modern day, and set Louie Love into the future of music. Brent barely had to edit the stems, the raw power boiling off the tracks.

He uploaded it, lowkey. Just a tight circle at first, enough to gauge whether his instincts were correct.

His friends couldn't believe it. They had never in their lives heard something like this. Sure, they knew Brent was solid, but this...this kind of sound was something else. People took notice, especially when Brent told them exactly what the drama in the song was about.

As the storm brewed, an unexpected summons arrived. Brent was invited to Ceru's sprawling mansion. Last minute stuff, Brent swore that this would be his last. Ceru's staff offered pay-and-a-half for something like this, usually a showoff DJ set for a moviestar who wanted to play pretend DJ for a night, to gain some cred for their millionaire friends.

#CharlesWho #ALoveRedeemed #CeruExposed went global as he uploaded the track. The engagement rate went massive. Minutes in, and Brent knew he was taking more than just one step up the ladder.

"Fuck this!" Brent thought. Ceru would certainly know his name now.

Catching a ride to the mansion, Brent savored the moment, ready to tell this story, the moment before he caught the wave so huge it would change his life, especially with the tale of revenge that would make it so sweet. One set up of wires and soundboards and he'd be out, done, ready for the next step entirely.

Hyacinth, Ceru's formidable assistant, greeted him with an uncharacteristic smile at the door to the mansion. "Mr. Ceru is eager to hear your performance. It's your moment," she intoned.

Confusion crawled across Brent's face as he was led to the DJ booth. He quickly realized that the gig wasn't for some superstar flown in for the night, it was for him. He was now at control of the boards he had so often worked his fingers stiff setting up, and with Ceru's crowd of wine and tastemakers watching.

The room's ambiance shifted as "Echoes" filled the air. The crowd swayed to the groove, the track gripping them immediately. They were in his palm before the first hook dropped, but amid the sonorous waves, phones buzzed with notifications, attendees whispering and sharing Brent's explosive revelation.

Charles Ceru, always the picture of composure, now bore a look of ashen betrayal. Tears welled up, spilling over the rims of his eyes. His past had been exhumed, just as he was about to extend a hand to Brent's future.

The music swelled and then abruptly stopped, just three minutes in. Online, tastemakers exclaimed it was a #hustle, a #setup, an attempt by Ceru to #stayrelevant using Brent as a patsy. Fuck these guys, online critics typed, #victimizingtheLove Brothers yet again.

The room froze in an agonizing hush. "Echoes" had ended, and as Brent looked out at the crowd, the only noise left in the room was a silence as huge and as crushing as the sky.

# The Sapphire Scion

*Tyson*

His brain buzzing like a neon sign, Tyson discovered a treasure unlike any other at the bustling gaming convention. Between VR booths and cutting-edge consoles, he found a retro-themed stall offering relics of computer gaming past. A series of vintage floppy disks, their dot-matrix label faded but legible, read: "Sapphire Scion".

At home, a lavish suburban dwelling where pink and yellow flowers stood high and proper in glazed pots, and the aroma of fresh cut grass lingered in the air, Tyson lived a good life. He had cats that he doted on with his partner Makalah, and the couple's globe-spanning vacations came easy and enjoyable.

Tyson's job was both lucrative and esteemed; his colleagues respected him, and his promotions came easily. But with every comfort, there came a subtle gnawing—a longing for a challenge, a hunger for something more interesting, engaging, intellectually exacting.

The first challenge was finding a computer that could run Sapphire Scion. Installing an older virtual machine and buying an external hard drive was his first step. He'd forgotten how long it took these kinds of games to install, the laborious process all part of the anticipation and fun.

But soon, Tyson was thrust into control of a fantastic empire teetering on the edge. Its pixelated landscapes were rich, evoking a sense of enchantment and peril. The game's depth seemed almost otherworldly, as if a real world had been compressed into bits and bytes.

His empire was not merely at risk of invading armies hungry for territory and treasure, no, the game took time to balance the citizens' tolerance for empty stomachs and internal strife. No detail seemed too small for Sapphire Scion. Should he quash an internal rebellion with an iron fist, or let it take its course and burn out? Should he ally himself with the wild and independent tribesmen in the hinterlands against the invaders, knowing that it may be a devil's bargain in the end? Should he allocate the lucrative crops to his vanguard troops, or deliver them to his capital city to ensure loyalty at his doorstep?

These decisions, always made at the razor's edge, were assisted by the enigmatic advice of the Seer, an in-game advisor who imparted wisdom through strange but clever aphorisms. Tyson soon found his wisdom to be a profound strategy in life, in addition to the game.

"Stay hungry to sharpen your senses," the Seer would often murmur. Tyson, intrigued, began to skip meals. The bite of hunger made the world seem sharper, colors more vivid, and his decisions less clouded. In the game, he would keep his armies hungry, seeing them battle harder.

In life, he found himself incredibly focused at work, his focus after fasting resulting in yet another promotion, his superiors astonished that he could gear up to yet another level of performance.

"To find abundance, you must embrace the void." came the Seer's next advice, when asked how to negotiate a tangle of treaties and smoldering battles that threatened expansive wars. By the simple act of ignoring these treaties, and allowing the resulting quagmire of wars and battles to draw his neighboring kingdoms leaving his own untouched, Tyson found he could always prove himself the benefactor. Whether selling food, weapons, supplies, or leveraging offers of peace, removing himself entirely reaped untold benefits later on.

In his home life, the same rang true. Tyson excised himself of all but the essentials, becoming near ascetic in his dress, foods, and belongings. Why own what was not essential? why bother with family members not necessary? Why engage with others destined to draw you into their own selfish drama and struggles?

Tyson found himself exceedingly relaxed in his new life. More time to focus on his own needs. More money to set aside for the future. Every future day seemed more like a gift, unburned from the worries of unnecessary people, meals, and concerns. It was becoming clear that the Seer's advice was proving just as true in life as it was in the Sapphire Scion.

The game's relentless challenges mirrored the rhythmic pulse of Tyson's increasingly rapid heartbeat. If he saw his friends anymore, they would have noticed the neglect shown to his house, and how Makalah's once loving voice turned to one of concern, then desperation. But in his tunnel vision, Tyson saw only the cascading threats to his empire in the Sapphire Scion.

The advice came so clearly. "The brightest flame casts the darkest shadow, ignore the periphery."

Of course. The endless wars, battles, and bloodshed over lines on the map were pointless to the man on the throne, so long as he controlled the heartland. So it was decided in the game, he would focus entirely on his kingdom, the rest of the empire be damned.

At work, he began to apply the Advisor's counsel, resulting in his team breaking new ground in key performance benchmarks. But while the bottom line reported success, his coworkers and managers both signed onto a report noting his utter disdain for teamwork and mutual respect, and his inability to function any longer within the norms of corporate policy.

The zenith came when, after endless eons of attrition, Tyson's virtual kingdom stood uncontested. Plagues, cataclysms, religious zealotry and inquisitions had shattered the competing realms and empires. But the trade routes were haunted highways, the once-bustling ports full of broken ships and beggars, the once-glittering streets of his capital now covered with a patina of grime, his citizens too scared and superstitious to leave their doors in all but the highest hours of the sun.

And this sullen victory revealed a haunting scene: his in-game avatar, gaunt and isolated, presided over silent halls and empty, twilight chambers. The empire was his, but it echoed with doomed loneliness.

Tyson looked around. His once pristine house now languished in disrepair. His phone, long silenced, blinked with a thousand unread messages and emails. Envelopes from work, bills from the power company and water mains piled up in the entryway. And on the dining table lay a letter, in Makalah's handwriting, expressing heartbreak and a desperate plea for the man he once knew to return.

Tyson returned to the Seer once again to ask him for advice on how to move forward yet again, to cut through this knot of impossible complexity with a solution so simple it would seem revelatory.

But the Seer had few wise words to offer.

"Congratulations to the Sapphire Scion! And it is my duty to remind you whatever my wise words may have proffered, it was your decisive hand that allowed you to conquer!"

www.ingramcontent.com/pod-product-compliance
Lightning Source LLC
Chambersburg PA
CBHW020457310726
48979CB00016B/2688/J

* 9 7 9 8 9 8 8 7 9 9 5 0 4 *